"A haunting thriller in which ancient evil and modern tech intertwine in streets of a dying city—and where the darkness hides things much older and more frightening than the darkness itself."
—*Richard Kadrey*, New York Times bestselling author of *Sandman Slim*

"[A] gripping supernatural thriller . . . Terrific pacing and detailed police work mixed with supernatural elements will serve well horror and urban fantasy fans alike."
—*Library Journal*, starred review

"Smart, tough, and scary as hell. Roberson delivers authentic-feeling police action while spinning us down into a pit (or mineshaft) of horrors."
—*Mike Mignola*, creator of Hellboy

"A novel that's part *True Detective* and part Lovecraft. . . . The plot is engaging, and Roberson really shines in building the relationships and dialogue. . . . The end will have horror fans ready for the sequel."
—*Publishers Weekly*

"As entertaining as can be, filled with humor and a satisfying depth of plot. Peering around the corners in Recondito is wicked good fun."
—*Shelf Awareness*

"Lefevre, Tevake and their supporting cast, not to mention the fictional location Recondito, are compellingly drawn . . . . memorably creepy and tense."—*RT Book Reviews* Top Pick (4.5 Stars)

DISCARD

"*Firewalk* turns the police procedural on its ear. Recondito is a simmering melting pot of diverse characters and long-buried evil."
—*Michael J. Martinez*, author of *The Daedalus Incident* and *MJ-12: Inception*

"Fans of the Agent Pendergast series will find a lot to love here, but Roberson takes things a few steps further: by introducing an inclusive cast of characters, and by bringing together Haitian Voodoo, ancient Mayan mythology, cosmology, and even a South Pacific cargo cult. If you're looking for a cop story with a heavy dose of the supernatural, *Firewalk* is the book for you."—*Matthew Sturges*, author of *Midwinter* and *The Office of Shadow*

"*Firewalk* is X-Files for grownups: weird doings in Lovecraftian caverns, Mayan mythology coming to life, and more. A spine-tingling treat from a consummate pro."
—*Dennis O'Flaherty*, author of *The Calorium Wars*

"Chris Roberson is always surprising you because you thought you knew where he was going and what he was going to do, but his plots are always a bit deeper than you thought, the knife a bit sharper. In *Firewalk*, he twists that knife like a drill."
—*Paul Tobin*, author of *Prepare To Die!*

"A scorching thriller that expertly blends horror, science fiction, and urban fantasy, *Firewalk* is an excellent launch to what promises to be a spellbinding series."
—*Richard Cox*, author of *The Boys of Summer*

FIREWALKERS

ALSO BY CHRIS ROBERSON

NOVELS

BONAVENTURE-CARMODY
Here, There & Everywhere
Paragaea: A Planetary
Romance
Set the Seas of Fire
End of the Century
Book of Secrets

CELESTIAL EMPIRE
The Dragon's Nine Sons
Three Unbroken
Iron Jaw and Hummingbird

Further: Beyond the Threshold

COMICS

Cinderella: From Fabletown
With Love
Cinderella: Fables Are Forever
with Shawn McManus

iZombie
with Michael Allred

Memorial
with Rich Ellis

The Mysterious Strangers
with Scott Kowalchuk

Sovereign
with Paul Maybury

EDISON REX
with Dennis Culver

Hellboy and the BPRD
with Mike Mignola and
various

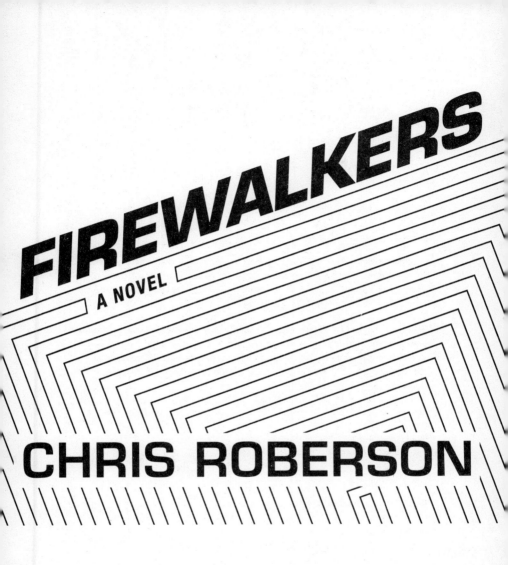

FIREWALKERS

A NOVEL

CHRIS ROBERSON

NIGHT SHADE BOOKS
NEW YORK

Night Shade books may be purchased in bulk at special discounts for sales promotion, corporate gifts, fund-raising, or educational purposes. Special editions can also be created to specifications. For details, contact the Special Sales Department, Night Shade Books, 307 West 36th Street, 11th Floor, New York, NY 10018 or info@skyhorsepublishing.com.

Night Shade Books™ is a trademark of Skyhorse Publishing, Inc.®, a Delaware corporation.

Visit our website at www.nightshadebooks.com.

10 9 8 7 6 5 4 3 2 1

Library of Congress Cataloging-in-Publication Data

Names: Roberson, Chris, author.
Title: Firewalkers : a Recondito novel / Chris Roberson.
Description: New York : Night Shade Books, [2018]
Identifiers: LCCN 2017052763 | ISBN 9781597809122 (softcover : acid-free paper)
Subjects: LCSH: Government investigators--Fiction. | Police--California--Fiction. | Paranormal fiction. | GSAFD: Fantasy fiction.
Classification: LCC PS3618.O31527 F58 2018 | DDC 813/.6--dc23
LC record available at https://lccn.loc.gov/2017052763

Cover design by Claudia Noble

Printed in the United States of America

PROLOGUE

The young woman was Mexican, and from her dress I took her to be a housekeeper, likely returning from a day's work cleaning one of the miniature mansions that lined the avenues of Northside. She was sprawled on the pavement, one shoe off, arms raised to shield her face. Two men stood over her, Caucasians in dungarees, workshirts, and heavy boots. The older of the two had the faded blue of old tattoos shadowing his forearms, suggesting a previous career in the merchant marines, while the younger had the seedy look of a garden-variety hoodlum. With hands clenched in fists and teeth bared, it was unclear whether they wanted to beat the poor girl or take advantage of her-likely both, and in that order.

The hoodlum reached down and grabbed the woman's arm roughly, and as he attempted to yank her to her feet she looked up and her gaze fell on me. Or rather, her gaze fell on the mask, which in the shadows she might have taken to be a disembodied silver skull

floating in the darkness. Already terrified by her
attackers, the woman's eyes widened on seeing me, and
her shouts for help fell into a hushed, awestruck
silence.

The prevention of crime, even acts of violence, is
not the Wraith's primary mission, nor did the situation seem at first glance to have any bearing on my
quest for vengeance, but still I couldn't stand idly
by and see an innocent imperiled. But even before
springing into action my Sight caught a glimpse of
the tendril which rose from the shoulders of the
tattooed man, disappearing in an unseen direction.
No mere sailor down on his luck, the tattooed man
was possessed, being "ridden" by an intelligence from
beyond space and time. And protecting the people of
Recondito from such incursions *is* the mission of the
Wraith-and if the Ridden was in league with those
whom I suspected, vengeance might be served, as well.

"Unhand her," I said, stepping out of the shadows
and into view. I Sent as I spoke, the reverberation
of thought and sound having a disorienting effect on
the listener that I often used to my advantage. *"Or
answer to me."*

The two men turned, and while the hoodlum snarled
at my interruption, there glinted in the eyes of the
Ridden a dark glimmer of recognition.

The possessed, or Ridden, can be deterred by running water and by fire, both of which tend to dis-
orient them, but neither is capable of stopping them
altogether. Even killing the Ridden's body is not a
permanent solution, since the Otherworldly parasite
will continue to move and operate the body even in
death. The only way to put down one of the Ridden

is to introduce pure silver into the body, by bullet or by blade, which serves to sever the connection between the parasite and host.

That's where my twin Colts come in.

The hoodlum released his hold on the woman's arm, letting her slump back onto the pavement, as the Ridden turned to face me, his eyes darting to the silver-plated .45s in my fists. I wondered whether the hoodlum knew that his companion was more than he seemed to the naked eye.

Typically the Ridden I encounter in Recondito are lackeys of the Guildhall, working as muscle for a political machine whose methods and reach would have eclipsed Tammany Hall in its heyday; the demon parasites from beyond are offered the chance to experience the sensual joys of reality in exchange for their services, while the hosts are most often thugs-for-hire who have disappointed their employers once too often. That one of the two attackers was Ridden suggested strongly that these two were Guildhall bruisers enjoying a night away from roughing up the machine's political enemies.

"Now step away," I ordered, aiming a pistol at each of them.

After I recovered Cager's body from the jungle, I took his Colt M1911 and my own and plated them with silver from the daykeeper's secret mine, and cast silver bullets to match. I usually carry a pistol in either hand, but make it a habit never to fire more than one at a time. Despite what the pulp magazines would have readers believe, no one can hit the broadside of a barn firing two guns at once. The first time I tried it, honing my skills in the forest above

Xibalba, the recoil drove the pistol in my left hand crashing into the one in my right, with my thumb caught in-between, the skin scraped off like cheese through a grater. And though the gloves I wear as the Wraith would save me from another such injury, I've found that the second Colt is much more useful as a ward against attack-the silver serving to keep any Ridden from venturing too close-and then ready with a full magazine to fire if the seven rounds in the other pistol run out before the job is done.

The silver of the Colt in my right hand was enough to make the Ridden think twice about rushing me, while the bullets in the Colt in my left were sufficient to give the hoodlum pause-I wouldn't fire on a man who wasn't possessed unless it was absolutely necessary, but it was clear that *he* didn't know that.

"Por favor . . ." the woman said in pleading tones, scuttling back across the pavement from me, seeming as frightened of the Wraith's silver mask as she'd been of her two attackers' fists only moments before. *"Ayuda me . . ."* I knew it wasn't me she was asking for help. But then, who? The shadows?

I intended to end the suffering of the Ridden's host-body, a single silver bullet driving the parasite back to its home beyond the sky, and to chase the hoodlum into the night with enough fear instilled in him that he wouldn't soon menace another girl walking alone by night.

"Now," I said and Sent, gesturing toward the hoodlum with the Colt in my left hand, *"one of you I shall send back to your Guildhall masters with a message . . ."*

The hoodlum began to turn away, shifting his weight as he prepared to take to his heels and flee.

I smiled behind my mask, raising the pistol in my right hand and training it between the eyes of the Ridden. "*. . . and the other shall be that message . . .*"

CHAPTER ONE

Izzie sat bolt upright, gasping for breath, her heart pounding in her chest. She looked down at her hands and had to stare at them for long seconds to assure herself that they were whole and unmarked, and hadn't been eaten away to nothing. She could still feel a sensation of emptiness, of the darkness pressing in . . .

She swung her feet to the floor and sat on the edge of the couch, elbows on her knees and her head in her hands. Everything that had happened in the last twenty-four hours came rushing back to her all at once. They had spent the night in the abandoned lighthouse, after finding the bodies in the subbasement of a warehouse, with rubber tubes snaking from shunts buried in their spines; bodies that were neither fully alive nor entirely dead. She remembered the unearthly smell and the feeling of disorientation in that dimly lit room. And the horror and revulsion that she'd experienced when the neither-dead-nor-alive bodies climbed with jerky, inhuman motions to their feet and began to shamble toward her.

The night before, Izzy hadn't had the chance to question the reality of what was happening. But now, in the stark, cold light of day, she had to ask herself—had all of that really happened? Were they really facing hordes of people whose minds had been destroyed while their bodies were being taken over by intelligences from another world? From another dimension? The mere fact that she knew how crazy that sounded didn't discount the possibility that it *was* crazy. Not when the simpler answer would be that *she* was the crazy one. Not when it was easier to accept that she had dissociated from reality and fabricated the whole thing, rather than believe that everything that she and Patrick Tevake had uncovered over the last few days was really true.

"Come on, girl," she said out loud to herself, "get it together."

"Izzie?" came a voice from the open doorway across the room.

From the other room she could hear sizzling and the clatter of pots and pans. She lowered her hands and lifted her head, sniffing the air. It smelled tantalizingly of bacon, and her stomach rumbled in response. If this was a delusion, it smelled delicious.

"Was that you talking just now?" Patrick stuck his head around the corner. He was wearing a grey t-shirt with *Recondito Police Athletic League* printed on the front, and a dishtowel draped over one shoulder. "Oh good, you're awake."

"I guess I am." Izzie shrugged. "Mostly."

Patrick smiled, looking relieved. "I was a little worried. You were thrashing around pretty bad just a minute ago."

"Yeah?" Izzie reached up and rubbed the inside corners of her eyes with her finger tips. Judging by the angle of the light shining through the window, she knew that she couldn't have slept for more than an hour or so, and if anything felt more tired than when she'd lain down.

"Bad dream?"

She nodded.

"Not surprised. Rough night." He pulled the towel off his shoulder and used it to dry his hands. "Well, breakfast will be ready by the time Joyce and Daphne get done with their showers, so just hang tight."

"Copy that," she answered as Patrick went back through into the kitchen. She sighed, and ran a hand through her braids, which were still damp from the quick shower she'd taken before lying down. They were getting so fuzzy that she was half-tempted to cut the whole mess off, rather than go on messing with them. But she had other things to worry about. "Rough night, he says. . . ."

Her feet were cold against the hardwood floor, and so she pulled on her socks and stomped into her boots before getting up and going in search of her phone.

Calling what they'd all just been through a "rough night" was like saying that World War II was a "minor disagreement." That the four of them had lived to see the sun rise again was just a little short of a miracle. Not that the nights ahead promised to be much better.

But they had survived. Of course, Officer Carlson hadn't been so lucky.

Izzie found her phone in the pocket of her jacket, hanging on a hook near the front door along with her FBI credentials and holstered firearm. But before she turned the phone on to check her messages, she had second thoughts. Whatever was waiting for her, whatever texts or emails or missed calls, could wait until after she had some coffee and food in her, in that order. Then, as her stomach growled audibly, she realized that she hadn't eaten since lunch the day before, so maybe food *before* coffee.

She slipped the phone into the pocket of her jeans, and turned to glance around the room. She wasn't quite sure what she had expected Patrick's place to look like, but this? This wasn't it.

There was an electric bass guitar in one corner on a stand, beside a small portable amplifier, a boombox, and a turntable sitting on top a shelving unit filled with vinyl LPs. Stacks of old comics and magazines were piled atop a bookcase crammed with paperback and hardcover books. On the mantle above the fireplace were dozens of Pez dispensers arranged in careful rows, and on either side hung movie posters framed behind glass, mostly action films from the eighties and nineties. Opposite the fireplace, in a place of prominence, hung what appeared to be a hand-woven tapestry with a tessellated geometric design. Below the tapestry, on a narrow table of lacquered wood, was a small collection of framed photos, including one showing an old Polynesian man in denim overalls, standing next to a small boy wearing a Power Rangers t-shirt and sporting a gap-toothed grin. Other than the couch there was a low table and a couple of chairs, but no TV or computer to be seen, and while the furniture seemed a little threadbare and old, it was in good repair.

They had been trying to get here the night before, until the road was blocked and they were forced to find another refuge. Making it to the Ivory Point lighthouse had been a lucky break in more ways than one, but still Izzie wished that they had made it to Patrick's place the night before. This would have been a much more comfortable spot to ride out a terrifying night than the cold, dusty living quarters attached to the lighthouse.

The shambling horde that had stood vigil on the boardwalk across from the lighthouse had fled with the sunrise, thankfully before the tide rolled out and the muddy land bridge once more connected the white rocks of Ivory Point with the shore.

It had been Patrick who suggested that they come home with him to get cleaned up and get something to eat before tackling everything that lay ahead of them. Daphne had driven them over in her bureau car, which had survived the night without so much as a scratch, and Patrick had given directions from the backseat. From the passenger side window Izzie could see the spiraling whorls of the engraved markings that Patrick had shown her when he had described how his great-uncle had carved swirls into the houses in the neighborhood

Patrick's house was a two-story Victorian row house, with a living room, bedroom, bathroom, and kitchen on the first floor, and on the second floor another bedroom, sitting room, and a second bath. But when Izzie had gone to use the upstairs shower the second floor turned out to be mostly filled with junk—old furniture, moving boxes, stacks of yellowing papers, battered musical instruments, and broken toys. The shower in the upstairs bath was functional, but the bathroom itself didn't look like it had been used in ages.

Considering how fastidious and organized the first floor was, Izzie had been surprised by the chaotic clutter upstairs, and had meant to ask Patrick about it when she came back downstairs. But he was on the radio when she walked in, probably checking in with the duty officer back at the 10th Precinct Station House, so she decided to lay down and close her eyes for a minute while she waited for him to finish up, and then . . .

She shook her head, trying to knock loose the memory of the nightmare she'd just had.

Her stomach growled again, and she turned and made for the kitchen.

"Is there any . . . ?" she began as she stepped through the doorway, to find Patrick reaching over and picking up a steaming mug from the counter and holding it out to her. "Coffee," she finished with a sigh as she took the mug in both hands.

She took her first sip, eyes closed.

"Cream and two sugars, right?" Patrick flashed a faint smile as he turned his attention back to the stove. "See, I remember things."

"Close enough." Izzie lowered the mug slowly from her lips. "I usually use the no-calorie sweetener stuff these days, but you won't hear me complaining."

Patrick was carefully folding an omelet in the skillet with a spatula. "I haven't had a chance to get to the market this week. . . . You know, with all of this mess going on. . . . So I had to make do with what I had."

"What, the impending apocalypse is interfering with your grocery shopping?" Izzie went to stand beside him, taking a deep breath in through her nose. "Well, it smells fantastic. Like I said, you won't hear me complaining."

She took another sip of the coffee, as a brief pause stretched out between them. Then she put the mug down on the counter and straightened up.

"You don't think we're crazy, right?"

Patrick looked over in her direction, quirking an eyebrow. "Excuse me?"

"This . . ." Izzie took a ragged breath. "This is all really happening, right?"

Patrick put the spatula down next to the stove top, and then turned to face her. "What, you think we're just imagining all of this? Like, this is one big hallucination that we are all sharing?"

"Maybe," Izzie said half-heartedly. She looked at the floor for a moment, then back up at him from under her eyebrows. "Or maybe *I'm* the one imagining all of it, and none of the rest of you are really here?"

Patrick's face cycled through a number of expressions quickly—the first hints of a smile, interrupted by a sudden shadow of doubt, and finally coming to rest on a look of resigned concern.

"Look," he said, reaching out and resting a hand on her shoulder. "You're exhausted, sleep deprived, and strung out. So I get why that would make sense to you right now. But I *promise* you that this is really happening. As much as it would be nice to think that we could just, I don't know, wake up and all of this wouldn't be real, we don't get that choice." He sighed heavily. "Those things really are out there, and we have to deal with it."

"Do I smell coffee?" said a voice from behind Izzie.

She turned to see Daphne standing in the open doorway, drying off her short blonde hair with a towel. Seeing her there, a smile spread across Izzie's face, as she remembered the hours that they had spent together earlier that morning, waiting for the sun to rise. Their personal rules about getting romantically involved with fellow FBI agents were completely forgotten, as they sought what comfort they could in the warmth of each other's embrace, sharing their most intimate secrets.

At least there was *one* thing about last night that Izzie was glad to know hadn't been a delusion. . . .

CHAPTER TWO

Patrick dug around in the cabinet until he came up with a couple of additional coffee mugs. He rarely had company over these days, and seldom had need for more than one mug at a time, and so he usually used the same insulated plastic travel mug every day. The ceramic coffee mug that he'd given Izzie was the only other one in regular use, most often used if he wanted hot tea later in the day. So the only options he had on hand to offer Daphne Richardson were two mugs that were normally buried way in the back of the cabinet.

"You've got two choices," he said a little sheepishly, turning back from the cabinet and holding a mug in either hand out to Daphne. On one was printed a blue Smurf holding a flower with the caption "Have a Smurfy Day," that had probably belonged to one of his older cousins when they were kids, and on the other was printed *SO MANY MEN, SO FEW CAN AFFORD ME.* He watched as Daphne read the text on the second one and then looked back at him, raising an eyebrow. He shrugged, and explained, "It was my mom's."

Daphne grinned, and opted for the Smurf. "I've got a Snoopy mug in my apartment," she said, as she walked over to where the coffee pot sat on the counter. "It's got a bonsai tree growing in it, though."

"I guess Joyce can use *that* one." Izzie nodded toward the other mug, and then leered suggestively at him. "If you think you can handle it."

Patrick rolled his eyes, and, picking up the spatula, turned back to the stove. "This should be done in just a few minutes. Eggs are okay for everyone, I hope?"

He glanced back over his shoulder when no one answered, and saw that the two women had drifted off to the far side of the kitchen, huddled close and talking in low voices as they sipped their coffees.

"I'll take that as a yes," he said, returning his attention to the omelets.

Izzie had told him in the car the other day that she might be interested in someone, romantically. Patrick hadn't suspected at the time that she was talking about another FBI agent, much less another woman. No wonder Izzie had accused him of having a blind spot where romantic matters were concerned.

Through the thin walls he could hear the sound of the sink running in the downstairs bathroom, and knew that Joyce must be almost finished up after her shower.

Speaking of blind spots . . .

Izzie had been giving Patrick a hard time for days about being oblivious to the fact that the city medical examiner was obviously interested in him—and that he was clearly interested in her, too. Patrick had objected, and insisted all along that she was imagining things. Then the night before, in the small hours of the night, he had found himself huddling for warmth under a dusty quilt with Joyce, and it turned out that what was between them was more than just a mild infatuation.

Patrick hadn't devoted much attention to maintaining a social life the last few years, much less romance. Ever since he transferred from Homicide to Vice he'd been keeping different hours, with more time spent on late night stake outs or under-cover operations. What little free time he had left over was usually taken up with volunteering at his old middle school, where he taught the neighborhood kids the Te'Maroan traditions that he had learned from the older islanders when he was young. Seeing the kids play a game of konare or learning the move-ments involved in Te'Maroan stick fighting always made Patrick feel like he was passing on something special that had been entrusted to him. There were times when he wondered what it would be like to have a serious relationship and kids of his own, but things just never seemed to come together for him. He'd dated in the past, but in the end the work always got in the way.

But now? In the midst of all of this strangeness, to find that he might have a chance with a woman as smart, funny, and beautiful as Joyce Nguyen?

Of course, that was assuming that they both survived the mess that they found themselves in.

Patrick cracked open the last of the eggs and poured it into the hot skillet. It had been a while since he cooked for so many people, and in fact most of the meals that he made were single servings. But when he was little, his mother would cook enough for a small army over this same stove, as aunts and uncles, cousins and siblings from all over the neighborhood crammed into the house for Sunday dinners. His great-uncle Alf had spent the last few years of his life living upstairs, until he died suddenly of a heart attack on the street when Patrick was just twelve years old.

Patrick always felt a little guilty that after the old man had died he'd quickly come to dismiss everything Uncle Alf had taught him as silly superstitions. By the time he was in high school, Patrick had decided that the real world didn't work that way, and that the old folks were just fooling themselves.

But now, after the last few days that he and Izzie had spent investigating the connection between Ink and the Fuller murders, Patrick had no choice but to accept that there was some truth to those old beliefs, after all.

At the moment, it appeared that Patrick and his friends were the only ones in a position to recognize the Preternatural forces that seemed to be engulfing Recondito.

"Something smells good."

Patrick turned to see Joyce standing in the open doorway, leaning on her cane. She was wearing one of Patrick's old t-shirts and a pair of sweat pants, having asked if she could run her own clothes through the washer and drier before putting them back on. Her hair, normally worn in a precisely sculpted asymmetrical undercut, was combed back straight from her forehead and tucked behind her ears.

"Hey, you," Patrick said, as Joyce walked across the floor toward him, her cane *tonk*ing on the hardwood underfoot.

"Well, my boots are *ruined*." She frowned, shaking her head ruefully. "I loved those damned things, too."

Patrick grimaced in sympathy. When they had been forced to wade across the rising waters to reach Ivory Point the night before, Joyce's boots with their elaborate buckles and straps had been a necessary sacrifice.

"It's okay, though," Joyce added with a sly grin. "It's the perfect excuse to waste a bunch of money on a brand-new pair that I'll love even more."

"Breakfast is almost ready." Patrick slid an omelet from the skillet onto a plate, and nodded toward the coffee pot. "There's coffee if you want some."

Joyce headed for the counter, pulling her phone out of the pocket of her sweatpants and checking her messages. "Got an update from security at the Hall of Justice, about the bodies missing from the morgue. They're reporting it as a break in."

"So they think that someone broke in and *stole* the bodies?" Patrick arched an eyebrow.

"That's an easier explanation than what *really* happened, isn't it?" Joyce picked up the mug on the counter and read the words printed on it before glancing sidelong at Patrick. "How many men *can* afford you, huh?"

Patrick rolled his eyes. "Just pour the coffee and help me get these plates to the table, okay?"

CHAPTER THREE

They ate in silence, and for a long while the only sound in the room was the clatter of knives and forks on plates as they made short work of the meal that Patrick had prepared. Izzie sat on one side of the table with Daphne, while Joyce sat across from them, next to Patrick, making it feel like some kind of surreal double date, but since they'd started eating no one had really spoken. It was as if they all welcomed the chance to take a break, however small, from the overwhelming strangeness that they were facing. Or maybe, Izzie thought, none of them knew exactly what to say.

When they were all on their second cups of coffee, it was Daphne who finally broke the silence.

"Okay, look," she said, dropping her fork so that it clattered onto her empty plate, "I'm just going to say it. Maybe I'm the only one, but I'm still pretty freaked out about all of this. You all seem pretty okay with dead bodies wandering around and invaders from another dimension or whatever, but if you ask me . . . this is crazy, right?"

Izzie and Patrick exchanged a look.

"Believe me," Izzie said, turning back to Daphne and laying a hand on her knee, "you're not the only one having a hard time with this."

Daphne let out a ragged sigh. "Well, at least the FBI's Resident Agency is closed on Saturdays and Sundays, so we've got a little time to work out how we're going to spin this with Agent Gutierrez." Seeing Izzie's frown, she hurried to add, "Look, I told you that I'd help keep the Bureau off your backs while you try to figure this out, but he knows that we both went down to assist with a Recondito PD investigation last night, so we have to give him *something*."

Izzie tried not to scowl as she took another sip from her coffee mug. Her experiences with Gutierrez were limited, but the Senior Resident Agent struck her as the type who wouldn't likely be satisfied with anything other than an airtight story. He was already bristling that she'd come to town in the first place, for fear that her investigations might reopen the books on a murder case that the local authorities would very much prefer remain closed.

"We'll figure it out," Izzie answered brusquely, then turned to face Patrick. "You were on the radio with the station house earlier, right? Where do things stand with the Recondito PD?"

"Things aren't great." Patrick shook his head, a morose expression on his face. "Chavez sent a couple of uniforms down into that warehouse subbasement after I didn't check back in, and they found what was left of Officer Carlson. Everyone knows that a police officer was murdered in the line of duty last night, though the department has been able to keep the exact details away from the press, so far."

"The EMTs have already delivered his remains to the city morgue," Joyce said, talking around a mouthful of bacon. She held one finger up, wiped her mouth with a napkin, and then pulled out her cell phone. She thumbed it on and opened up her text messages, displaying an automated notification sent to her at the medical examiner's office. "The request for an autopsy came through the system this morning."

As Joyce reached for another piece of bacon, she caught the glance that passed between Patrick and Izzie.

"You're worried about what I'm going to say, aren't you?" Joyce said. She narrowed her eyes, glaring at Patrick.

He gave her a pleading look. "You *know* that the authorities aren't prepared to deal with this, Joyce. Not yet."

"So, what, you want me to just make something up? Look, I'm the city medical examiner, damn it. I'm not going to falsify an official report and *lie* about the cause of death. I don't care *what* kind of weirdness is going on." She took a bite of bacon and crunched angrily on it for a moment, fuming. Then she sighed, calming visibly. "But I can, I don't know, be a little *vague* in the way that I record the details, and go with a watered-down version of the truth. Something that frames the results so that they're less likely to raise any red flags about what happened down there until we know what we're doing."

"Thanks, Joyce," Izzie said. "We'll have enough trouble explaining away the rest of what they found down there."

"Well, that's just it," Patrick said, chewing the inside of his cheek. "They might have found Carlson, but what they *didn't* find was anything else. No other bodies, none of that equipment that we found, none of the Ink supplies . . . nothing. It was all gone by the time they got there."

The fact that the half-dozen *bodies* they had seen the night before were gone didn't come as much of a surprise. After all, they had gotten up off the tables and chased Izzie and the others out of the building, and then joined the horde that pursued them all the way to the Ivory Point lighthouse. But the missing medical equipment was another matter entirely. Someone with resources was covering up their tracks.

"So what's the official story on what happened?" Daphne asked. "What did you tell them?"

"It's like she said." Patrick indicated Joyce with a quick nod of his head. "A watered-down version of the truth, basically. I told the duty officer that Carlson and I found what appeared to be an Ink lab down there, and that in the course of our investigation we were attacked by unknown individuals. After Carlson was down, I engaged in a high-speed pursuit, and was unable to radio for backup due to technical malfunctions."

All of which was essentially true, leaving aside the fact Patrick and the others were the ones being pursued. And the minor detail that the "unknown individuals" pursuing them were half-dead drug users who had been taken over by an entity from another universe.

"I've got to go to the station house and submit a full after-action report today," Patrick went on. "The captain will write me up for not filing it sooner, I'm sure, but otherwise it doesn't sound like they doubt my story."

"What about all of those people on the street? The . . ." Daphne looked from Patrick to Izzie. "What did you call them, again? The Riders?"

"The Ridden," Izzie answered. She thought of the horde of men and women who had pursued them through the streets, their skin almost completely covered by the black blots associated with long-term use of the street drug Ink. Men and women whose minds had been eaten away, both figuratively and literally, leaving them little more than puppets being controlled by an intelligence from a higher dimension that Izzie had dubbed the *loa* the night before.

The loa that, to all indications, was either controlling or being controlled by Martin Zotovic, self-made millionaire and founder of the software company Parasol.

Patrick shook his head. "Not a word. Nothing about the bus driver, either."

Izzie rubbed her chin, thoughtfully. "Aside from those kids who were tagging that wall on the boardwalk and that homeless guy, I don't remember seeing any other civilians out on the street. And they ran off before the Ridden got there. So maybe no one else saw them?" Even as she said it, Izzie knew she didn't really believe it.

"Yeah." Patrick had a skeptical look on his face. "Or maybe someone saw it but *couldn't* tell anybody about it, or call for help. No cell service, remember?"

"That broadcast van on the boardwalk was probably blocking our phones, right?" Izzie glanced around the table. "Who knows how big of a radius that thing covered."

"It was probably a stingray," Daphne said, almost like an afterthought. "Sorry, I was still trying to process all of this last night in the lighthouse and didn't think to mention it."

"Damn!" Patrick slapped a hand to his forehead. "I should have thought of that."

"Don't beat yourself up," Izzie said. "I've used the damn things on investigations before, and I was too distracted to think of it."

"Um, hello?" Joyce held up a hand, looking like the only one not in on the joke. "What the hell is a stingray?"

"It's a cell site simulator." Daphne explained. "It mimics a cell phone tower's signal, in other words. They're used to track cellular devices, or intercept signals, or even just to boost cell signals. But they can also be used for jamming. The stingray broadcasts a stronger signal than any of the legitimate cell phone towers in the area, forcing all of the compatible devices in range to connect to it, instead. But if the stingray isn't set to passively transmit that data on to the network, then any of the connected devices are basically useless. You've got full bars, but no real signal."

"Recondito PD has one," Patrick said. "We used to bring it out on stakeouts to scan the cell phones of suspects we were monitoring, pulling their call logs and text messages without them ever knowing about it. But there were a whole rash of lawsuits in the courts, with people suing the city and arguing that it was an invasion of privacy, or overreach. That kind of thing. It was a mess."

"Wait." Joyce sat up straighter. "So that thing wasn't just blocking our phones, but it could have been *scanning* them, too?"

"Could be." Izzie frowned. "There's no way of knowing for sure."

Joyce crossed her arms over her chest, scowling.

"Okay, let's think this through," Patrick said, leaning back in his chair and rubbing his temples with his fingertips. "Those . . . those 'Ridden' guys came down to the warehouse because they knew we were there."

"They knew because the loa knew." Daphne glanced around the table, and then turned to Izzie. "That's what you called it, right?"

Izzie nodded. "Don't ask me *how* it knew, though. Those people were barely alive when we got there."

"Well," Joyce said, "what we've been calling Ink is just part of this higher dimensional . . . whatever, if your theory is correct. And the Ink appears to highjack the host's nervous system, which is how it's able to direct their movements. So it obviously would have access to their senses, as well. So even if the hosts were dormant . . . like those six bodies we found in the basement . . . the Ink in their brains would still be receiving any incoming sensory data."

"You're all missing my point," Patrick interrupted, an impatient edge to his voice. He stood up from the table and began to pace across the floor. "The Ridden knew we were there last night. More importantly, Martin Zotovic and his people had to have known we were there, too. He had to have been the one to send the broadcast van to block our radios and phones. So we can't dismiss the possibility that he knows *who* we are, too. Hell, he could be tracking us right now."

Izzie couldn't help but steal a glance down the hallway at the front door, as though a horde of shambling Ridden might burst through at that very moment.

"Crap," Joyce said softly, looking down at the phone in her hand like it had suddenly turned into a poisonous snake. Then she suddenly set it down on the table at arm's length before hurriedly leaning back away from it.

"But these Ridden guys, they can't go out in the daylight," Daphne said. "So even if they did know where we are right now, they wouldn't be able to come after us."

"Yes and no," Izzie answered. "Malcolm Price had enough Ink in his system to turn Ridden after he jumped out a third story window, but before that he was walking around in the daylight without any trouble at all. So I'm not sure how that works."

"I have a theory about that." Joyce pushed back from the table, perhaps to put even more distance between herself and her phone. "You described how Price's skin changed after he got back up from the pavement. How quickly the blots spread."

Izzie nodded. She could still remember the way that the inky blots had bloomed across his skin from one instant to the next, until he looked like a walking shadow, staggering toward her with murderous intent.

"And the blots on those six bodies in the warehouse *moved* in response to external stimulus," Joyce went on. "They aren't bruises or blemishes. I think that the blots are *Ink*, the substance itself. We assumed that the Ink was somehow being manufactured in the hosts' bodies, and extracted from their brains and spinal columns by those hoses and pumps. And that fits the available evidence. But if the blots *are* Ink, then where did it go when Malcolm Price died? There was no trace of it when I examined him postmortem. More Ink *appears* in the host's system over time, but I don't think it's being *produced* there. I think it's arriving in their bodies from somewhere else."

"From ana to kata," Izzie muttered. Seeing Daphne's confused glance, she explained. "Two terms that keep cropping up in the weirdest places. A nineteenth century mathematician made them up, or borrowed them from the Greek or something, to describe movement in the fourth dimension. North and south, east and west, up and down, ana and kata."

"I was thinking in terms of 'in' and 'out,'" Joyce said, nodding, "but the terminology doesn't really matter. The important thing is, I think that the place the Ink is coming *from* as it appears in the hosts' body is the same place it *goes* when the host body is killed. When you described it as 'tentacles,' Izzie, I think you were pretty close to the mark. The Ink is still connected to the main body, wherever that is, through the fourth dimension, and it pushes more of itself *into* the body, consuming more and more of the host's grey matter as it does, and it can pull itself back *out* of the body, as well, leaving vacuoles behind. We know that the more pronounced side-effects of Ink use, like photophobia, only show up after prolonged usage. But maybe that's just because there's more of the stuff in their system. It could be that it's the Ink that's reacting to the light, not the host."

Izzie scratched the back of her neck, thinking it through. "So, what...? Maybe the loa can draw enough of itself out of the Ridden that those side-effects go away? At least temporarily?"

Patrick was leaning against the wall, arms crossed, a skeptical expression on his face. "Doubtful. It's chewing up their *brains*, right? That's where it starts. Would there even be enough up there left to operate if the Ink was gone?" He turned to Joyce. "What was it you said the other day about the effects of that much of the brain being missing? Their personality would be gone, and even if they were moving around, from a medical standpoint it wouldn't be *them* calling the shots? Isn't that how Ink works?"

Joyce held up one hand, palm toward the ground, and wiggled it back and forth in a "yes and no" gesture.

"Sure, that was the case with Malcolm Price," she answered, "which was in line with the pattern of brain damage that we found in Nicholas Fuller's victims five years ago. In all of those cases, the majority of the vacuoles were located in the frontal lobe, and yeah, with that much grey matter missing, they would have been incapable of independent thought or moving on their own volition. The car might have been driving, in other words, but they weren't the ones behind the wheel anymore. But the brains of the other Ink users that I've examined didn't display that same pattern. In each of those cases, the vacuoles were more evenly distributed throughout the entire brain. So they would still have been capable of some level of independent thought and agency, but it would have been impaired to one degree or another."

"Maybe it just affects different people in different ways," Daphne put in.

"Or maybe we're looking at two separate things," Izzie suggested. "What if the reason that we saw different kinds of damage in the brains of Nicholas Fuller's victims was because the Ink was doing something *different* to them? The damage is more precise, maybe even surgical, because it needed to control them without causing all of those other side effects. Fuller claimed that his victims showed signs of personality loss, so there's that, but none of them had black marks on their skin or had a problem walking around in broad daylight. Maybe it was using Malcolm Price the same way, until he threw himself out a window and ended up basically as good as dead anyway. So that was the point where enough Ink was pushed down into his system to cause the blots to appear on his skin."

"So let's assume for the moment that it's a one way street," Patrick said. "Once someone is totally taken over, and the blots are on their skin, then they can't go out in daylight. But until that point, sunlight isn't a problem."

"So, if they know where we are right now," Daphne asked, "what's stopping them from coming after us? There's got to be some of them that aren't that far gone, right?"

"Well, we know that there are other ways of stopping the Ridden, short of sunlight," Izzie pointed out. "They can't cross running water, we saw that last night. Loud, discordant noise or music confuses their senses. They are repelled by salt and other crystals, or can't come into close contact with crystals, or something like that. And silver disrupts their connection with the loa, somehow. At least, that's what Robert Aguilar wrote in his journals. So maybe some of those side-effects apply to the Ridden like Fuller's victims and Price, who are under the Ink's control but aren't completely far gone yet."

"Uncle Alf's marks." Patrick turned to Izzie. "Remember?" Izzie nodded slowly.

"Uncle who's whats?" Joyce raised an eyebrow.

"Symbols of protection that my great-uncle carved into Te'Maroan houses all over this part of Oceanview," Patrick explained. "I noticed that there hadn't been any reported cases of Ink-related crimes in this part of the neighborhood. No Ink deals, no users, nothing. People from these blocks were using the stuff, but only in other parts of town, and once they started using they never came back home again."

"Then we found a map of the city in Fuller's effects," Izzie added. "And he had put these little spiral marks all over the southwest corner of Oceanview, and another similar mark over the Ivory Point lighthouse."

"Where the Ridden can't go," Daphne said.

"Exactly," Patrick answered. "Uncle Alf always told me that the marks were there to prevent evil influences from entering a house. To keep away things that lived in the shadows. Looping spirals carved into the pavement, or the brick, or even wood, and filled with a paint that was mixed with sea salt." He gestured over his shoulder toward the rear of the house. "There's one on the back of this place, and on at least a third of all the houses in a six-block radius from here."

"So maybe they haven't come after us because they *can't* come after us." Joyce glanced again at her phone, as though it had betrayed her. "Not here, anyway."

"That's why we were trying to get here last night," Patrick went on. "But then when we were cut off by that bus that the Ridden had stopped in the street . . ."

"The lighthouse was the only other option," Izzie finished for him.

"But Ivory Point is only safe at high tide, I'm guessing," Patrick said. "That's when Fuller committed all of his murders, so far as we were able to work out. Presumably so that the other possessed individuals couldn't come and interfere."

Daphne was thoughtful for a moment, a worried look on her face.

"So are we going to be okay going back to the Resident Agency? Or even back home, for that matter?" She finally said, looking around the room at the others. "My apartment is on the other side of Hyde Park, and there's no magic markings on *my* building, so far as I know. If they know who we are, couldn't they be waiting for us?"

"Maybe there's a way to make something portable that would serve the same purpose." Izzie frowned, rubbing her chin. "My grandmother never left the house without her mojo hand, a gris-gris bag that she made to protect herself against evil. Could be we need something like that to keep us safe, only using the stuff that we know is effective against the

Ridden instead of the camphor and roots and bits of bones that Mawmaw Jean used."

"I've got tons of sea salt, and we can probably do something with my mom's wedding silverware, or maybe some of her old jewelry." Patrick glanced over at the pantry and the cabinets. "It's worth a shot, anyway."

"I'll see what I can do." Izzie nodded.

Daphne was thoughtful. "I wish there was a way to know who was Ridden and who wasn't, short of them going all blotchy and mindless. Would help to defend against them if we could see them coming."

"Well," Izzie rubbed her jaw, "there is the 'ilbal.' It was a drug that Nicholas Fuller took that supposedly helped him to see the Ridden for what they really were."

"What, you mean those vials of powder that were found at Fuller's apartment?" Patrick gave her a skeptical look. "You really think one of us should try that stuff?"

Izzie shrugged. "It might be worth a shot, is all I'm saying."

"So what's the plan?" Joyce asked. "Where do we go from here?"

"We still need to figure out what the hell they found down in that mineshaft," Izzie answered. "Was it just the stuff we're calling Ink, or was there more to it than that? What happened the other times this kind of thing cropped up, like with the Guildhall fire in the forties and the Eschaton Center murders in the seventies, and is there anything from those cases that might be useful for us to know now? Strategies, tactics, defenses, whatever. And finally, how does Martin Zotovic and Parasol fit into all of this, and just what is it they're trying to achieve?"

"And then?" Daphne looked a little dubious.

"Then we figure out how to stop them."

CHAPTER FOUR

It was past noon before Joyce's clothes were finished in the dryer, by which point Daphne and Izzie had already left together, each carrying one of the "gris-gris bags" that Izzie had assembled: Ziploc sandwich bags filled with sea salt, random bits of quartz that Patrick had found in a drawer, and a piece of silver cutlery from the silverware drawer or silver jewelry that had belonged to his mother. The idea was that, if cornered by one of the Ridden with no way out, they could use the salt to form a ring around themselves, and hope that either the quartz or the silver might be enough to keep the Ridden at bay. If nothing else, they could throw the sea salt in an attacker's face and hope for the best, or try stabbing them with a fork. Daphne and Izzie were driving back to the FBI offices to retrieve some of the things they needed, and would pick up clothes and supplies at Izzie's hotel and Daphne's apartment before returning to Patrick's house for the night. They'd all agreed that it was safest to spend the hours between sunset and sunrise in a place that they knew to be secure, at least until they could work out other forms of defense.

Patrick had finished cleaning up the kitchen, clearing away the dirty dishes and washing up the pots and pans, and then changed into something a little more appropriate for the cold weather outside, ultimately opting for flannel shirt, jeans, and hiking boots. His quilted jacket was in the dryer with Joyce's things, a little scuffed up after the evening's excitement, but still serviceable.

While he was getting dressed he heard the timer on the dryer buzzing down in the basement, and by the time he finished lacing up his hiking boots and returned to the living room, he found Joyce was already dressed in her own clothes again. She was looking at the framed photos on the table beneath the spot where he had hung the tapa cloth that his maternal grandparents had brought with them from Kensington Island back in the seventies.

"Is this you?" Joyce picked up the frame that was sitting front and center, showing a little boy standing beside an old man in overalls.

"Yeah, that's me and my great-uncle, Alf Tevake. That was taken when I was about three years old, I think? Right around the time that he moved in with us."

"He was your dad's uncle, then?"

Patrick nodded. "My dad died when I was little, and after that it was just me and Mom in the house for a while. Uncle Alf used to have his own apartment in the neighborhood, but when he got older and needed a little more help, he moved in with one of my aunts. When they had another baby on the way, he went to stay with her sister, and then a few years after that moved in with another. He spent the last years of his life moving from one relative's house to another. But he stayed the longest here with us, and this was where he lived for the rest of his life." He took the photo from Joyce and looking at it for a long moment before continuing. "I was just a baby when my dad died, and I guess Uncle Alf figured that my mom and I needed him around as much as he needed a place to stay. He helped raise me, really."

Patrick set the photo back on the table.

"He looks like a sweet old man," Joyce said, gently.

"Sometimes." Patrick smiled. "He was kind of a bastard sometimes, too. He'd never had kids of his own, and there were times when he could be hard to live with. But that's just how families work, I guess."

Joyce rolled her eyes. "Remind me to tell you about my sisters sometime. If you want to talk about 'hard to live with,' I've got you beat."

Patrick looked over and saw that Joyce had brought his quilted jacket up with the rest of the laundry, and left it neatly folded on the couch.

"Well, I guess I should be going," Joyce said, jerking her thumb toward the door. "I'm hoping that my car is still where I parked it last night. And that those Ridden jerks didn't mess with it."

"Hang on, I'll walk with you." He went over and picked up his jacket. "My car is parked over there, too. It's only a ten, fifteen minute walk from here."

He picked up the two makeshift "gris-gris bags" that Izzie had left for them, and handed one to Joyce.

"We really thinking a bag of salt, rocks, and a silver spoon is going to do anything to these guys?" She looked sidelong at it, tucked it into the pocket of her leather jacket hanging on the wall, and then picked up her boots from the floor.

"It's worth trying," Patrick answered, and shoved his own bag in the pocket of his jacket.

Joyce sat down on the edge of the couch and set the boots on the floor in front of her. They made little squelching sounds as she pulled them on, an annoyed expression on her face, and it was clear that they had dried marginally since their trudge through the tide the night before, but not enough.

"The offer to buy you another pair still stands," Patrick said, zipping up his jacket. He clipped his holstered service weapon to his belt, and shoved his Recondito PD badge on its neck chain into his jacket pocket.

"Don't sweat it, I'm just giving you a hard time." She paused, and looked down at his hiking boots. "Besides, you could probably use the money to get *yourself* a nicer pair. Those kicks are looking a little ragged."

Patrick rolled his eyes. "Come on," he said, grabbing his keyring from the hook and pulling open the front door. "Let's get going already."

"Okay," she said with a sly smile. "But if you ever need any fashion advice, I've got some ideas."

Patrick's place was near the corner of Almeria and Mission, in the southwest corner of Oceanview, and the warehouse that they'd visited the night before was in the northeast corner of Oceanview, just off of Bayfront Drive in an industrial area not far from the fish market.

Patrick had parked his car a few blocks away from the warehouse, over by the docks, and approached the rest of the way on foot. Later that night they'd left Joyce's car parked on the street when they'd fled the warehouse. So unless anyone had made off with them in the hours since, they should both still be parked within a couple of blocks of each other.

The skies overhead were grey and cloudy as they walked east along Almeria toward the intersection with Mission. The Church of the Holy Saint Anthony had evidently just finished Saturday Mass services, as there was a steady stream of cars pulling out of the metered spaces on either side of the street.

"So have you lived your whole life in that house?" Joyce asked as they waited for the walk signal, glancing back the way that they'd come. "I mean, I'm not judging you or anything, but still . . ."

"Nah." Patrick shook his head. "I moved out when I went to college, and then had my own place in the Kiev when I came back to town, a second story walkup up on Odessa Avenue. But I was down here all the time anyway, looking after my mom. When she died a few years ago, she left the place to me, and it didn't make any sense to keep paying rent on my tiny apartment across town when I could live here for free."

The light changed, and they crossed Mission heading east.

"I don't blame you," Joyce said. "And that was before the rents got so crazy too, I guess. If I hadn't bought my place when I did, well . . . I'd never be able to afford it now, the way the housing market keeps going up." She turned, and saw Patrick's inquisitive glance. "I've got a condo in City Center, just a few blocks from work. If not for needing this thing—" she shook her cane "—I probably wouldn't even have a car. But it would just take me too long to walk to work every morning, and my knee gives me enough trouble as it is." She sighed, and shook her head ruefully.

Patrick nodded, a sympathetic expression on his face. He'd never asked Joyce why she needed the cane, but gathered it was something that she didn't much enjoy talking about. He momentarily considered asking her now, but then she quickly moved to change the topic.

"Seriously, though," she said, glancing over at him, "what's the long-term plan here? I know that, as things stand, neither you nor Agent Lefevre want to take this to your superiors. And I'll keep things vague in my reports as long as possible. But *eventually* you're going to bring in backup on this, right? Are you hoping to build a solid enough case that they'll listen to what you've got to say, and not just order psych evaluations for the both of you?"

Patrick thought about it a moment before answering. "I'm not sure, to be honest. That was the plan when I called Izzie in, definitely. I knew she would hear me out, wouldn't dismiss my suspicions out of hand. But the deeper we dig into this, the bigger it gets." He chewed the inside of his cheek thoughtfully. "When I thought that it was just a matter of there being a connection between the Reaper murders and the Ink, that was one thing. But it's so much *more* than that. I mean, whatever we've uncovered, it's been going on in this town for a long, long time. Or else this kind of thing keeps happening, over and over again. Somebody *must* have tried to take this to the authorities before, right? So why wasn't anything ever done about it?"

"What, are you saying there have been cover-ups? Conspiracies, that kind of thing?"

Patrick turned to meet her gaze before answering. "What other explanation could there be? I mean, Izzie thinks that the Guildhall fire back in the forties was part of all this, and those guys practically ran the town back then. So sure, if there was something hinky going on, they could probably keep it out of the newspapers and the courts for a long time. Maybe somebody found out about what they were doing and got fed up trying to get it through the system without any luck, and took matters in their own hands."

"Wait." Joyce reached over and took hold of his elbow, stopping him. He turned to look in her direction, and saw a worried expression on her face. "Is that what *you're* planning to do?"

Patrick let out a ragged sigh before answering. "Like I said, I'm not sure. But with someone like Martin Zotovic mixed up in this, I'm not ruling out the possibility that he might be gaming the system. Ever since Zotovic got the mayor reelected, the city has been cutting all sorts of sweetheart deals, both to Parasol and to his real estate outfit, Znth. He even managed to buy the Undersight mineshaft out from under Ross University, and the Ivory Point lighthouse, too." He rubbed his eyes, exasperated. "So let's say I manage to convince my captain that this is a real case we're working. And say that *he* is able to convince the Deputy Commissioner. All it would take would be one word from Zotovic to the mayor, and the whole case could be thrown out and I'll be busted back down to issuing parking tickets."

"That's a lot of ifs and maybes, Patrick." Joyce's tone was supportive, but there was a harder edge underneath. "And it sounds like you've already talked yourself into taking matters into your own hands."

"No, I haven't. Seriously." He reached forward and took hold of her shoulders, locking eyes with her. "I honestly haven't decided anything yet."

"But it's still on the table." She narrowed her eyes, her jaw tightening.

"I just . . ." He lowered his hands from her shoulders, looking away from her hard gaze. "I'm just not dismissing the possibility that we might have to work outside the system, is all."

Joyce stood looking at him for a long moment, without speaking, and then turned and continued walking up the sidewalk, her cane tick-tacking on the pavement with each step.

They walked in silence for the next few blocks. Aside from a few places that were open for brunch, the majority of the restaurants and bars that this part of the Oceanview was known for weren't yet open for the day, and so there were few people out on the streets. The occasional jogger braving the chill air, or people out walking their dogs, but not the sorts of crowds that spilled out onto the sidewalks in the evening hours. Which, Patrick felt, made the silence that stretched between them that much more awkward. He knew that Joyce was disappointed in him, and to be honest he was a little disappointed in himself. He hadn't joined the police force to work outside the law; he'd joined up to be a good cop. But what they were facing was nothing that they'd covered at the academy.

When they were crossing Delaney, he became acutely conscious of the fact that they were now outside the "Little Kovoko" corner of the Oceanview neighborhood, and that the nearest of his Uncle Alf's protective markings were some distance behind them. Whatever defense was offered by those spiral whorls with the sea-salt embedded within, they were outside that sphere of protection now.

As each new person came into view, rounding a corner with a dog on a leash, or carrying recycling out to the curb, he studied their faces for any sign that they might be under the influence of Ink. Was the man stepping out of that taqueria up ahead one of the Ridden? Was that woman putting coins in a parking meter being controlled by an intelligence from another dimension?

When they reached Bayfront Drive without incident, Patrick realized that he was probably being paranoid. But if a little paranoia served to keep him observant and alert enough that he was ready for an attack when it *did* come, then it would have been worth it.

A few minutes later they reached the block where the warehouse stood, and parked a short distance up the street was Joyce's vintage Volkswagen Beetle. It was still sitting where she had left it the night before, and appeared to be untouched.

"Thank god," Joyce said, her keyring jangling as she pulled it out of her purse. "I don't know if I would've been able to handle losing my boots *and* Buggy in the same day."

"Buggy?" Patrick raised an eyebrow as Joyce unlocked the driver's side door.

"What?" Joyce looked back over her shoulder at him. "Doesn't *your* car have a name?"

Patrick shrugged. "'Car,' I guess."

"Yeesh." She threw her purse into the passenger seat, rolling her eyes. "I can see I've got my work cut out for me."

Straightening up, Joyce leaned in close and gave Patrick a quick peck on the lips. Then she pulled back and poked her index finger hard against his chest.

"Do *not* do anything stupid without talking to me first, you understand?"

Patrick knew that he had a silly grin plastered to his face, but he didn't care.

"I promise," he said, mooning. And then, in a more serious tone, repeated, "I *promise*."

She gave him an appraising glance for a second, and then tossed her cane into the floorboards on the passenger side and folded herself down into the driver's seat. "I'm going to go home and grab some things, and then head into work to take care of Officer Carlson's remains. I'll meet you guys back at your place later?"

"Copy that." He nodded. "And be careful, okay?"

As soon as she turned the key in the ignition, the Dead Milkmen's "Punk Rock Girl" started blaring from the car stereo's speakers. Without turning the music down, she looked out the window at him, a grin on her face, and winked. "See ya, cutie."

Then the Beetle pulled away from the curb and sped up the street, tires screeching, kicking up gravel in its wake.

Patrick shook his head, grinning.

And then his grin fell as he glanced back at the warehouse down the street. There had been a point the night before when he hadn't been sure he would ever leave that subbasement again.

He wasn't going to do anything stupid, he told himself. That hadn't been a lie. But he would do what he had to do, and try to be smart about it.

Hands shoved deep in the pockets of his quilted jacket, head down and shoulders hunched, he turned and continued walking down the street in the direction of the docks where his own car was parked. He had work to do.

Patrick drove with the window down, the chill air bracing him, keeping him alert. He drove west on Howard, skirting the northern edge of the Oceanview neighborhood, until he reached the 10th Precinct station house at the corner of Howard and Albion. Turning into the entrance to the underground parking garage, he swiped his access card against the reader, and when the barrier gate lifted, he eased his car down the ramp.

Moments later, when he stepped off the elevator on the second floor, he almost collided with another officer walking in the other direction.

"Hey, watch it!"

Patrick stepped back, starting to apologize, until he saw who it was. "Oh. Hey, Harrison."

Detective Harrison was wearing the same rumpled suit from the day before, but his jawline and cheeks were freshly shaved and his mustache precisely trimmed. This was a man who'd gotten a full night's rest.

"Damn, Tevake, you look like you got run over."

Patrick rubbed the stubble on his chin and grimaced. His eyes had been bloodshot and raw when he'd last looked in a mirror, with dark circles underneath. He was tired, and he knew that it showed.

"What the hell *happened* out there?" Harrison crossed his arms over his chest. "You and Carlson found our guys?"

Patrick's jaw tightened. "More like they found us."

"I heard from the uniforms who found him that Carlson was *messed* up. Beaten to death, with his sidearm in reach. What was *that* about?"

"We had split up to search the subbasement, so I didn't see the attack." Which was true, as far as it went. "Carlson was already down by the time I reached him."

"The duty officer said something about a pursuit?"

Patrick nodded. "I tried to radio for backup, but couldn't get through." He glanced around the squad room, which was pretty quiet for a day shift. "I lost them in the end, and wasn't able to get in to file an after-action report before now."

"Damn." Harrison shook his head, whistling softly. "I'd like to get my hands on the sons of bitches who beat him down like that." He paused for a moment, and a pained look flitted across his face. "It was my fault you guys were down there. I was the one handing out the search details. Maybe if I'd sent more uniforms with you . . ."

Patrick was a little surprised. He'd always considered Harrison to be something of an ass, and had found his police work to be mediocre at best, and so he would never have expected that sort of reaction from him.

"I don't know that it would have made any difference," Patrick said, somberly. "You made the call based on what we knew at the time. I wouldn't have done it any differently myself."

"Yeah, maybe." Harrison looked uncharacteristically vulnerable for a brief moment, and Patrick found himself sympathetic to him. Then the moment ended as Harrison's accustomed arrogant expression settled back into place and he reached up and smoothed his mustache with thumb and forefinger, his signature tic. "Well, at least I don't have to be the one to write up all that paperwork."

And just like that, Patrick's newfound sympathy for Harrison quickly dissolved.

"Where do we stand with the surveillance?" Patrick said, redirecting the conversation.

"Chavez has a rotating crew of undercover officers in unmarked cars watching the suspects IDed from the Fayed kid's computer," Harrison answered, a little surly, "but so far all they're coming up with is a whole bunch of long distance photos of a bunch of computer geeks doing regular old computer geek stuff."

During the raid at Malcom Price's house on Wednesday they had arrested two of his associates, Ibrahim Fayed and Marissa Keizer, both of them employees of the Parasol corporation, and both suspected to be involved in the manufacture and distribution of Ink. When they searched Fayed's apartment, they found that he had left his personal laptop computer powered up and running, with a "Find Friends" application active. Cross referencing emails and contact information, Patrick and the others had been able to identify an additional half-dozen Parasol employees who were also believed to be involved in the Ink traffic, and had begun to monitor their movements. It was a pattern that was identified in the daily movements of all six that had led Patrick and Officer Carlson to the warehouse down near the docks the night before.

"Chavez wants to keep the surveillance in place, and is pushing to get the district judge to sign off on wiretap and pin register for each of them," Harrison went on, "but the captain doesn't think we've got enough on the table to justify a link between them and the goons that jumped Carlson yet. Even so, the captain has called for a Monday morning all-hands-on-deck meeting of the different narcotics squads working the Ink trade. My guess is that he's going to push for us to start making some arrests, starting with those six computer geeks, and see if we can't lean on them to give up the names of the people higher up the ladder."

"What would we charge them with, though?" Patrick asked. "All we've got on them is a few emails, but in those they only talk about the 'product' and the 'launch' and that kind of thing. Never any direct mention of Ink, and they don't refer by name to any of the known dealers. That's pretty flimsy stuff. I don't see the judge buying any of it."

"You won't get any argument from me." Harrison shrugged. "But if the captain wants arrests, we can bring them in. What happens after that is out of my hands."

Patrick scowled. That kind of thinking wasn't going to do them any favors, considering what they were *really* up against. And what would happen if the precinct lockup were to be filled with men and women with enough Ink in their systems to turn Ridden?

Before Patrick could follow that train of thought much farther than that, Harrison stepped past him, slugging him lightly on the arm as he went by.

"Anyway, see you on Monday, Tevake," Harrison said, chuckling. "And good luck with the typing. Better you than me."

Watching Harrison's retreating back, Patrick shook his head, and then turned and headed for his desk. The sooner he was able to file his report and get back to his investigation, the better. The last thing he wanted was to be stuck here when the sun went down. There were too many things lurking out in the shadows of the city.

CHAPTER FIVE

The time that Izzie spent in the passenger seat as Daphne drove them across town from Oceanview to City Center had felt like a perfect little break from all of the strangeness that swirled around them. Just two colleagues who had quickly become friends, and seemed to be on their way to something more than that even quicker, talking about anything but what was really worrying them. They were playing songs on Daphne's car stereo, talking about old sitcoms and their favorite movies, past loves and old heartbreaks, just as they had done the night before on the dusty old couch, and again that morning in Patrick's kitchen over their first coffees of the day. With traffic it had taken them no more than fifteen minutes to reach their destination, but for that brief time it was as though the weight on Izzie's shoulders had lifted.

But when Daphne pulled over to the curb on Hauser Avenue in front of Izzie's hotel, that weight came crushing back down. It was one thing to spend idle time with frivolous distraction, and quite another to waste valuable time that could be better spent pursuing their agenda.

"I just need to run up to my room and grab some things," Izzie said as she opened the passenger side door, "and then I'm heading over to the RA." She pointed with her chin across the street at the building that housed the offices of the FBI's Recondito Resident Agency.

"I'm going to swing by my place, and then I'll meet you back here." Daphne leaned to one side to look out the window at Izzie as she closed the passenger-side door. "You need me to bring you anything? Clothes, maybe? I know you didn't bring much with you in your go-bag, and I think my stuff would fit you."

Izzie put a hand on her hip and cocked her head to one side. "I'm not sure we're at the 'borrowing each other's clothes' stage of things just yet, Agent Richardson. I can make do with what I've got."

Daphne stuck out her tongue. "Okay, meet you at the offices in a bit."

As the compact hybrid pulled away from the curb and merged back into traffic, Izzie hurried into the hotel. She didn't want to waste any time.

Fifteen minutes later, she was back downstairs with her go-bag slung over her shoulder. She'd packed up just about everything she had brought with her from home, including toothbrush and clothes, and had supplemented it with the complimentary toiletries that the hotel cleaning staff had left in the room. She wasn't sure when she would be coming back, but if she ended up showering at Patrick's place again, she didn't want to have to rely again on that sad sliver of soap that she'd been forced to use in his upstairs bathroom that morning.

As Izzie walked over to the crosswalk to get to the east side of Hauser, a car parked further up the street caught her eye. It was idling, the parking lights on, and her first thought was that it was an Uber or Lyft driver waiting to pick up a passenger. But she didn't see any of the usual stickers or markings in the windows, and no one on the sidewalk was making a move toward it. Someone was sitting in the driver's seat behind the wheel, but their face was almost completely obscured by wraparound sunglasses and a hoodie.

Keeping the car in the corner of her vision without making it obvious she was looking, Izzie stood at the curb by the crosswalk and waited for the light to change. She felt as though the driver in the parked car might be watching her, but she couldn't be sure.

When the light changed, Izzie felt a momentary chill of fear. Stepping out into the road to cross to the other side would put her directly in the path of the parked car, if the driver were to suddenly put it into gear and gun the accelerator. Was she putting herself at risk? What if this were how Zotovic or his subordinates planned to eliminate any threat she posed to their operation, while making it appear to be an everyday traffic accident?

The numbers on the crosswalk light started counting down from ten. If Izzie wanted to get across, she needed to go now.

Hiking the strap of her go-bag higher on her shoulder, Izzie steeled her nerves and stepped off the curb onto the tarmac.

From the corner of her eye she could see the parked car, but from this angle she couldn't get a clear look at the driver without turning her head, so she kept her eyes straight ahead and continued walking.

The numbers had counted down to six by the time she reached the middle of the street. If the driver intended to hit her, he'd now have to drive into oncoming traffic to do so. Which didn't make Izzie all that much safer, but would make any accident she suffered look less like an accident and more like the driver was going out of his way to hit her intentionally.

A few seconds remained on the count as Izzie approached the eastern side of Hauser, and so intent was she on paying attention to the car down the street behind her that she almost didn't notice the truck barreling down the street from north to south, heading directly for her.

She heard the growl of the diesel engine just in time, and dove for the curb just as the truck roared right through the crosswalk.

If she hadn't jumped over those last few feet, the truck would have run right into her. And at the speed it was surging down the street there wouldn't have been much left of her but a bloody streak down the tarmac.

Still clutching the strap of her go-bag, teetering on the edge of the curb, Izzie wheeled around and looked in the direction of the parked car. The driver in the sunglasses and hoodie was looking directly at her, there was no question of that. Then he put the car in drive and sped off down Hauser to the north.

There hadn't been time to get the tags on the truck, which she'd noticed didn't have any logo or markings on its plain white exterior, but she got her phone out just in time to snap a photo of the license plate of the car as it sped away from her. Maybe it was just a coincidence that it had driven off just as she had narrowly avoided being run over by a truck? After all,

the light *had* just changed. Or maybe the parked car was acting as a spotter, letting the driver of another vehicle, one more
capable of inflicting serious injury, know when it was time to
strike?

It seemed more plausible to think it was just a coincidence,
Izzie knew. But given how many unlikely connections they'd
uncovered in their investigations this past week, she wasn't
willing to rule out anything at this point.

The offices of the Resident Agency were closed, so after Izzie
signed in with the security guard at the front entrance of
the building, she used the keypad beside the office door to
enter the access code she'd been assigned, and the door buzzed
open.

"Jiggity jig," she muttered to herself as she made her way
into the silent offices. This was familiar territory. When she
had been in Recondito five years before working on the Reaper
task-force, there had been many late nights and weekends
when she had found herself working alone in the RA offices,
whether doing research or combing through forensic evidence
or simply catching up on the mountains of paperwork that
such an intensive investigation required. Spending so much
time during the daylight hours canvassing for witnesses or
searching for material evidence, the off hours were often the
only opportunity she had to catch up.

She was overdue in filing a report on her current investigations, of course. But that was less a question of a lack of opportunity, and more a desire not to have her security clearance
revoked and her sanity questioned. Daphne had offered to provide what assistance she could in her own reporting, helping to

provide justification for Izzie's continued presence in the city, and the need to continue liaising with the Recondito Police Department. But Izzie would have to give something to her superiors in Quantico to account for her time here.

The laptop that she had borrowed from the office's equipment supplies was still on the desk that Izzie had been assigned, and after turning on the lights and dropping her go-bag on an empty chair, she sat down and turned it on.

After logging into her work email account, she quickly scanned through a few threads from her colleagues at the Behavioral Analysis Unit about other ongoing investigations, replied to a couple of requests for clarification on a few reports she had filed before leaving for Recondito, and then began to compose a brief summary of the last forty-eight hours for her supervisor. When she'd last checked in on Thursday morning, she had covered the highlights without going into great detail, explaining how she and Lieutenant Tevake had met with the chief medical examiner, interviewed a professor at Ross University named Hayao Kono who provided some background on Nicholas Fuller's scientific research, and then had observed a tactical unit of the RPD carry out a drug raid.

As she prepared her summary of the events since that update, she was conscious of the fact that in the broad strokes the new update followed much the same lines. She and Patrick had met with Joyce Nguyen to get the results of an autopsy of a suspected drug dealer, then returned to Ross University to meet with another professor who had some background on Fuller, and finally she and Agent Richardson had accompanied officers of the RPD on a raid. The differences, though, were that the autopsy results indicated that the drug dealer Malcolm Price had already been dead before he got back to his feet and tried to

attack Izzie, the background the university professor had provided had largely been concerned with a secret society of Mayan
warrior priests, and the raid had ended not with any arrests but
with an attack by dozens of the shambling undead and the murder of a police officer. Izzie felt that it was prudent to be as vague
about those differences as possible, at least for the time being.

She still told herself that she fully intended to reveal the
entire truth of the situation to the Bureau when the time was
right. And yet every time she omitted key details from an official account, or failed to notify her superior about a crucial bit
of evidence, or was coy when explaining the nature of her current investigation, an internal war was being waged in the back
of her head. Part of her still insisted that it was vital to observe
regulations and procedures, if perhaps not in an entirely timely
manner. But there was another voice in her head, faint at first
but growing in volume, that questioned whether it was necessary to report on this at all.

But she would have to worry about that later. She had
much more pressing concerns in the short term. Like staying
alive long enough to figure out exactly what they were dealing
with, for one thing.

After emailing the sanitized summary to her supervisor,
Izzie pulled up the photo she'd taken of the license plate of the
car outside a short while before. She ran the plates, and within
moments discovered that a car with that license plate number, of the same make and model, had been reported stolen
the month before. And while she seriously doubted that the
elderly retired gentleman in San Diego who was listed as the
vehicle's owner had any connection with the hooded person
behind the wheel, she made a note of his name and pertinent
details, just for the sake of thoroughness.

Exasperated, Izzie shut the laptop and slid it across the desk. Then she opened the drawers in the desk until she found the one where she had put her things the previous day, and pulled out a stack of hardcover journals, an academic paper, and a legal pad.

The previous day, Izzie had spent several hours reading through the journals of Roberto Aguilar, using his granddaughter-in-law Samantha Aguilar's academic paper as a skeleton key to help her decipher what it was the old man had been writing about. Izzie had filled page after page in the legal pad with her notes, before being interrupted by Patrick's call to come join him in the warehouse near the docks.

Roberto Aguilar claimed to have been inducted as a young man into the "daykeepers," a secret order dating back to the ancient Maya who protected humanity from threats from beyond. The daykeepers believed that entities that Aguilar referred to as "daimons" and "shades" invaded our world from another space which he called "the Unreal." The daykeepers believed that it was possible for daimons to make use of the bodies of the dead and nearly dead as vessels, and called to those controlled by daimons as "Ridden," just as those possessed by spirits were called in the Haitian Voudou tradition. Aguilar wrote that the daykeepers believed it was necessary to dismember the bodies of the dead, in order to make them unsuitable as vessels for the daimons.

Five years before, Izzie and the rest of the taskforce had assumed that the "Recondito Reaper" butchered the remains of his victims in order to satisfy some kind of aberrant psychological gratification. And even after they had identified Nicholas Fuller as their primary suspect, and found the mountain of books on mythology and religion in his apartment, among other obscure and arcane topics, it was believed that Fuller had simply cobbled together a delusional rationalization to justify his own actions and drives to himself.

But the day before, Izzie and Patrick had learned that Fuller had actually been following in the secret traditions that he had been taught by Roberto Aguilar. He had syncretized and synthesized elements from other religions and mythologies along the way, but the core of his personal belief system derived from the Mayan daykeepers.

Already the little that she had been able to glean about the daykeepers from Aguilar's journals had proved to be invaluable. Had she not read in the early evening that they believed that the Ridden could not cross running water, it was likely than Izzie and the others would not have survived the rest of the night. She questioned the efficacy of the Ziploc gris-gris bag that she'd cobbled together that morning, but if it worked at all it was because she had read in Aguilar's journal that crystals and silver were inimical to the Ridden.

Silver could disrupt the connection between the Ridden and the daimon, she had noted on the legal pad. What she and the others had taken to calling the loa could be forced out of host's body if silver was present in the system. Which perhaps explained why Fuller executed his victims with a silver-plated blade?

And then there was the "key."

That night five years ago, as Izzie had lain bleeding on the metal floor of the lighthouse lantern room, Fuller had talked about the "old daykeeper" giving him a key that finally allowed him to understand, and that allowed him to walk through the fire and see the shadows for what they were. It wasn't until she read Aguilar's journals that Izzie understood that the "key"

Fuller had referred to was the substance the Maya had called ilbal. Samantha Aguilar had assumed that it referred to some kind of crystal or mirror, but Izzie was certain that it was much more than that.

Izzie and Patrick had learned from some of Fuller's surviving colleagues at Ross University that toward the end of his time there, when his behavior became increasingly erratic, that he had begun to take some sort of psychotropic drug. Among the evidence that the CSI unit had removed from Fuller's apartment five years before had been a few small glass vials filled with a crystallized powder. The analysis of the contents conducted by the Recondito Police Department's Office of Forensic Science had been fairly inconclusive, but their findings had suggested that it was likely derived from some unknown plant species, with a chemical structure similar to hallucinogens like DMT.

Izzie was convinced that the powder in the vials, the drug that Nicholas Fuller had been taking during the last months of his life, was the substance that the elder Aguilar referred to as ilbal. Fuller believed that it was the key that allowed him to perceive directly the presence of invaders from a higher dimensional space.

Was that simply a delusion brought on by Fuller's repeated hallucinogenic experiences, colored by the myths and legends that the old daykeeper had taught him? Or was it a verifiable fact?

Izzie couldn't help but wonder what she would experience if she took the ilbal herself. What would *she* see?

She picked up the journal on the top of the stack, flipped the legal pad to where she'd left off, and started to read.

CHAPTER SIX

Patrick felt like he had been working on his after-action report for ages. But when he finally typed the last entry, and clicked the link to file it, he glanced at the corner of the screen and saw that it had only taken a little more than an hour. It was the middle of the afternoon, with a few hours to go until sunset. So perhaps not ages, Patrick thought, but longer than he would have liked.

As he pushed back from the desk, Patrick felt his stomach grumbling, and realized that he hadn't eaten anything since breakfast. He was sure that Izzie would have given him a hard time for thinking about food when there were so many other pressing concerns at hand, but he told himself that he functioned better on a full stomach. He'd be sacrificing productivity and effectiveness if he *didn't* take a break to get something to eat.

He was rationalizing, he knew, but he was going to do it anyway.

Logging out of his computer, Patrick tucked his phone in

his pocket and clipped his holstered pistol on his belt, then shrugged into his quilted jacket and headed for the elevator.

He didn't want to waste more time than was necessary, rationalizations aside. So rather than going all the way down to the garage and driving his car to one of his usual lunch spots, he pressed the elevator button for the ground floor. There was a decent taco truck that was usually parked a couple of blocks up Albion, and if it wasn't open, there was a Korean barbeque across the street that would do in a pinch.

When the elevator doors opened, he was assaulted by a din of shouting voices. From the looks of it, a fight had broken out between a couple of prisoners in the intake area, and a group of uniformed officers were attempting to break things up. But other prisoners were shouting, urging the two brawlers to continue, whether because they had a stake in the argument or just for their own entertainment; it wasn't clear.

Patrick walked over to the officer manning the intake desk. "Everything okay down here, Anderson?"

Sergeant Anderson turned in his direction, an expression of brief annoyance on her face that faded when she saw it was him. "Oh, hey, Tevake." She turned back to look at the processing area where the commotion was going on. "Yeah, I'm giving them another thirty seconds to knock it off and then the Tasers come out." She shook her head. "Couple of hopped-up crackheads like them, though, might have to zap them a few times until they take the hint."

"Well, good luck with that," Patrick said, and continued walking toward the door.

After badging out through the security gate, he pushed open the door and stepped outside, and wondered what effect a Taser would have on one of the Ridden. Or just electricity in general? If the loa or whatever they were calling it was controlling the body through the central nervous system, would an electrical shock interfere with that? If a bullet couldn't take down one of the Ridden, would electrocution do the job?

It was worth considering, though Patrick wasn't sure that he wanted to get close enough to one of the Ridden to find out one way or the other.

As he walked along the sidewalk heading west on Albion, Patrick couldn't help but feel as though there were eyes on him, watching his every move. He'd spent enough time working undercover to know better than to simply turn and look, so he paused in front of a storefront, pretending to window shop, but in reality, using the reflection in the glass window to check to see if there was anyone following him. Then at an intersection he paused, as if undecided about which way to turn, and scanned his surroundings out of the corner of his eye as he turned to look first one direction up the connecting street and then the other. But he could see no sign of anyone following him, and no one seemed to be in any of the cars parked along either side of the street.

He kept on walking up the street, and was pleased to see that the taco truck was parked in its usual spot, and open for business.

But as he got in line behind the other patrons waiting to place their orders, he felt anxiety itching at him again, and felt exposed and vulnerable, even in broad daylight.

Twenty minutes later Patrick was walking back into the station house with a paper bag filled with tacos in one hand

and a bottle of Mexican Coke in the other. The tumult in the intake area had subsided, and the prisoners had been transferred to holding cells.

As he passed the intake desk, he held the paper bag against his chest with the hand holding the Coke bottle, and with his free hand reached in and pulled out a taco wrapped in aluminum foil.

"For you, Anderson," he said, holding the taco out to her. "With Carlos's compliments. He said it was your usual."

"That old smoothie." A blush rose on her cheek as she took the taco from him. "I swear he's trying to fatten me up. Probably has a thing for big girls."

Patrick shrugged, a sly grin on his face. "I wish *I* had someone that can cook like that flirting with me."

"Don't give up, Tevake," she said around a mouthful of taco al pastor, as Patrick pushed the call button for the elevator. "There's a taco truck out there for everyone."

"You're a regular poet," he called back to her as the elevator doors clanked open.

Anderson was nearly finished with the taco already, chewing contentedly. "What can I say? I'm a romantic."

Patrick smiled at her as he stepped onto the elevator, but the smile quickly faded as soon as the doors shut behind him.

"Damn it," he said softly to himself.

He couldn't help feeling like he was putting his fellow officers at risk by not telling them about the Ridden. Uniforms routinely pulled in blots for public intoxication—it had been cops who had coined the term for users of Ink in the first place—but those encounters so far had not escalated to the point where the user had gone full-on Ridden. But assuming that the step between run-of-the-mill Ink user and full blown

possession was as simple as Patrick and the others had theorized, then how long until a blot being processed at intake or
just riding in the back of a squad car made that transition?
How would the officers involved respond to a prisoner who
couldn't be subdued and was impervious to even the deadliest
of force?

He tried to tell himself that his theory about Tasers might
pan out, in which case the officers could at least contain the
situation. But what if he was wrong? What if one of the Ridden
shrugged off a jolt from a Taser as easily as it could shrug off
a bullet? Was Patrick then responsible for any casualties that
resulted, because he failed to warn the others in time?

Just three days before, Chavez, Harrison, and the others
had watched the lifeless, Ridden form of Malcom Price get
up off the pavement after a three-story fall, with three bullets
already in his chest, and attack Izzie. And even seeing it with
their own eyes, they hadn't had any problem accepting that it
was just a question of a man so out of his head on drugs that he
didn't feel any pain. If Patrick had tried to tell them what had
really happened, what were the chances that they'd believe him?

The elevator chimed as the doors opened on the second
floor, followed by a grumbling from Patrick's stomach.

"Well, I function better on a full stomach," he said to himself, savoring the smell of the tacos wafting up from the bag.

Stopping by the squad room to grab his laptop computer,
Patrick came back out and turned the corner toward the community room that was at the end of the corridor. Snagging the
top of the paper bag with the fingers of the hand holding the
Coke bottle, the laptop tucked under his elbow, he fished his
keys out of his pocket with his other hand and unlocked the
door.

He flicked the light switch with his elbow as he stepped inside, and the fluorescents overhead flickered and buzzed as they warmed up, bathing the room in a wan, antiseptic light. The boxes that they had recovered from the Property and Evidence warehouse in the South Bay were still piled to one side of the room along with most of the furniture, and the table was stacked high with papers, books, maps, academic journals, and all of the other material evidence that had been taken from Nicholas Fuller's apartment five years before. The dry erase board at the front of the room was covered with a constellation of names and places and facts, those associated with the Fuller murders on one side and those associated with Ink on the other, with a web of lines connecting one to another, the physical manifestation of the thought processes that he and Izzie had worked their way through in the previous days as they had tried to figure out how it all fit together.

Patrick put the laptop down on one end of the long table, and booted it up while he sat down, taking a long sip from the bottle. By the time he got to the log-in screen, he was already halfway through the first of the tacos he'd pulled from the bag. He'd had better carne asada, but rarely from a street vendor.

Punching in his password one handed, the other occupied with keeping the taco from falling apart before he could maneuver the rest of it into his mouth, Patrick glanced over at the dry erase board. He'd chosen to eat in the community room rather than at his desk so that he could spend some time going back over their work, seeing if there was any connection or angle that he and Izzie might have overlooked.

That's when he noticed something out of place. When he and Izzie had set up shop in the community room earlier that week, the first thing that they had done after bringing in all of the boxes of evidence had been to move almost all of the upholstered chairs that were normally positioned around the table over to the far side of the room, leaving just two in place at the table for them to use. And when he and Izzie had left the day before, that was still the case. But now there was a third chair that was parked right in front of the dry erase board, facing it, like someone had sat down and studied what was written on it for a while.

Patrick looked around the room, slowly chewing a mouthful of grilled steak. Was anything else out of place? Who had been in there since they were last here? There was only one key to the community room available to check out, and Patrick had it with him the whole night. The only other people in the building with access in the meantime were the cleaning staff and the captain. But the cleaning staff had been instructed not to enter the room while it was being used to store evidence, and the captain always avoided the room like the plague because he said it reminded him of too many unpleasant memories of interminable meetings with disgruntled community members. Which was not to say that a member of the cleaning staff *couldn't* have entered the room, or the captain too, for that matter, but that neither of them would have had a reason to. And if someone *had* been in here, which seemed to be the case, what had they made of the things that Patrick and Izzie had written on the dry erase board?

Looking around the room, it didn't appear that anything had been taken away, though he couldn't be sure whether anything had been moved. The mountains of books on history, the occult, science, and mythology appeared no smaller than they had when he and Izzie had unpacked all of them three days before. And the boxes containing the rest of the material evidence they'd requested from storage, including the murder weapon and silver-skull mask that Fuller had used in the killings, were still sitting where they'd left them at the far end of the table.

Patrick got up and closed the door to the hallway outside before sitting back down and pulling the second taco out of the bag. He savored a bite of al pastor and tried not to worry about the chair. The worst-case scenario was that the captain had come in to check on their work, and had spent some time looking over what they'd written, in which case he had probably walked away mystified. But the fact that Patrick hadn't been ordered to the Medical Unit to see one of the departmental psychologists suggested that he didn't have much cause for concern.

The one thing missing from the web of associations written on the dry erase board was the spider at the middle: Martin Zotovic. His software company, Parasol, was prominently represented, as was the Pinnacle Tower building where it was headquartered, and any number of its current and former employees who had been identified as being involved in the manufacture, distribution, or sale of Ink. But not Zotovic himself. Up until the night before, it had been impossible to imagine that such a high-profile figure could be involved in anything as sordid as trafficking in street drugs, and they hadn't known that he had any connection to the Fuller murders. But his name belonged on the side of the board that listed all of the members of the Undersight team that had been the victims in the Reaper killings, even if the Reaper hadn't lived long enough to get to him. And they now knew that the Ink trade was being directed by the highest levels of Zotovic's company.

But what did they know about Zotovic himself, beyond what appeared in the newspaper headlines?

Tucking the last of his taco al pastor into his mouth and wiping his fingers on a paper napkin, Patrick brought up a browser window on the laptop and did an online search for "Martin Zotovic." Then he pulled the third and final taco from the bag while the search results loaded.

The top results were mostly links to news pieces about Zotovic's various business dealings, or announcements about product launches from his company, Parasol. As he savored his grilled chicken taco, Patrick worked his way through the links, building a larger picture of the self-made millionaire's business dealings.

Zotovic had first started making headlines a few years before when he launched a photo-sharing app for smart phones that quickly became one of the most popular software applications of its kind. Free to download and driven by sponsored ads, it was also one of the most profitable. Flush with capital from the success of that first launch, Zotovic founded Parasol, which originally operated out of a small office block in a converted warehouse in the South Bay. But within a year Parasol had outgrown that space, with a steadily increasing workforce and an ever-widening catalog of new apps on offer, and the company continued to move to increasingly larger spaces over the course of the next two years. Zotovic founded a second company, a private equity firm called Znth, to handle the increasingly complex real estate dealings that those subsequent moves involved. And finally, the year before, Znth had closed a somewhat controversial deal to purchase the landmark Pinnacle Tower outright from the holding company that had owned the property since the eighties. All of the existing tenants, some of them long-established Recondito businesses and firms who had occupied their respective spaces in the building for decades, had been effectively evicted on the spot, with Znth refusing to extend or renew any of the existing leases when they expired at the end of their contractual terms. By the beginning of the current year, Parasol, Znth, and various other Zotovic-founded subsidiaries were the sole tenants of the Pinnacle Tower.

The sale of the Pinnacle Tower to Znth had been controversial in part because the building was on the registry of Recondito historical landmarks, and the graceful art deco spire of the skyscraper had been widely viewed as a symbol for the city since the building was first completed in the early 1930s. The main elevator lobby with its ornate bas relief featuring symbolic depictions of the history of the city and the surrounding countryside was described on one website Patrick visited as "a timeless monument to Recondito's rich cultural heritage and all that the Hidden City has meant to so many of its denizens." Which, while perhaps a little flowery, pretty accurately summed up the esteem with which many in the city held the building and its fixtures.

When it was first announced that Znth planned to purchase the building, however, it was discovered by the local press that Zotovic intended to substantially renovate the interior of the structure, but had no intention of letting the board of Recondito Historical Register review the plans. Outrage among local historical societies and concerned citizens groups put pressure on the mayor's office to enforce the provision requiring that any substantial changes made to a historical landmark would first need to be approved by the board. And at the outset the mayor's office signaled that it would indeed be requesting that be made a prerequisite for the sale. When at the last minute the mayor reversed course, and issued an executive order that the transfer of ownership to Znth could go ahead without impediment, and that the new owners would be free to make any alterations to the structure that they desired without the need for any official approvals, even going so far as to relax to standard permitting required of any large construction project, many in the local press believed that a backroom deal had been struck between the mayor's office and Zotovic himself.

There had been some simmering outrage in the editorial pages and community websites for several weeks, but when the lobby of the Pinnacle Tower was once again opened to the public after the renovations were completed, and the signature golden bas relief in the foyer was pristine and untouched, looking the same as it ever had, the controversy quickly died out.

Otherwise, Zotovic's brief career as a software mogul was largely free of controversy. Though he appeared regularly at tech conferences and charity events, he was rarely seen in public in social settings. In the photos that Patrick found online, Zotovic looked more like someone who would be working in a coffee shop or behind the counter of a comic book store than the head of a billion-dollar company, with a shaggy mop of dark hair and five o'clock shadow on his chin, favoring jeans and hoodies over suits and ties. There were no mentions in any of the articles Patrick could find of Zotovic being romantically involved, or of maintaining anything like a social life in general. There were no paparazzi photos of him at clubs with supermodels on each arm, or palling around with Hollywood stars, or carousing drunkenly with his friends. Zotovic kept a condominium in a City Center high rise and a veritable mansion way up on the hills of Northside, but seemed to spend the majority of his time inside the Pinnacle Tower, day and night.

There was no mention anywhere of Zotovic's involvement in Ross University's Undersight research project years before, though it was a standard element in the puff piece write-ups to mention that he was a "college dropout." It was a nice bit of mythologizing, Patrick thought, emphasizing the humble origins from which this mighty titan of industry had arisen, but it wasn't entirely true. Zotovic had been a graduate student when he joined the Undersight team, and while he had left before completing his master's degree, that made him a "college dropout" in only the loosest of definitions.

Patrick was unable to find any major scandal or controversy, beyond the flap over the Pinnacle Building purchase and renovation. Even after logging in and searching various law enforcement databases resulting in nothing more serious than a few parking violations when Zotovic had been a teenager.

But when he found a link to a video playlist entitled "Parasol's Dark Secrets," a lengthy series of YouTube postings that all appeared to revolve around some shady doings involving Zotovic and his software offerings, Patrick was certain for the moment that he had hit pay dirt.

Five seconds into the first video in the playlist, that certainty began to falter.

All of the videos in the playlist were the work of the same man, who identified himself only as "Bitstreamer 9000" and wore a robot-like helmet that obscured his features, using electronic effects to disguise his voice. But as Patrick watched further past the first few seconds, he found that despite his outlandish look and cartoonish persona, the man gave the impression that he had some expertise. The first video began with a discussion of steganography—the art of hiding information and messages within images, audio, or video—and then went on to discuss spectrograms: graphic representations of the frequencies that make up a sound and how they change over time. These were illustrated throughout with graphics that appeared on the screen, showing textbook examples of each topic in regular usage. Patrick failed to see how any of it pertained to software applications that had been released by Zotovic's companies, or what they might have to do with Parasol's "dark secrets," but he was learning things about the ways in which different kinds of data could be concealed, revealed, manipulated, or analyzed.

The second video began to apply that kind of analysis to various Parasol products, beginning with the photo-sharing app that had made Zotovic his first fortune. "Bitstreamer 9000" claimed to have discovered that many of the filtering effects that users could apply to their uploaded photos altered the images in more ways than were immediately obvious. And he claimed, further, that what appeared at first glance to be nothing more than "noise," like the visual equivalent of static, in fact contained encoded data that was effectively hidden from the user. He showed a few examples, with lots of red circles and arrows and lines indicating where on the images he felt that this data was hidden, but Patrick wasn't exactly convinced.

The next video in the playlist began with the suggestion that this additional encoded data, while not noticeable to the user, might be exerting some kind of subliminal effect. Even if people couldn't consciously perceive what was hidden in the image, some part of their brain might be picking up on it. The analogy of sounds outside the range of human hearing being sometimes perceived as a kind of pressure on the ear drum or other disquieting effects made sense to Patrick, even if he wasn't quite prepared to accept the premise.

But when the next video opened with the assertion that the true purpose of the encoded data was for mind control, and that Parasol was secretly brainwashing the users of their software products to engender brand loyalty, Patrick couldn't help but roll his eyes.

The rest of the videos in the playlist veered ever deeper into the realms of conspiracy theories, arguing that Zotovic was secretly part of the Reptilian Illuminati, lizard people who disguised themselves as human and secretly controlled all of the major governments and financial institutions of the world, and that Zotovic had been instrumental in engineering the global warming that would render the planet Earth more suitable for a full-scale invasion by his fellow lizard people from outer space, and on and on and on.

Cursing under his breath, Patrick slapped the lip of the laptop shut, berating himself for devoting so much of his time to watching what were clearly the ravings of a deranged lunatic.

Glancing at his phone, he saw that there was only a little more than an hour left until sunset. Grabbing his laptop and his quilted jacket, he started for the door. But he stopped short as a thought struck him, and walked over to where the file boxes were stacked. He was alone in the room, but couldn't help glancing around nervously to make sure no one was watching as he reached inside one of the boxes, and quickly slipped his closed hand into his pocket. Then he turned off the lights and locked the door of the community room behind him. He had just enough time to stop by the grocery store on the way home to pick up supplies and be safely back in his neighborhood before the Ridden were free to roam the city streets.

At least they didn't have to worry about an invasion of lizard people from outer space.

CHAPTER SEVEN

Back at the FBI's Resident Agency, Izzie was making notes on the legal pad when her phone chimed in her coat pocket, indicating a new message. She pulled it out and tapped the power button. The text was from Daphne.

"DOING OKAY?"

Izzie tapped out a quick response: "GREAT. FINISHING UP SOME RESEARCH AT THE R.A., SHOULD BE READY TO ROLL SOON. YOU?"

She watched the ellipsis pulse in a text bubble on the screen as Daphne composed her response on the other end.

"COOL. I'M HEADING THERE SHORTLY. I'M BRINGING YOU SOME CLOTHES I THINK WOULD LOOK GREAT ON YOU. ;)"

Izzie rolled her eyes, but couldn't help but smile. She texted back an emoji of a smiley face with its tongue sticking out, then returned the phone to her pocket.

She stacked the journals, academic paper, and legal pad

on top of the closed laptop, then bent down under the desk to unplug the laptop's adapter cord. Then she picked up the carrying case that the laptop had been in when it was issued to her, and shoved the whole stack inside. She was zipping it shut when she heard footsteps behind her.

"Agent Lefevre, this is a surprise."

She turned, and saw Senior Resident Agent Manuel Gutierrez standing in the doorway. He was dressed casually, in a plain t-shirt, jogging pants, and running shoes. It was a stark contrast to the dark, somber suit and tie that he'd worn every other time that she'd seen him. He had a coat draped over one arm, and under his other arm was tucked a vinyl case that appeared to contain a tennis racket.

"Agent Gutierrez," Izzie managed, nodding in greeting. "I didn't think you were coming in today."

He hung his coat on a hook by the door, and held up the vinyl case.

"Had a squash game with the Deputy Mayor at the athletic center," he explained. "Figured I'd drop by and catch up on some correspondence."

"Did you win?" Izzie was trying to keep her tone light, but wasn't sure she was succeeding.

"Not this time." The Senior Resident Agent shrugged. "I find it helps to let the deputy win a few, from time to time. Keeps him amenable."

He set the racket case down on an empty desk.

"The Mayor's office was keen to hear any updates about your investigation. I told them that so far you hadn't turned up anything of substance." He crossed his arms over his chest. "Is that an accurate assessment, would you say?"

"Do you mean," Izzie replied, unable to keep a somewhat

defensive, even combative tone out of her voice, "have I found anything that would indicate that the books on the Fuller case need to be reopened?"

Agent Gutierrez narrowed his eyes, his jaw tight. "I know I don't need to remind you that the local authorities would just as soon forget that the 'Recondito Reaper' ever existed. Dragging it back through the courts again—or worse, the media—would make for some very unhappy people down at City Hall. The Mayor is dealing with the bad publicity that surrounds a police officer killed in the line of duty. I would hate to see him face more unnecessary stress at a time like this."

He paused for a moment, giving her a hard stare. "And I can assure you that they would want to make the Bureau understand the full measure of their unhappiness, too. Especially with respect to the enterprising young agent who was responsible."

Izzie stood up straighter, hands at her sides. "With all due respect, sir," she said, in a tone that was far from respectful, "let's assume for the moment that I *did* discover something that we missed five years ago. Some crucial bit of evidence that would mean that the Fuller case *did* need to be reopened. Are you suggesting that I should *ignore* it? Are you attempting to *order* me to do so? Because I would have to check the chain of command to be certain, but I'm pretty sure that you would be—"

"Hold on, hold on." He put his hands up in front of his chest, palms forward, in a defensive posture. "I'll go on record as saying that the last thing I'd do would be to suggest that you conceal evidence of a crime. Okay? That's not what I'm saying."

Izzie arched an eyebrow suggestively, inviting him to continue.

"What I'm saying is that Nicholas Fuller is dead, the families of his victims have found whatever peace with that they're going to find, and the city has done its level best to move on. Anything that you find, whatever detail about those killings that you uncover, isn't going to bring Fuller back so we can take him to court again. The man's dead. So unless you've found that he wasn't acting *alone*, and that there's another suspect out there . . ."

He trailed off, an expression blooming slowly across his face.

"You haven't found evidence of an *accomplice*, have you?" he asked, horrified.

"No, no," Izzie answered, shaking her head furiously. "Nothing that Lieutenant Tevake and I have found contradicts the established conclusion that Nicholas Fuller carried out the Reaper killings on his own."

Not exactly, anyway, she thought to herself.

"Good." He breathed a literal sigh of relief.

"In fact," Izzie continued, taking on a more conciliatory tone, "the bulk of our investigation has been focused on the production and distribution of a new street drug, and the inquiries into Fuller's background and the background materials we've gathered from his former colleagues have primarily been gathered in support of the RPD's ongoing narcotics investigation. It's true that we have uncovered some information about Fuller that didn't come to light in the taskforce's original investigation, but it's all in line with what we already knew." She paused, and then managed a wan smile. "No surprises."

Agent Gutierrez seemed somewhat mollified. He nodded slowly, and then went to pick his racket up from the desk. As he turned, his gaze landed on Izzie's go-bag sitting in the chair across the room, and he straightened back up, leaving the racket where it lay.

"Planning on leaving us soon, Agent Lefevre?" he said, giving her a quizzical look.

She looked from Agent Gutierrez to her bag and back again, thinking fast. "I'll be joining Lieutenant Tevake on an extended stakeout," she said matter-of-factly. "It's not clear how long we'll have to remain in position, so I figured I'd bring along my things to keep as comfortable as possible."

He nodded. "My first stakeout was down in Biloxi, back in '98," he said, a little wistfully. "We thought we'd be in and out in a couple of days, but ended up having to stay in position for an entire month. And then the *hurricane* hit and it all went to—"

"Are you decent in there, Izzie?" a voice from the hall outside shouted. "Because I'd be okay if you're not, because then maybe we could—"

Daphne stopped short as soon as she stepped through the open door and saw the Senior Resident Agent standing there.

"Oh," she said, quickly regaining her composure. "Agent Gutierrez." She glanced at the racket case. "How'd the match with the Deputy Mayor go?"

"I let him win," he answered, and then gestured to the overnight bag hanging off Daphne's shoulder. "Going somewhere, Agent Richardson?"

"I, um . . ." Daphne clutched the strap of the bag, and Izzie could almost see the thoughts racing behind her eyes.

"I've requested that Agent Richardson assist me in the surveillance team," Izzie quickly put in. "Lieutenant Tevake's vice squad has already committed so many resources to this narcotics investigation that they're a little short-staffed, so I suggested that we might be able to offer some backup."

"And it won't interfere with my current workload," Daphne hastened to add, following Izzie's lead. "My caseload is pretty light at the moment, and what little I do have on my plate I can handle remotely. And I'll be close enough that I can get back to the office quickly if needed." She paused, studying Agent Gutierrez's expression. "I was coming in to write it up for your approval, sir."

He chewed it over for a long moment before answering, giving them each a hard stare in turn.

"All right, I don't have any strong objections to that," he finally answered. "So long as I don't end up having to pick up your slack."

He picked up his racket, and then crossed the floor to his office door. Pausing in the open doorway he turned and gave them a curt nod, and then shut the door behind him.

"Stakeout, huh?" Daphne said in a low voice, turning to face Izzie.

"I had to improvise." Izzie shrugged. "But it'll cover us if we need to go to ground."

Daphne glanced over at the door to Agent Gutierrez's office. "There's a chance he could follow up on it. Not saying he doesn't trust us, but he's a stickler for documenting any Bureau involvement with local law enforcement."

"Yeah, we'll have to see if Patrick can put in some paperwork on his end, get it on the books with Recondito PD. Between the ongoing Ink investigation and a police officer killed in the line of duty while working the case, I'm sure he can put together a strong enough case to justify a surveillance team, at least on paper."

Daphne nodded, then gestured to the laptop carrying case on Izzie's desk. "You get everything you need?"

"I think so." Instinctively, Izzie patted her pockets in sequence, making sure she had all of her equipment on her, even though she had just done so a short time before when leaving her hotel room. It was somewhere between a ritual and an obsessive tic. Phone, FBI credentials, firearm? Check, check, and check. Ammunition and handcuffs? "It probably wouldn't be a bad idea to get some more ammo before we go, though."

"I got you covered." Daphne headed toward the gun vault door, and Izzie followed her over. As she punched in the code on the electronic door lock, Daphne hummed thoughtfully. "I'm wondering if we shouldn't tool up."

She pushed the door open, and then held it for Izzie to step inside.

"What do you have in mind?" Izzie asked.

Daphne followed her inside, and gestured to the locked cages that lined the walls. "Bullets might not be enough to take those Ridden guys down, but maybe something with a little more stopping power could slow them down a bit."

Izzie looked around the cages while Daphne pulled a keyring from her pocket and unlocked the locker where the ammunition was stored. A Resident Agency like this didn't maintain the kind of armory that a Field Office supporting a Special Weapons and Tactics Team would, but what they did have might come in handy.

"You don't think Agent Gutierrez would have a problem with that?" Izzie asked.

"I'm responsible for the inventory." Daphne had a sly grin on her face as she passed her a few clips worth of ammunition for her semiautomatic. "We'd have it all checked back in before he even noticed, I'm guessing. And if we have to use any of this gear, and I have to write up any shots fired reports, well, the fact we needed it will justify the fact we took it, right?"

"Okay, then." Izzie nodded, sliding the ammunition into her pocket. "Let's tool up."

A short while later the two left the offices, Izzie with her go-bag slung over her shoulder and the laptop carrying case in her hand, and Daphne with her overnight bag on one arm and a vinyl duffle bag containing a couple of tactical shotguns, two bulletproof vests, and several boxes of shells on the other.

"Come on," Izzie said, glancing at the sky as they stepped outside. The sun was barely visible over the tops of the sky-scrapers of the Financial District to the west. "We need to get moving. There's some things I want to pick up on the way there."

CHAPTER EIGHT

Patrick was in the produce section of the grocery store, loading his basket with the ingredients for the stew he'd decided to fix for dinner, when his phone buzzed in his pocket. He pulled it out and swiped it on, and saw that he had an incoming call from Joyce.

"Hey, you," he said, holding the phone to his ear. "Where are you?"

"I'm at the morgue," came the reply over his phone's speaker. "I just finished up my report on Carlson, and as soon as I file it I'll be heading down to your place. Are you there now?"

"No, just making a quick stop at the store." Patrick tossed a bag of potatoes into the shopping cart.

"Okay." She sounded a little preoccupied.

"Everything alright?"

He could hear her sighing on the other end of the call. "Yeah, I'm just a little spooked. Ten years working with dead bodies every day and I never really had a problem before, but now . . ." She trailed off.

"That was before one of them got back up off the slab and came after you," Patrick said, his tone sympathetic.

"Yeah." She paused for a moment. "Oh, hey, I finally got back the lab analysis of the stuff I found under Tyler Campbell's fingernails."

It was Campbell's unexpected death in a holding cell, and the discovery of the vacuoles in his brain in the subsequent autopsy, that had first given Patrick the suspicion that there might be a connection with the Fuller murders.

"And?" he asked.

"Haven't had a chance to dig too deeply into it, but it's . . . weird." He could hear papers rustling in the background. "I'm bringing it with me, so you can look it over yourself tonight, if you want. But like I say . . . it's weird."

"So, noted." He steered the shopping cart out of the produce section and headed toward the butcher counter. "Can I get you anything at the store?"

She barked a quick laugh before answering. "How about a case of wine? After all that's happened, I think I need at least that much."

"I'm on it," Patrick answered, chuckling.

"Okay, I'll see you in a bit." She paused, and added, "And Patrick? Don't do anything stupid."

"Never."

The call ended, and he slipped the phone back into his pocket.

He might need to stop by the liquor store down the street from his place on the way, as well, Patrick decided. If the rest of them were as anxious about all of this as he was, wine might not cut it.

Patrick was unloading grocery bags from the trunk of his car when a car pulled to a stop at the curb a few car lengths behind him, and he felt himself tensing defensively as he turned at the sound of the engine switching off and the car doors opening. He glanced over his shoulder, his free hand slipping to his side toward the handle of his holstered pistol, but when he saw that it was Izzie and Daphne climbing out of the car behind him and not some blot-marked shamble come to kill him, he relaxed visibly. Intellectually, he knew that, even though the sun had just set, the marks his great-uncle had made around the neighborhood would keep the Ridden at bay, but there was still a skeptical voice in the back of his head that felt vulnerable and exposed being outside after dark.

"Evening, ladies," he said with a nod in their direction and, picking up a paper bag of groceries in either hand, headed toward the front door of his house.

"Such a gentleman," Izzie said, voice dripping with sarcasm as she pulled a backpack, computer carrying case, and shopping bags from the back seat of the car.

"Wouldn't a gentleman offer to help with the heavy stuff?" Daphne replied, struggling a little with the weight of a heavily loaded duffle and an overnight bag.

"Yeah, yeah," Patrick answered as he balanced one of the paper bags on his hip and unlocked the front door. He held the door open with his foot, stepping to one side to let Izzie and Daphne enter past him. "Put your stuff anywhere. I'll clear out one of the rooms upstairs as soon as I get the stew cooking on the stove."

"Don't sweat it, we can handle the mess upstairs." Izzie was already climbing the stairs to the second floor, and Daphne was depositing the duffle bag on the floor in the living room before following her up.

Patrick felt the same pang of embarrassment that he'd felt that morning when they'd gone to shower in the second-floor bathroom. He was self-conscious that anyone was seeing the sorry state of the rooms upstairs, and he was sure that Izzie must have taken him for some kind of hoarder. But the truth of the matter was that the "mess" up there, as she had described it, represented all that Patrick had left of his mother and great-uncle, and the only physical reminders he had left of his own childhood with them. He had tried many times over the years to tackle the almost Herculean task of clearing all of it out and making those rooms usable again, but each time he started in on it he ended up losing hour after hour lost in nostalgia, following a seemingly endless web of associations that led from one childhood memory to another, some pleasant and some less so, but all of them cherished in one way or another.

After putting the grocery bags on the kitchen counter next to the supplies he'd already brought inside, Patrick headed back to the car to get the next load.

He was carrying in the bottles of wine that he'd got at the grocery store and the rum he'd picked up at the liquor store when a Volkswagen Beetle pulled up beside him, with Bauhaus's "Bela Lugosi's Dead" blaring from the car stereo.

"Have I come to the right place for the zombie-hunter slumber party?" Joyce called out over the din from the stereo speakers, leaning out the open driver-side window. "I brought my fuzzy pajamas."

"Very funny," Patrick dead-panned. He hefted the wine. "I got your order."

"Good thing." She turned and lifted up a reusable bottle bag that had been sitting on the passenger seat beside her. "I picked up a few bottles, too, just to be on the safe side."

She drove past Patrick's car, rolling up the window as she went, and parked by the curb. Patrick waited on the sidewalk as she climbed out, leaning heavily on her cane. She was wearing her leather jacket over a Joy Division t-shirt, faded denim jeans, and a pair of bright-pink eight-holed Doc Martens boots.

"Want some help with that?" Patrick asked as she reached into the back seat.

Joyce straightened up and shrugged. "Sounds good to me."

Leaving the rest of her things in the car, she pulled a single bottle of wine out of the bag from the passenger seat, and then turned and simply walked toward the open front door of the house, leaving her car door standing open. As she walked inside, she glanced back over her shoulder at him and smiled.

"Just be sure to lock it up when you're done." She held up the bottle of wine, waggling it back and forth. "I'm going to have a drink."

Patrick smiled as he set his load of bottles down on his front steps and went to fetch Joyce's things from the car. Then he felt a chill, and glanced up at the darkening sky overhead. He knew that they were probably safe here, but he didn't want to be out in the open any longer than he had to be. He hurried to pull the bags from the Volkswagen so he could get back inside as quickly as possible. It was almost as if he could feel eyes on him, watching from the shadows.

As Patrick worked in the kitchen, browning the cubes of chuck roast before stirring in onion and garlic, he could hear the sound of Izzie and Daphne walking across the floor upstairs, back and forth, no doubt moving boxes and shifting old furniture. On the other side of the kitchen wall he could hear Joyce's cane *tonk*ing on the floor as she went about unpacking her things in his bedroom. His intention was that he would offer to sleep on the couch while she took his bed, thinking it forward to assume that they would share a bed again just because circumstances had forced them to do so the night before in the abandoned lighthouse. Or maybe he was just overthinking things.

Patrick added diced potatoes, chopped carrots, tomato sauce, and chicken stock, then seasoned the pot liberally with salt and pepper. He was putting the cover on the pot when Joyce came in from the other room, holding a half-empty glass of wine in one hand, leaning heavily on her cane with the other.

"Smells good," she said, sniffing the air.

"It's my mom's recipe," Patrick answered, washing his hands in the sink. "Pretty standard island style."

"My mother was a horrible cook." Joyce shrugged. "So at least I come by it honestly."

"What?" Patrick dried his hands on a dish towel. "Don't enjoy cooking?"

She shook her head, miming a shudder with her lips pursed in a moue of distaste. "Not really. I mean, I *do* cook. You can't eat out every meal, right?"

"You could try."

"Not on my salary." Joyce circled the kitchen, heading toward the open bottle of wine she'd left on the counter earlier. She poured herself a full glass, and shrugged. "So I cook when I have to. Just very badly, is all."

Patrick fetched a tumbler from the cabinet and reached for the wine bottle. "Mind if I . . . ?" He glanced in Joyce's direction.

"Be my guest," she said, with a welcoming gesture like a hostess showing a restaurant patron to their table.

"I'm a decent cook at best," Patrick admitted as he splashed wine into the tumbler. "But I had good teachers."

Joyce leaned over the stove and took in a deep breath through her nostrils.

"I didn't think I was all that hungry, but smelling this . . . ?" She turned to look back over her shoulder at him. "I think I could just about eat the whole pot by myself."

"Well, don't get too eager," Patrick said, leaning his hip against the counter and taking a sip of the wine. "It needs to stew for at least another hour. My mother would smack me with a wooden spoon for cooking it even that quickly. She'd start a pot of stew simmering over a low flame in the morning and wouldn't let anyone touch it until sundown. The house was filled with the smell of her cooking almost every day, for hours and hours."

He put the tumbler down on the counter and bent down to pull another pan out of the cupboard.

"I usually serve the stew over rice, if that's okay with every-body." He set the pan next to the sink and then headed for the pantry to get out a bag of rice.

"Your slumber party, your rules," Joyce said, raising her glass and smiling.

Patrick put the rice and the empty pan on the counter, and set a timer on his phone to remind him to start the rice cook-ing when the stew was almost finished. Then he picked up his tumbler from the counter and nodded toward the living room.

"Let's go sit down. I want to hear about these test results you were talking about."

"Right." The smile faded from Joyce's face, and a more serious expression settled into place. She nodded toward the wine bottle as she walked to the door, her cane *tonk*ing against the kitchen floor like a drumbeat with each step. "Bring the wine. We're going to need it, I think."

J oyce was joining Patrick on the couch, having gone to grab some files from her bag in his bedroom, when they could hear the sound of footsteps coming down the stairs, and Izzie and Daphne rounded the corner, each of them carrying shopping bags.

"What's that?" Patrick glanced at the bag Izzie was carrying.

"Arts and crafts," Daphne answered for her.

Izzie elbowed her in the ribs and then dropped the bag on the far end of the coffee table. "I'll explain after we eat. I'm *starving*."

"And here I thought *I* was the one obsessed with food," Patrick said, smirking.

"I forgot to eat, okay?" Izzie rolled her eyes. "And I could smell whatever that is in the kitchen all the way from upstairs, which only made matters worse."

"Well, you'll have to wait, I'm afraid," Patrick answered. "Needs to simmer for a while longer."

"I could settle for *that* in the meantime." Daphne pointed at the wine bottle on the coffee table.

Izzie started for the kitchen, waving Daphne toward an empty chair.

"Sit," she said, "I'll get us a couple of glasses."

As she eased into the chair with a weary sigh, Daphne

turned to Patrick and Joyce. "It doesn't seem like anyone tried to kill either of *you* today, then?"

Patrick sat forward, raising an eyebrow.

"I'll take that as a no." Daphne glanced over at the kitchen door. "Izzie says that she nearly got run over by a truck in the street, right in front of the RA offices."

"Did she get the plates?" Patrick asked, putting his glass down on the coffee table. "I could run them through the system and see if . . ."

He trailed off when Daphne shook her head, lips pursed.

"No markings, either," she went on. "She *did* get the plates of a car she thought was being used as a spotter up the street, that took off as soon as the truck drove by."

"But when I ran the license number I came up empty," Izzie said as she walked back into the room from the kitchen carrying a glass in either hand. "Stolen last month from an old guy down in San Diego."

She put the glasses down on the table, filled each from the wine bottle, then handed one to Daphne and carried the other to the only remaining chair in the room.

"But you think this spotter was involved in all of this?" Joyce asked, looking worried. "That they were targeting *you* specifically?"

"It tracks." Izzie took a sip of wine, and lifted her shoulders in a slight shrug. "If Zotovic and his people know that we're onto them, a hit-and-run would be a good way of getting rid of one of us. Even if he *does* have people that can walk around in the daylight, Ridden or otherwise, they can't just go around killing federal agents in the street without raising a few eyebrows. But a garden-variety traffic accident? That's a little easier to get away with."

"I did some digging on Zotovic's background," Patrick said, leaning back on the couch. "News accounts, public records, law enforcement databases, you name it."

"Find anything useful?" Izzie asked. "Or interesting, at least."

"Not really." Patrick shook his head. "Only that he is part of a secret cabal of lizard people using phone apps to brainwash the human population."

All three women turned and gave him confused looks.

"A nutty conspiracy theory I found on the internet," he said. "Total waste of time."

"A week ago, that's what I would have thought about *this*." Joyce leaned over and bent down, to pick up the files that she'd brought over from the bedroom. "After everything that's happened the last few days, though . . . ?"

"This is about the stuff you found under Tyler Campbell's fingernails?" Patrick asked.

"Yep." Joyce nodded.

"That was the drug dealer I was telling you about," Izzie said, turning to Daphne. "The one whose body Patrick took me to see the first day I was in town."

"I remember," Daphne shot back, and then looked back to Joyce. "So was it Ink? Under the dead man's nails?"

"That's a little hard to say," Joyce answered, "given that we've never had a verifiable sample of Ink that we could compare it to. But then, it's easier to say what that stuff *isn't* than what it *is*."

"Mind clarifying that?" Patrick asked, and then hastened to add, "In layman's terms, please."

Joyce took a deep breath and let out a ragged sigh.

"The lab techs thought that this was a prank," she said. "Or some kind of test. I think they're still waiting to see if I show up to deliver the punch line, or give them gold stars for passing with flying colors. You see, the thing is, the stuff that I sent them to test didn't turn out to be *anything*."

Patrick looked around the room, and saw that the others were just as perplexed as he was.

"You mean it vanished?" he asked.

"No, it was still there," Joyce answered with a shake of her head. "It just . . . *wasn't* anything. They were completely unable to identify its chemical makeup. The stuff was completely nonreactive. Its surface texture was completely featureless, even under an electron microscope. They even put a small sample of it into a mass spectrometer, and all that they were able to prove conclusively was that it *had* mass. The electrons just passed right through it. Heck, it had volume, but it didn't appear to have any appreciable *weight*."

Something was itching at the back of Patrick's thoughts, an echo of something that he'd heard recently.

"So why did they think it was a prank?" Izzie asked.

"Because after spending three days wracking their brains trying to figure out what the stuff was," Joyce answered, "the other night one of the techs left the sample sitting on a workbench under a window, and when he came back the next morning . . ."

"It was gone," Izzie finished for her.

Joyce nodded. "They think I had someone come in and switch out the sample trays in the night, just to mess with them. They've got a small wager going about what was *really* in that sample that I sent them, and they want me to fess up so they can settle the bet."

Patrick's brow was furrowed as he rummaged through his memories, trying to find the one that echoed what Joyce had said.

"I'm guessing that there was sunlight through the window?" Daphne asked.

"That's my thinking, yeah." Joyce put the file on the coffee table and reached for her wine glass. "The stuff was buried pretty deep under Campbell's nails, which were *pretty* grimy, so it's possible that was the first time the sample had been exposed to daylight."

"Weakly interacting particles . . ." Patrick finally said under his breath.

The others turned to look in his direction.

"You remember what Professor Kono told us the other day?" Patrick asked Izzie. "About what Undersight was designed to look for?"

"The leaked gravity stuff, you mean?" Izzie said, and then turned to Daphne and Joyce. "Nicholas Fuller had this idea that gravity is weaker than the other forces like magnetism because most of the gravity is leaking out into the higher dimensions."

"No, that's not what I'm thinking of." Patrick shook his head. "Or not exactly, anyway. I meant the type of matter that should be there but that we don't detect." He thought for a moment, knowing it was on the tip of his tongue. "Dark matter."

"Oh, right," Izzie said. "And there was dark energy, too. But Fuller thought they were all part of the same phenomenon. The missing energy, the missing matter, the missing gravity . . . all of it the result of the higher dimensions."

"Wait, I've read a few articles about dark matter," Joyce said. "I thought the whole point of it was that we couldn't detect it, we just see its effects. Like, we wouldn't be able to see it, even if we were looking at it, because it doesn't emit or absorb light. Right?"

"Yeah, I guess," Patrick said, feeling out of his depth. "But maybe . . . I don't know, maybe whatever this stuff is, it shares similar properties?"

"It certainly lines up with what we know about Fuller's research." Izzie had her hand on her chin, a thoughtful expression on her face. "I don't know that any of that helps us any, in practical terms, but I guess it gives us a little bit of a better idea what we're dealing with."

Daphne had finished off her first glass of wine, and reached to grab the bottle on the table. "I think the real question is . . ." She paused, and then hefted the empty bottle. "The real question is, do we have any more wine?"

"Just a second." Patrick hopped up from the couch and walked to the kitchen. He picked a bottle of decent pinot noir, and then fished around in the drawer until he found his corkscrew.

He couldn't quite hear what they were saying in the living room, but when he came back in carrying the open wine bottle, the conversation stopped suddenly and all three women turned to look at him with abashed expressions on their faces. Izzie even held her hand over her mouth as she stifled a laugh.

"What?" Patrick couldn't quite keep a note of defensiveness from creeping into his voice. He walked over and handed Daphne the bottle. "Seriously, what?"

"It's nothing," Joyce said quickly, fighting a smile. "Let's get back to it. Daphne, you were saying?"

"Well, I did some checking today, made some calls from my apartment, that kind of thing." Daphne finished filling her glass almost to the rim, and then set the bottle on the table. "Through the course of a few different investigations, I've gotten to know people at city works, and the Recondito Bureau of Transportation, and a few other city agencies. And I wanted to find out if anything about last night had been picked up on automated surveillance systems. Traffic cameras, security feeds, that kind of thing. Because I just couldn't accept the fact that there hadn't been *anything* in the news or online or anywhere today about all of those . . . those people filling the streets last night."

"And?" Patrick asked.

"Nothing. Not. A. Thing." Daphne took a sip of wine, and eyes looking out over the top of her glass, added in a mock casual tone, "But I did learn something interesting, though."

She paused, looking around the room, as if for dramatic effect.

"Just tell us already," Izzie said, reaching over and kicking Daphne's foot.

"Okay, okay." She lowered the glass and held it in both hands in her lap. "One of my contacts with the Bureau of Transportation was complaining about still getting used to this new software that they'd just upgraded on all their computers. And then a guy I know at City Works mentioned that *they'd* just had to install some new software on their computers, too. I started asking around, and it turns out that it was a city-wide initiative spearheaded by the mayor's office, supposedly to increase efficiency and eliminate budgetary overruns, by standardizing the computer systems across different departments. So all of the software that controls the traffic cameras, security feeds, alarm monitoring systems, you name it . . . it's all been upgraded this year. And want to guess what company *made* all of that new software?"

"Parasol, obviously," Izzie said.

"Oh." Daphne deflated, a disappointed expression on her face. "I didn't think it was obvious."

"Not when you were doing the investigating, no," Izzie answered, conciliatory. "But the fact that you're telling us in this dramatic fashion, like the answer is going to surprise us. . . . With that kind of set up, of *course* the software that you've found out about would turn out to be made by the software company that's been on all of our minds this whole time."

"Ignore Izzie," Patrick said. "Seriously, I work in a city office and had no idea. But the mayor's office doesn't have the same degree of oversight and control over the Recondito PD as he does the departments that are run out of city hall, so maybe it just hasn't hit us yet. But knowing that Parasol wrote the code that controls all of the city's cameras on the streets . . ."

"My theory was that they might have put in some kind of backdoor," Daphne went on. "Something that would allow Parasol to get into the system without the city knowing about it, and get rid of any footage that they didn't want to be recorded."

Patrick was about to reply when his phone's alarm went off. It took him a moment to remember why he'd set it in the first place.

"Stew's almost done," he said, standing up from the couch, "so I need to go put the rice on the stove."

He started toward the kitchen.

"You guys just hang out here and I'll let you know when . . ."

He trailed off, and glanced back over his shoulder, eyes narrowed suspiciously. Sure enough, Izzie and Daphne were already leaning in closer to Joyce, and looked at him with slightly guilty expressions.

"Wouldn't it be easier to talk about me behind my back when I'm in the other room?"

"Maybe," Joyce said. "But probably not as much fun."

CHAPTER NINE

Izzie wasn't sure whether it was just because she had been so hungry, or was due to the glasses of wine she had while waiting for dinner to be ready, but after the first bite of Patrick's beef stew she was prepared to state categorically that it was the best thing she had ever tasted. Not that anyone was asking. They were all too busy eating. It was clear that she wasn't the only one to have skipped a meal that day.

All except Patrick, of course, who seemed never to miss a meal if he could at all help it. While the rest ate, he picked at his plate while summarizing the results of his online investigations into Martin Zotovic's background, and his theory about the possible effect of a Taser on one of the Ridden. He talked for far too long, hardly touching his food. For a while Izzie wondered if he'd simply lost his appetite. But then while she caught everyone up to speed on what she had pieced together from revisiting Roberto Aguilar's journals about the history of the Mayan daykeepers, Patrick proceeded to work his way through a second helping. And when Izzie asked whether he would be able to file the necessary paperwork with the Recondito Police Department to back up the "extended stakeout" that she and Daphne were using to justify their absence from the Resident Agency offices, Patrick said that he didn't think that would present any significant difficulty, all while serving himself a third helping of the beef stew and rice.

Along with what Joyce had told them earlier about the lab results on the Campbell sample, and the information that Daphne had supplied about the city's new computer systems, it seemed to Izzie as if everyone had been brought up to speed on what the others had learned that day.

The question remained: Where should they go from here?

A fter helping clear away the dishes and opening another bottle of wine, Izzie led the others back to the living room.

"Okay, let's see where we stand." She turned to Daphne, and gestured to the duffel bag that they'd brought with them from the RA offices. "What do you think about unpacking the gear, just so we can get a good visual check of what we've got to work with?"

"Seems as good a plan as any," Daphne said, and knelt down beside the bag. Unzipping it, she pulled out the two tactical shotguns and boxes of shells, and arranged them on the floorboards along the far wall.

"I grabbed a few things on my way out of the 10th, too." Patrick stepped into the kitchen and returned with a hard-sided gun case that was about the height and width of a businessman's briefcase, but two or three times as thick. Setting it down on the floor, he worked the combination locks to pop open the latches, and then lifted the lid. He reached inside and pulled out a stun baton in one hand and a Taser with a pistol grip in the other. "Like I said, I wondered whether they'd work on one of the Ridden, so I figured I'd bring along a couple from the precinct armory, just in case they came in handy."

He put them back in the case, but left it open on the ground beside the tactical shotguns.

"I've got my service weapon and ammo, of course," Patrick went on, patting the holster at his side. He turned to Izzie and Daphne. "I'm assuming you two have yours, as well?"

"Naturally," Izzie nodded, speaking for them both.

"I picked up one last thing, too." Patrick reached into his pocket, and held out his hand. There were two small glass vials on his palm, which Izzie recognized immediately.

"The ilbal," she said. It was the drug that Nicholas Fuller had taken, which he believed helped him to "see" the Ridden for what they really were.

Patrick nodded, and then bent down to put the vials in the gun case along with the stun baton and Taser.

"But weren't you the one worried about taking evidence out of the station without permission?" Izzie chided.

"Well, none of this is exactly by the book, is it?" He shrugged. "But it was slated to be destroyed anyway, right? And I figured maybe it would come in handy at some point."

Izzie chewed her lower lip, casting a glance at the vials.

"What, is no one going to ask the medical examiner if she came armed?" Joyce adopted a tone of mock outrage. Leaning heavily on her cane, she walked over to where her leather jacket hung on a hook by the front door. "Shows what *you* know."

She reached into the pocket of her jacket, and pulled out

a small case. It looked almost like the kind designed for eye-glasses, but was narrower and more squared off than most that Izzie had seen.

"Come at the queen of the underworld—" Joyce gave Patrick a sly look, and then snapped open the small case and held it out for their inspection "—you best come correct."

Izzie and the others leaned over to see the interior of the case, in which a dainty-looking long-handled blade rested on a lining of purple silk.

Joyce looked from face to face, and saw the confused expressions that Izzie and the others wore. "What don't you get?"

She reached in and plucked the blade from the case, hold-ing it up in front of her with the handle pinched between her thumb and index finger.

"My grandfather gave it to me when I graduated from med school," she explained. "It's an antique, dating back to Victorian England."

Izzie was trying to follow what Joyce was saying, but was sure that the confusion on her own face was as evident now as it had been a moment before, and glancing at the others she saw that she wasn't the only one.

"Look." Joyce sighed. "The blades of most surgical scalpels these days are made out of steel. But back in the olden days, they made them out of *silver*."

"Ooooh." Izzie nodded, the realization of what she was hearing slowly dawning.

"I mean, it's not *much*," Joyce said, shrugging, "but if silver introduced into the body of one of the Ridden *does* disrupt the possession, I thought this would be a useful thing to have on hand."

Izzie thought about the long, curved blade that Nicholas Fuller had used in the Reaper murders, sitting now wrapped in plastic in a box back in the 10th Precinct station house community room. Would *that* blade be a useful thing to have on hand now, too? It felt gruesome to consider using a serial killer's favorite murder weapon for their own defense, but if it meant the difference between surviving an encounter with one of the Ridden and living to see another day, she could cope with feeling a little bit gruesome.

"Probably more useful than a silver spoon in a sandwich bag," Patrick said, then turned to Izzie and quickly added, "No offense."

"No, I think you're completely right." Izzie walked over to the coffee table. "Those bags I gave you this morning were a long shot to begin with, I'll be the first to admit. Which is why I think we need to come up with something a little more reliable."

Izzie picked up one of the shopping bags that she'd brought in from Daphne's car.

"What do you have in mind?" Patrick asked.

"Like I said . . ." Izzie upended the bag, and the contents spilled out onto the surface of the table—necklace chains, bits of wood and metal, a soldering gun, costume jewelry, carving knives, jars of paint, and more. She looked up, taking in Patrick and Joyce's confused expression and the slight smile on Daphne's face. "Arts and crafts."

Izzie tossed the empty shopping bag to the corner, and then emptied out the other one she'd brought on the table, as well. Spools of string rolled out, along with bits of leather and fabric, containers filled with crystal beads, scissors, and the like.

"What . . . what is all this?" Patrick looked at the chaos sprawled out across the surface of the coffee table.

"It's amazing what a little motivation and a couple hundred bucks can get you at a crafts supply store," Daphne said, dropping into a chair.

Izzie turned to face Patrick and Joyce.

"Mawmaw Jean didn't just take a gris-gris bag with her everywhere she went, she also made all sorts of charms. She thought they protected her from evil spirits, or invoked the aid of good ones. And that got me thinking about the marks that your great-uncle made, Patrick. If that's really what's keeping the Ridden out of this neighborhood, what if we made portable versions that we could take with us when we leave? What if we carried that protection wherever we go?"

Patrick turned back to look at the table, his eyes narrowed.

"I don't know," he said, thoughtful. "I mean, it *could* work . . . but . . ."

"Didn't your great-uncle teach you how to make them?" Izzie pressed on.

Patrick raised his eyes to meet her gaze, a somewhat stricken expression on his face.

"No! I mean . . . not really. He was going to, but . . ." He lowered his eyes, trailing off, and when he continued a note of sadness crept into his voice. "There wasn't time."

Joyce reached over and rested her hand gently on his arm, a comforting gesture.

"Well," Izzie said, plowing ahead, "in that case we'll just have to copy the ones that he left behind."

She started toward the stairs to the second floor.

"Where are you going?" Patrick asked, raising an eyebrow.

Izzie glanced over, hand on the rail and already several steps up the stairs.

"I'm going to get my jacket," she said, as if it were the most obvious thing in the world. She pulled out her phone and held it up. "I've got some pictures to take, and it's *cold* outside."

"What?" Patrick stepped forward, holding up his hand for her to stop. "You want to go outside *now*?"

Izzie stopped on the third step up, leaning back and looking over the railing at them. "Why not? We're wasting time if we don't, I figure."

"But . . ." Patrick glanced over at Joyce.

"Don't look at me," Joyce said. "You two are the mumbo-jumbo experts around here. I'm the science one, remember?"

With a sigh, Izzie went back two steps on the stairs so she could see everyone in the room more clearly. "Look, we *need* to be able to move freely around the city without worrying all the time that we're going to get caught too far away from this neighborhood when the sun goes down. And there's no way of knowing if we're still not exposing ourselves to risk when the sun is *up*, since some of the possessed people can still walk around in daylight. So if there's a chance that a charm—or amulet or whatever you want to call it—with those markings on it is going to keep us safe out there, then we're wasting time *not* doing it right now."

She looked around the room at the three of them.

"Besides, the markings will keep us safe here, right? So, I'll do it by myself if I have to, but we'd be done a whole lot quicker if I had help."

By the time she came back downstairs with her jacket, the rest of them were already wearing their own jackets and coats.

"All right, then," Izzie said with a grin, heading for the door. "Let's get to it."

Fifteen minutes later, the four of them were in the alley behind Patrick's house, using their phones to take pictures of the markings on the various houses on either side of the alleyway. In the distance they could hear the low murmur of the nightlife on Almeria a few blocks away on the other side of Mission, the low thrum of the music from the bars, the susurrating murmur of people talking and laughing as they walked down the sidewalks, or gathered to talk in small groups beneath the eaves. Though the air stirred with a faint breeze, the skies overhead were cloudy, and the light from the houses and streetlights below suffused the clouds, so that it seemed as if the four of them were moving through the shadows of the alley beneath a dimly lit ceiling far overhead.

Izzie had already snapped off a dozen or so high-definition images of the spiraling whorls etched high up on Patrick's house, both with the flash and with what little usable light reached this far down the alley from the streetlight on the corner. Now she was a few dozen feet further down the alley behind another house that had been marked with the sign of the old man's protection.

"This one is different," she said, as she carefully framed the spiral markings in the shot. "I mean, it's *pretty* similar, but it's not identical."

She glanced over her shoulder at Patrick, who was standing in the middle of the alley with Joyce, looking uneasy.

"It was an art, Uncle Alf always used to say," Patrick answered, glancing from one end of the alleyway to the other, warily. "Knowing just what mark to put in a particular spot, to get a particular result."

"Mmmm." Izzie brought up her phone's photo gallery and swiped through the images that she'd captured so far. "Tied to a specific geographic location, maybe?"

She looked back at Patrick, who was still shifting his gaze all around them, his eyes narrowed.

"Maybe," he answered, sounding preoccupied.

Izzie put her hand on her hip, head cocked to one side.

"Listen, *Lieutenant*," she said, tone dripping with sarcasm, "I thought the marks kept us safe from the Ridden here, even after dark. That was the whole reason that we all came back at your place tonight, right? So what's got you so spooked?"

"I'm not sure." Patrick spared her the briefest of glances before continuing to scan their surroundings. "Something doesn't feel right. It's like we're missing something."

Izzie noticed that Patrick's hand was hovering near the handle of the semiautomatic holstered at his hip, and that he kept shifting in place, as if trying to remain between Joyce and whatever threat he imagined out in the darkness.

"Too many shadows," Patrick added, looking down the alley. Then he turned his attention back to Izzie, and added in a low, urgent voice, "Let's wrap this up and get back inside."

Izzie gave him a curt nod, and went looking for another spiraling mark that she could photograph. The shadows grew larger and more diffuse the farther away she moved from the mouth of the alley.

"Hey, Izzie," she heard Daphne calling from the shadows ahead of her, "is this what we're looking for?"

Izzie turned and looked in the direction of her voice, and saw that Daphne had already gone another thirty or forty feet further down the alley, using her phone's flashlight function to scan the backs of the houses. At the moment, her attention was on a spot illuminated by her phone's light on the rear exterior of a house five or six doors down from Patrick's.

"I *think* it is. . . ." Daphne turned from the spot overhead to glance over in Izzie's direction. "But I'm not sure."

Izzie walked down the alley toward Daphne, conscious of the audible crunch of her boots stepping across broken glass and rock on the alley's tarmac. The sounds of the revelers over on Almeria grew fainter and fainter the deeper into the alley she moved, almost as if the noise were being swallowed up by the shadows themselves. She couldn't help but think of the dream she'd had that morning, briefly dozing on the couch in Patrick's living room, and the way that the surrounding darkness had seemed like a solid medium through which she had struggled to move. Before the shadow had begun to consume her flesh bit by bit, that is.

"It looks like one of the markings," Daphne said when Izzie reached her side. "But it's got vines or some kind of brambles growing over it, so . . ." She trailed off, shrugging. "I can't be sure."

Izzie looked up at the spot illuminated by Daphne's phone light and squinted. It *did* look like one of the old man's marks might be hidden beneath the foliage, but it was hard to say for certain.

"It probably is. Must be a lot of them in that state, I'd guess. Patrick said that his great-uncle used to pay him and his cousins to keep the marks clean and clear." Izzie turned to glance back toward the mouth of the alley, where Patrick was huddled protectively near Joyce. They seemed to be talking to each other, but the sound of their voices was little more than a dull murmur from this distance. "Every weekend, he'd be out here pulling crawling vines off the ones on the walls, or sweeping away dirt or trash from the ones on the ground. Sounds to me like . . ."

"Wait," Daphne interrupted, reaching out to touch Izzie's elbow. "Did they *have* to?"

"I suppose not." Izzie looked back at her, and lifted her shoulders in a faint shrug. "The old guy paid them a quarter each for it, so it doesn't sound like he *made* them do it."

"No." Daphne's tone was more insistent now, and she took hold of Izzie's upper arm, squeezing tightly. "Did they *have* to keep the marks clean and uncovered? For them to *work*?"

Izzie's eyes widened as the implications of what Daphne was saying sunk in.

"Come on," she said, taking hold of Daphne's hand. "Let's get back inside, okay?"

They turned to head back toward the mouth of the alley.

But the shadows in front of them had grown so thick that they could barely *see* the mouth of the alley.

"Izzie?" She could only faintly hear Daphne's voice, even though she was right beside her.

Izzie felt a wave of nausea grip her insides, and a strange, unpleasant taste spread across her tongue. She had experienced this before. She knew what this was.

"Daphne?" She kept a firm grip on Daphne's hand, squeezing it tightly, and for an instant savored the weight and warmth of it as Daphne squeezed back. "I think that we should . . ."

But before Izzie could finish, figures began to detach themselves from the shadows on either side of them, advancing on the two of them. Izzie could just barely make out the black spots that marked the skin of their faces and hands, darker still than the shadows around them.

They were the Ridden.

CHAPTER TEN

Patrick had been unable to stop glancing over at the mouth of the alley, where it met Almeria. He kept thinking about the car that Izzie had seen parked on the street earlier that day, and the truck that had nearly run her over. And he was reminded how he had felt like he was being watched earlier that day, when he ventured out from the 10th Precinct station house to get some lunch. Were they being watched? Was someone following them? Maybe Uncle Alf's marks were protecting them here, but even then, there was something about that lurking just at the edge of his thoughts, an anxiety that wouldn't stop nagging him, though he couldn't bring it into clear focus.

"I'm cold," Joyce had said, huddling close to him for warmth. "Do you think we've got enough to work with, so we can get inside already?"

"Yeah, we probably do," Patrick had answered. "We just need to convince Izzie that . . ."

The sound of shouts issuing from the far end of the alley behind them interrupted him, and Patrick wheeled around, hand instinctively moving toward the semiautomatic holstered at his hip.

He saw Izzie and Daphne, some twenty yards away, menaced on both sides by figures emerging from the shadows. Was it just a couple of tweakers or crackheads, desperate for some easy money and thinking that two women walking down a dark alley made for easy marks? Or were they . . . ?

"Ridden!" Izzie shouted.

Patrick's gaze shot up to the spiraling mark carved into the rear of his house, the same one that he'd spent countless weekends as a kid tending and cleaning. There were marks on every second or third house on this block, so why would the Ridden not be repelled from approaching?

And the anxiety that had buzzed at the edge of his thoughts slid clearly into focus.

There was a reason that his Uncle Alf had insisted that the marks be tended to on a regular basis.

As Patrick watched, two more figures emerged from the shadows in front of Izzie and Daphne. The two women were now surrounded, ahead and behind on either side, and the Ridden were closing in fast.

Izzie gave Daphne's hand one last squeeze and then let go, reaching for her semiautomatic, which sat in a holster slightly behind her right hipbone. As she drew the pistol, with her other hand she reached into the left pocket of her suede jacket, fingers searching for the Ziploc bag that she'd stuffed in there that morning, hoping against hope that it was still there.

"Izzie?" Daphne stood shoulder to shoulder with her, and had already drawn her own pistol out of its holster. "Any ideas?"

"I'm working on it," Izzie answered, and felt a brief surge of triumph as her fingers closed on the plastic bag in her pocket.

Izzie raised her left hand out in front of her, the makeshift gris-gris bag hanging from it, and held it out toward the nearest of the approaching Ridden.

But the Ridden seemed unaffected by the salt, quartz, and silver in the lumpy bag, and continued to shuffle toward her, its eyes seeming cold and lifeless in a face that was so marred by blots that it was practically a walking shadow.

"Izzie?" Daphne hissed through gritted teeth.

Izzie spared the briefest of glances down toward the mouth of the alley, where Patrick stood with his pistol in hand, Joyce right behind him. The Ridden seemed uninterested in either of them, which suggested that the unobscured and unobstructed marks on the building in that end of the alley were keeping the Ridden at bay. But how could she and Daphne reach that spot of safety? There were six Ridden approaching them slowly but inexorably, three on either side, blocking their escape down either end of the alleyway.

"Stay back!" Daphne shouted to the Ridden on her side, punctuating her words with a sharp jab of her pistol's barrel. "I *will* shoot if you come any closer."

One of the Ridden opened its mouth, jaw hanging open at unnatural angle, and an inhuman-human sounding noise shuddered forth. It sounded almost like "Ke-ke-ke-ke . . ."

Were the Ridden attempting to communicate? Was this their best approximation of human speech? Or was it just a voiceless threat?

The Ridden with the open mouth lurched forward, arms out and grasping toward Daphne only a few short paces away.

"Stay *back*!" Daphne shouted, pulling the trigger. Her pistol rang out as she fired a round into the Ridden's torso, but the blot-covered shambler seemed unfazed.

Bullets weren't the answer, Izzie knew.

"Hang on," Izzie said, holstering her own pistol and then zipping open the mouth of the plastic bag. "I've got an idea."

Simply holding the salt in her hand wasn't going to be enough, she realized. She had to be smarter, use the tools at her disposal the way that she already knew would work. Her mind raced as she thought back to what she had read in Roberto Aguilar's journals, taking a step *toward* the nearest of the Ridden.

"Izzie, what are you *doing*?" Daphne shouted.

"Did you bring yours?" Izzie bent down and tipped out a line of salt on the tarmac between herself and the Ridden, then continued in a slow clockwise arc as she moved in front of Daphne. When Daphne didn't answer, she clarified, "The gris-gris bag? The Ziploc I gave you this morning?"

"Oh," Daphne said in a quiet voice, sounding abashed. "No, I left it inside."

"We'll have to hope this is enough," Izzie answered, eyes still on the ground as she carefully continued to mark out a tight orbit around the spot where they stood, leaving a faint circle of sea salt glittering on the dark tarmac underfoot.

By the time she reached the point where she had started, and closed the circuit around them, there were only a few grains of salt left in the plastic bag. She stood up, pocketing the Ziploc, and moved to stand close to Daphne at the center of a circle of sea salt roughly four feet in diameter.

Izzie remembered the circle that Nicholas Fuller had marked out on the metal floor of the lighthouse's lantern room where he dismembered his victims, a final barrier against an attack. Would it be enough to protect her and Daphne now?

The nearest of the Ridden reached the edge of the circle and stopped short, as though it had hit a wall. The tips of its toes were mere inches from the salt, and if it had reached out its arms it could have grabbed Izzie easily. But the Ridden kept its arms at its sides, seemingly unwilling even to reach across the line.

As Izzie and Daphne huddled together, the other five Ridden approached the protective ring of salt, and all stopped short, just like the first one had. They stood, swaying slightly back and forth, feet planted on the ground just inches from the salt ring. And as one, they opened their mouths, impossibly wide, and that same horrible, inhuman sound shuddered forth.

"Ke-ke-ke-ke."

Izzie thought that they were safe for the moment, but she wasn't sure how long that would last. As the breeze picked up once more, Izzie could see some of the salt on the ground begin to stir, and she knew that it wouldn't last for long.

Patrick had watched as Izzie shuffled her way around Daphne, hunched over and pouring out salt, and realized immediately what she was trying to do.

"Are you okay?" he called out, cupping one hand by the side of his mouth to direct the sound of his voice.

"For the moment," Izzie answered, shouting to be heard over the unsettling sound coming from the mouths of the Ridden. "But this is only a short-term solution."

Patrick had approached as close as seemed advisable, with the closest of the uncovered markings just a short distance behind him. Joyce had followed close behind, her hand on his back as though she worried they might lose each other in the shadows, though they had not yet ventured farther than the pool of light that spilled across this end of the alleyway from the streetlight on the corner.

"We've got to get them out of there," Patrick said, thoughts racing. The night before they had been in close quarters with a pack of the Ridden, and had only narrowly escaped. The only thing that had saved them when things seemed at their darkest had been . . . "That's it!"

He wheeled around to face Joyce.

"The Ridden are disoriented by loud, discordant sounds," he reminded her. The night before, a few selections from ABBA's Greatest Hits playing on the speaker of Joyce's phone had been enough to keep the Ridden at bay just long enough for them to escape. "Do you have your phone on you?"

Joyce eyes widened as she met his gaze. "It's in my bag inside."

"Damn," Patrick cursed beneath his breath.

He turned back to see how Izzie and Daphne were faring. The Ridden were still holding their positions outside the ring of salt. For now.

"The wind is picking up!" Izzie shouted. "The salt is already starting to blow away!"

Patrick took a step toward them, then stopped. The bullets in his pistol were no good, that much was clear. There were the tactical shotguns back in his living room, but could he get there and back in time to help? Or should he just try to find enough salt in his kitchen to reinforce or even widen the circle of protection? Maybe he could create a path from the safety of the spiral markings down to where Izzie and Daphne were trapped, and then they could . . .

"Joyce, do you think . . . ?"

He glanced behind him, and saw that Joyce had taken off running and was already rounding the corner onto Almeria. With the din of the strange noises the Ridden were making, he hadn't been able to heard her footsteps as she left. Whether she was going to get her phone and then come back, or had decided just to run away, he wasn't sure. Would Joyce just run off and leave him without saying anything if she hadn't intended to come back?

"Patrick?" Izzie called out. "What are we thinking here?"

He turned back, considering their options. The Ridden that stood between him and the nearest side of the circle of salt were of average height, but with the thin, almost emaciated build of most Ink users. It was difficult to tell if they were men or women, or rather if they *had* been men or women before being taken over by the loa, because now they were little more than mindless suits of meat and bone. But Patrick figured that he had at least a couple of inches and a couple dozen pounds on each of them. Perhaps if he were to tackle one of the ones on this side of the circle, he could open a hole large enough for Izzie and Daphne to break through and run for cover. But what were the chances that he would be able to escape being grabbed by one of the Ridden himself before he could get back to safety?

He couldn't worry about that now. He had to act fast while there was still a chance. If he didn't make it back, then hopefully they would.

Patrick holstered his pistol. Then he bent low, one shoulder forward, and took a deep breath.

zzie was standing so close to Daphne that they were practically pushing against each other, shoulder to shoulder and turned to face the Ridden on either side, so that they were almost standing back to back now.

"As dates go, this could have gone better," Daphne deadpanned. "Next time, how about *I* make the plans, okay?"

Izzie glanced back over her shoulder, and met Daphne's eyes.

"Yeah, maybe we should have just gone dancing, after all," Izzie said.

"Hey, guys!" Patrick shouted from further down the alley. "Get ready!"

Izzie and Daphne exchanged a quick look before turning in his direction.

"Get ready for what . . . ?" Izzie began to say, but her words were drowned out by the tinny blast of a high-pitched car horn honking from far behind them.

She spun around, momentarily blinded by the glare of a pair of headlight beams swinging into the far end of the alleyway.

"What the hell . . . ?" Daphne said.

A heartbeat later and the alley was filled with the thumping sounds of a car stereo blaring out the Sisters Of Mercy's "This Corrosion."

The headlights' glare grew even brighter as the car barreled down the alley toward them.

The Ridden seemed instantly disoriented. They left off making that horrible sound, and flailed around, as if they were suddenly struck blind and left in an unfamiliar place. One of them placed a foot on the salt circle, and recoiled as if in pain. Another waved its arms in front of it, hands grasping.

Brakes squealed as the Volkswagen Beetle slammed to a halt just to the left of Izzie and Daphne, and the passenger side door swung open.

"Get in!" Joyce shouted over the music howling from the car's speakers.

Izzie pushed Daphne in front of her, keeping her eyes on the Ridden around them. They were disoriented, perhaps, but they were still trying to reach them. They grabbed the air blindly, hoping to take hold of them.

After Daphne was in the passenger seat, Izzie started to get in. There was no back door, and no time to crawl over Daphne into the back seat.

"Get *in* already!" Joyce urged.

Izzie folded herself down onto Daphne's lap as best she could. It was a tight squeeze, but workable.

As Daphne was pulling the passenger door shut, Joyce was working the gear shift.

"Okay," Joyce said, standing on the clutch and slamming the car into first gear, "now let's . . ."

What she was about to say next was lost when one of the Ridden reached through the open driver's side window and grabbed hold of Joyce's throat, squeezing hard.

"Joyce!" Izzie shouted.

The driver's side of the car was outside the salt circle, Izzie realized, even assuming that enough of the salt remained on the tarmac to provide any protection. One of the flailing Ridden, grasping at whatever was within reach, had by chance managed to grab Joyce. But now that it knew she was there, it wasn't letting go.

"Shoot it!" Daphne said.

Izzie had thrown herself across the interior of the car and

grabbed the Ridden's arm, trying to pry its hands loose from Joyce's neck. She knew that shooting it wouldn't do any good.

Joyce, struggling for breath, eyes bulging, batted at Izzie's arm, and at first Izzie thought she was just thrashing around in a panic. Then she met Joyce's determined gaze, and saw that Joyce was trying to tell her something. She was trying to *reach* something.

On the floorboards at Joyce's feet, a small case with squared off corners.

The Ridden still held tight to Joyce's neck, and was now forcing its own head and shoulders through the open driver's side window, eyes black and lifeless, mouth open and the same horrible sound shuddering from deep in its throat, audible even over the din of the music blaring from the speakers.

Izzie scrambled, ducking low and trying to reach the case. She was sure that she was kneeing Daphne in the face, but would have to apologize for that later. Muscles strained as she stretched her arm, shoulder wedged firmly against Joyce's leg, until finally her fingers nudged the case.

From outside the car, Izzie could hear gunshots ringing out.

She sat up as best she could, clutching the case in her hand, and then quickly flipped open the lid. There on the bed of purple silk sat the long-handled silver-bladed scalpel that Joyce had shown them a short time before.

Wrapping her fist around the handle of the scalpel, Izzie twisted and in one swift motion slammed the blade into the side of the Ridden's neck, just below the jawline.

Joyce gasped for air as the hand gripping her neck slowly loosened, and the Ridden slid backwards out of the open window like a marionette whose strings had just been cut. The dark blots that mottled its skin were quickly shrinking, like drops of water burning off a hot skillet, and the Ridden's eyes rolled up in their sockets, showing white. By the time the lifeless body hit the ground, the scalpel's handle sticking out of its neck, there were no visible signs that it had ever been possessed.

"Go!" Daphne shouted, somewhere behind Izzie's knee.

Without waiting for Izzie to get out of her lap, Joyce stood on the accelerator pedal and the Volkswagen Beetle lurked into motion, barreling toward the mouth of the alley.

Patrick barely had time to jump out of the way as Joyce's car roared past him. He'd stopped charging toward the circle the second that the Volkswagen had appeared at the far end of the alley, and had breathed a momentary sigh of relief as first Daphne and then Izzie had climbed into the passenger seat. But seconds later when the Ridden had reached through the driver's side window and grabbed hold of Joyce, he had rushed forward again, all thoughts about his own safety forgotten.

Patrick had ducked the grasping arm of one of the flailing Ridden, then skidded to one side to avoid colliding with another. But just when it looked as though he had a clear path to rush the Ridden who was slowly choking the life from Joyce, in the hopes of tackling it and prying loose its grip on her throat, a third Ridden shambled directly into his path. Patrick's forward momentum was too great to change direction in time, and his shoulder slammed right into the Ridden's bony chest.

The Ridden grabbed hold of Patrick's left arm just above the wrist, pinning it in a vice-like grip.

Patrick's first instinct was to try to wrest himself free by force, but his first attempt to budge the Ridden's fingers was met with failure, the thing's grip being too strong to break. He tried punching the Ridden in the throat, but got no response.

The Ridden might be impervious to pain, it still relied on the mechanics of the possessed body to function. And if he could impair the functioning of the body parts involved . . .

Trying to ignore the pain of the Ridden's tight grip on his left arm, with his right hand he drew his semiautomatic, and pressed the barrel right against the wrist bones of the Ridden's hand that gripped him.

Patrick fired three shots in rapid succession, ripping through the bones and tendons of the Ridden's wrist.

The Ridden's fingers still tried to keep their hold on Patrick's arm, but with the tendons that connected to those fingers left shredded, it was unable to maintain sufficient pressure, and Patrick was able to wrench his arm free.

Just then, Joyce's Volkswagen beetle barreled past him, blaring the Sisters of Mercy.

The Ridden lost track of where Patrick was, disoriented and confused, and Patrick took off running after the speeding car.

CHAPTER ELEVEN

Izzie's heartbeat was pounding in her ears as she and Daphne tumbled out of the passenger side door of Joyce's car.

"Joyce!" Patrick shouted, sprinting around the corner toward them.

From the driver's side, Joyce waved him away with one hand, the other held to her bruised neck.

"Door . . ." Joyce managed to croak, and then gestured toward the front of his house. "Inside . . ."

Without missing a step, Patrick pivoted and raced up the front steps, hand digging in his pocket for his keys. By the time Izzie and Daphne were helping Joyce up the steps, Patrick was flinging the door open to usher them inside.

Izzie glanced back over her shoulder, but from this vantage point all that she could see were the cars parked up and down Almeria, and the spire of the Church of the Holy Saint Anthony rising up above the roofs of the houses across the street. There were no shambling Ridden in sight.

When they were all through the door, Patrick slammed the door shut behind them, and quickly locked each of the locks. Then he turned to Izzie.

"The rear windows in the bedroom upstairs overlook the alley," he said in a rush. "I'll double-check the locks on the backdoor, you run up and see what you can see."

Izzie was racing up the stairs before Patrick had even finished talking.

She turned the corner at the top of the stair, and skidded down the hallway, narrowing avoiding a teetering stack of moving boxes. She hooked to the right, dancing through a maze of junk and old toys strewn on the floor, and then slammed open the door to the bedroom. Thankfully, this was the same room that she and Daphne had spent some time organizing earlier that evening, and so there was a clear enough path to the window on the far side of the room.

Izzie yanked the cord to raise the velour blinds, which clattered and bent with the force of her pull, and then she peered down through the streaked and grimed window at the darkened alleyway below.

It took a moment to orient herself, and to work out which direction she should be looking. But when she craned her neck she saw the mouth of the alley off to her right, and then swung her head around to lean over and look down the other direction.

She could just barely make out the glint of the light reflecting off the small sections of the salt ring that had not been blown away. But of the six Ridden who had attacked them there was no sign, not even the one who had gone down with the silver scalpel in its neck.

Turning away from the window, Izzie realized that her

heart was still racing, and she was breathing so fast and heavily that she probably ran the risk of hyperventilating. As she
headed back across the room and down the hallway toward
the stairs, she tried her best to still her fight-or-flight instinct.
She was safe now, she told herself. Assuming that the Ridden
hadn't broken down the back door and were even now attacking Patrick.

But no. As she descended the stairs, she hear Patrick's footsteps on the hardwood floor as he came back from the rear of
the house.

"It's all locked up and secured," he told Izzie as she reached
the first floor. "See anything from up there?"

Izzie shook her head.

"No, they're gone," she answered. "Even the one that I
stabbed with Joyce's scalpel."

"You think they took the body with them when they left?"
Patrick asked, as they went to join the others in the foyer.

"Maybe. Silver didn't seem to repel them, so maybe they
can get close to it? Maybe it's only when silver enters their bodies that it causes problems for them?"

"Could be," Patrick answered. "Either way, I think we're
safe for now."

Then he turned to Joyce, who was standing with her back
leaning against the wall, with her fingertips gingerly probing
the welts that covered either side of her neck, the marks left by
the Ridden's vice-like grip.

Izzie continued trying to slow her breathing, her pulse still
pounding in her veins. She bent over with her hands on her
knees, trying to regain her composure.

"You okay?" Daphne came over and put her hand on Izzie's
shoulder.

Izzie looked up to meet Daphne's gaze.

"I think so," she said, with less certainty than she had intended. Then she straightened up, took a slow, deep breath, and nodded. "Yeah, I'm okay. You?"

Daphne rubbed the left side of her jaw.

"You clocked me in the face with your kneecap," she said in mock offense, and then smiled slightly. "But yeah, I think I'll live."

Izzie turned, and saw that Patrick and Joyce were heading into the living room.

"Maybe just a glass of water?" Joyce was saying, as she sank down onto the couch.

Patrick hurried into the kitchen, and seconds later Izzie could hear the sound of the tap running.

"Quick thinking back there," Izzie said as she crossed the floor and sat down in a chair facing Joyce. "That salt ring trick of mine wasn't going to keep them off us for much longer."

"Yeah, well . . ." Joyce shrugged her shoulders fractionally, and then winced as the motion pulled at the bruised muscles of her neck. "I'm just glad that I had that scalpel in my pocket."

Izzie sat back in the chair, legs stretched out in front of her.

"If nothing else, we know that silver *does* work against the Ridden," she said, leaning her head back against the top of the chair. "Salt, too, obviously, but only if there's not a strong enough breeze."

"Well, we've learned what *doesn't* work, as well," Patrick said, coming through the door to the kitchen carrying a glass of water. After he'd handed the glass to Joyce, he rubbed his forehead, face screwed up in a grimace. "If it had been a snake it would have bit me. I can't *believe* I didn't think about what would happen if any of the marks were covered up."

"But they have been keeping Ink users out of the neighborhood, right?" Daphne sat down in the chair beside Izzie. She looked around, uneasily. "Are we going to be okay in here? If those spiral things aren't keeping the Ridden away, what's to stop them crashing in here after us?"

Patrick pulled his hand down his face, blinking hard, like someone trying to shake off fatigue.

"Well, they didn't seem to be able to approach the back of *this* house, or any of the other ones with unobstructed markings on them," he said. "So Uncle Alf's markings *are* keeping them at bay, but they only seem to work over short distances. We should be safe enough in here tonight, but we obviously can't make any assumptions that the rest of the neighborhood is safe." He shook his head in frustration. "What I can't figure out is, how did they end up in the alley in the first place?"

"Maybe now that they're motivated to come after us," Izzie suggested, "they started probing the neighborhood's defenses for weak spots. Looking for places that they could tolerate passing through, threading their way through the gaps until they reached that spot."

Patrick stood in the center of the room, arms crossed over his chest, his brow knit.

"If anything had happened to any of you—" his gaze darted over to Joyce "—it would have been *my* fault. All of the things my great-uncle taught me, and I forgot the one thing that might have mattered the most."

"Don't . . ." Joyce croaked a little, wincing, then took a sip of water. "Don't beat yourself up. We all survived."

Patrick slowly loosened his arms, letting them fall to his sides, his expression softening.

"Joyce, I just . . ."

She managed an abbreviated shake of her head.

"It could have been much worse," she said. "We're all still here to talk about it. So there's no point in wasting any more time with self-recrimination. We need to figure out what to do next."

Izzie pulled out her phone, and after powering it up swiped through the photos that she had taken in the alley before the attack.

"We need to make more of these, for one thing," she said, holding the phone up to show the others the images of markings on the screen. Then she gestured to the supplies piled on the coffee table. "Might as well get started."

"What about the marks out there that are covered up?" Daphne asked.

"I can clear off the ones in the alley tomorrow," Patrick answered, and went to sit on the couch beside Joyce. "And after that . . . ? I don't know, maybe I can get some of the students I teach at Powell Middle School to take care of the rest. Call it a 'cultural enrichment activity' or something like that, give them some extra credit."

"What, you aren't going to pay them?" Izzie said, unable to resist a sly smile. "Too cheap to kick in a quarter a piece?"

"Pretty sure the rates have gone up since I was a kid." The corners of Patrick's mouth tugged slightly upwards in a weary grin. "But I'll break open the piggy bank if I have to."

"Would probably be handy to have some more weaponized silver," Daphne said. "I mean, did you see the way that guy reacted to that scalpel?"

Joyce was taking a long sip of water, and seemed to be recovering somewhat from the ordeal. She lowered the glass, holding in her lap.

"The blots on the face began to diminish immediately after Izzie inserted the blade." Joyce paused, and then turned to Izzie. "Was that roughly the same rate of change that you saw with Martin Price the other day?"

Izzie couldn't help shivering at the memory of it. The dead man, skin all but completely covered in ink-black blots, advancing on her even after taking multiple bullets to the chest and a shotgun blast to the knee, not to mention the fall from the third story window onto pavement. Only when she had bashed his neck with a battering ram repeatedly until his head was severed from his body had he finally stopped moving, and the blots had vanished in a matter of eyeblinks.

"Yeah," Izzie answered, nodding. "Petty much exactly."

"Then it must be just like we theorized this morning." Joyce sat forward, an expression of intense concentration on her face. "The Ink, or loa, or whatever you want to call it . . . when the host is rendered unusable, in this case due to the introduction of silver, it pulls back out of the body and into the higher dimension." She glanced in Izzie's direction. "From ana to kata, or from in to out, or however you want to describe it."

She was thoughtful for a moment, and then deflated slightly.

"Damn, I really loved that scalpel, though," Joyce added. "First the boots, now this? This is really not turning out to be my week, you guys."

Izzie chewed at her lower lip, mulling over what she was about to suggest, thinking over the ramifications. When Joyce had first produced the scalpel, it had occurred to Izzie that there was *another* silver blade that they might make use of, but she couldn't help feeling like even the idea of it was too morbid to consider.

"Why silver, though?" Daphne asked, before Izzie had worked up the nerve to say what she was thinking. "That's werewolf rules again, right? But what's so special about silver that it causes them to react like that?"

"Mmm." Joyce pulled out her phone and, after bringing up a browser window, began typing with her thumbs. "Let me see . . ." she said in a low voice, and then sank deep into an online search.

Patrick stood up from the couch and walked over to Izzie's chair.

"Can I see that?" he asked, indicating the phone in her lap. She thumbed the power button and handed it over.

"Okay," Patrick said after studying the images of the spiraling marks for a moment. "Let's see what we can do with this."

Then he turned and knelt down beside the coffee table, and began to pick through the bits of metal and wood that Izzie and Daphne had brought.

"Here's something," Joyce said, eyes still on the screen of her own phone. "Silver has the highest electrical and thermal conductivity of all metals, and the lowest contact resistance." She looked up and glanced around the room at the others. "Perhaps that's a factor?"

Izzie and Daphne exchanged a glance, and then shared a shrug. It seemed as good an answer as any.

"Speaking of electrical," Patrick said, picking up a round wooden disc about the size of his palm, "I wish I'd thought to take the Taser out there with us tonight. Would have been a good opportunity to see what kind of effect it has on those bastards."

"Well, the next time one of them is choking your girlfriend," Izzie said with a lopsided grin, "I'll be sure to remind you to test out your Taser theory before we try anything else."

Patrick shot her a wounded look, but Izzie couldn't help noticing that Joyce was hiding a smile while she pretended to take a sip of water.

"Come on," Daphne said, getting up from her chair and nudging Izzie's shoulder. "Let's help out with the arts and crafts, already. This was *your* idea, after all."

Izzie slid off of the chair and sat on the floor between Daphne and Patrick. It felt like a faintly ridiculous way to end such a stressful evening, but if carrying portable versions of the markings could help make the days to come a little less stressful, it was worth it.

CHAPTER TWELVE

Patrick's sleep that night was fitful and full of unsettling dreams. When he woke, squinting in the glare of the morning sun slanting in through the bedroom window, all that he retained of the nightmares was a confusing jumble of imagery—menacing figures formed from living shadow, rooms engulfed in flames hidden deep beneath the earth, and the sense of being pursued by unseen eyes everywhere he went.

Something shifted on the bed beside him, pulling the bedsheets taut, and it took a few startled seconds before Patrick remembered that Joyce had insisted that he share the bed with her when they had finally turned in, deep into the small hours of the morning. They had been too tired to do much more than collapse on the mattress and hold each other until they fell asleep moments later, but Patrick had felt an unfamiliar sense of security and contentment in that warm, drowsy embrace.

Joyce snored loudly, almost a honking sound, and rolled over in her sleep.

Patrick smiled as he slipped out from under the covers, careful not to wake her. She probably needed the sleep. They all did, for that matter. But having been roused from slumber himself—quite possibly by her snoring, he realized—he knew that there was little chance that he'd be able to fall back asleep himself.

Dressing as quietly as he could manage, carrying his boots in one hand, he padded across the hardwood and into the hall-way in socks, closing the bedroom door behind him. There was no sign of movement from upstairs, no sound of footsteps in the guest room or running water in the upstairs bath, so it seemed likely that Izzie and Daphne were still asleep as well.

Patrick considered making breakfast again. He had pur-chased supplies at the grocery store the day before in antic-ipation of doing so. Standing in the doorway to the kitchen with his boots in his hand, though, he couldn't shake a creep-ing sense of claustrophobia. Staying holed up inside for the sake of protection was one thing, but with the coming of day it would be safe to go back outside, and at the moment the idea of getting out and stretching his legs a bit was too appealing to ignore.

And so, after brushing his teeth and splashing some water in his face, Patrick stomped into his boots, pulled on his quilted jacket, and prepared to go for a walk. But before leaving he made sure that he had the Ziploc bag of sea salt in one pocket and the wooden disc engraved with a copy of one of his great-uncle's markings in the other, with his holstered semiautomatic clipped to his belt. He wasn't anticipating any trouble by daylight, but preferred to be prepared.

At the last moment he realized that Joyce and the oth-ers might wonder where he'd gone if they woke up before he returned, and, considering the heightened stress that they had all been under lately, it would probably be a good idea not to let them worry needlessly. Ducking quickly back into the kitchen, he penned a hasty note and left it in plain view on the counter, then headed back to the front door.

Patrick had lived alone his entire adult life, never sharing a place with a roommate, and it had been some time since a date had ended up staying the night. It was an unfamiliar sensation, having to take someone else in his living space into consideration. An unfamiliar sensation, he thought as he stepped outside and closed the door behind him as quietly as possible, but not an unpleasant one.

Patrick's first instinct was that donuts were in order, island-style donuts, to be precise, and for a hot minute considered going to get them at his favorite donut shop in town. But that was in City Center, all the way across town on the other side of Ross Village, too far to walk if he wanted to get back home any time before lunch. And he wasn't much in the mood for driving, either, which limited his options to the offerings in this corner of Oceanview. But there was a bakery owned by another Te'Maroan family about a half-dozen blocks south on Mission that also served island-style donuts, and while they were not his absolute favorites, they would do in a pinch.

Sunday Mass at the Church of the Holy Saint Anthony was still in full swing, and as Patrick walked up the sidewalk past the building he could faintly hear the sound of the old pipe organ playing in the sanctuary, and the faint hum of voices raised in song. He was sure that most of his surviving aunts were probably in their usual pews, as they had done since he was a little boy. Like most Te'Maroan families, the Tevakes were nominally Catholic, while still adhering to the traditional island beliefs, and didn't see any contradiction between worshipping one god in the church while honoring others in the home. It hadn't been until after the death of his great-uncle that Patrick had begun to question any of it, but soon there were nothing but questions left in his mind, and by the time he felt like he had the answers he had turned his back on all of it. He had been done with the whole mess, and neither the Roman church nor the Te'Maroan rituals had held any attraction for him.

And now, all of these years later, Patrick found himself wondering if he'd been wrong to dismiss the lessons that his great-uncle had taught him. He couldn't help thinking about the last day that they'd spent together, and the things that the old man had told him that day, twenty-five years earlier . . .

Patrick was certain that the dead man had been staring at him.

As he hurried through the streets of Little Kovoko, eyes on the pavement in front of his feet and clutching his knapsack to his chest, Patrick tried his best not to cry. But while he successfully managed to stifle his sobs, he could still feel hot tears streaking down his cheeks. Already he burned with embarrassment at the thought that he might run into one of the older kids in the neighborhood, who routinely teased him mercilessly for being so much younger than the rest of his cousins. The fact that he was short for his age, nearly half a foot shorter than the rest of the sixth graders at Powell Middle School, only made matters worse. The other kids would call him much worse than the usual "Shrimp" or "Rugrat" if they were to catch him crying like a baby.

But Patrick couldn't help himself.

It wasn't the idea of death that had him so unsettled. He had seen dead things before. Once he'd come across a dog in a vacant lot, lying on its side in the tall grasses, and couldn't figure out what he was smelling until he saw the maggots wriggling and writhing in the gash in the dog's side where a car had struck it. He'd seen birds mangled and half-eaten by alley cats, left to desiccate in the sun. Once at the Founder's Day Parade he'd seen a horse fall down dead in the street, struck by a sudden heart attack. And each experience might have left him uneasy, or sick to his stomach, or simply sad, but never as upset as he was now.

And it wasn't that he hadn't encountered a dead person before. He had seen images of dead people in magazines and newspapers, or on the TV news of course. But the closest he had been to a dead body in person had been his Aunt Winnie's open casket funeral the summer before, and she had looked more like one of the statues in the Recondito Waxworks museum than the woman Patrick had known all of his life.

Before today, he had never looked death squarely in the face. Much less had death stare right back at him.

"Finished already?"

Patrick looked up, startled, nearly colliding with the old man in front of him.

"Better start watching where you're going, boy, or you're liable to run into someone who . . ." The old man broke off when he saw Patrick's face, the red eyes, the tear tracks down his cheeks. "What's wrong, Patrick?"

Patrick's eyes welled as he took a ragged breath and stifled a sob. Then he dropped his knapsack on the sidewalk and lunged forward to wrap his arms around his great-uncle's waist.

"Uncle Alf, there's a . . . a . . ." He choked on the word, eyes squeezed tightly shut. "In the alley . . ." The tears flowed faster, soaking into the fabric of the old man's denim overalls, and he began to sob.

The old man rested a hand on Patrick's back, patting lightly. "Come on, grab your bag and you can show me."

Patrick walked back the way he had come, clutching his knapsack to his chest, while his Uncle Alf followed along behind him, hands tucked into the front pocket of his overalls. Neither spoke a word, their only sound being Patrick's occasional ragged sob and the slap of the old man's sandals against the pavement with each passing step.

Finally, they came to the mouth of the alley that ran between two row houses facing in either direction.

Patrick's great-uncle turned to look down at him. "You were out this way, heading to check on the Kururangi house?"

Patrick managed a nod. Like most Saturdays, he'd spent the afternoon ranging all over the neighborhood, checking on the old man's marks.

"And that's when you found . . . ?" The old man trailed off, turning from Patrick back to the alleyway before them.

"Him," Patrick said, pointing a trembling finger toward the shadows ahead.

The old man nodded once, then stood silently, considering the matter. Then he ran a wrinkled hand across his forehead, brushing the ragged fringe of white hair to one side, and started to walk toward the dead man. "Come on, then. We can't just leave him lying there."

Patrick stood in the sunlight, at the edge of the shadows, afraid to venture any closer. "But Uncle Alf . . . ?" He paused, swallowing hard. "Shouldn't we . . . I mean, *couldn't* we just tell the police or something?"

The old man barked a laugh. "Of course we tell the police." He looked back at Patrick with lopsided grin on his face. "What do you think, boy, I want to bury some vagrant's body my own self? Find his people, let them know he's gone? From the looks of him, he probably drank himself to death, and that's a sadness, but we have our own people to look after. Which is why we can't just leave the body untended in the meantime. It's not safe." He glanced up at the sky, and then back down to the dead man. "Especially not so close to sundown."

Patrick hugged his knapsack tighter to his chest, and tried not to look at the wide-open eyes of the dead man.

"He was looking at me, Uncle Alf," he said, sniffling. "Right *at* me."

"Hhn?" The old man put his hands on his knees and bent down, craning his head to one side to look the dead man in the face. "Ah, nah, he's not using those eyes anymore. He's gone." The old man straightened up, wincing slightly and putting a hand to the small of his back, joints creaking, breathing heavily. "Course," he went on after he'd caught his breath, "something else could come along and use those eyes for themselves, which is what I'm worried about."

The old man turned to Patrick.

"You got the paint I gave you in there?" He gestured with a knobby finger to the knapsack in Patrick's arms.

Patrick blinked for a moment, then nodded, trying not to look at the dead man's face. "Y-yes, Uncle Alf."

"Bring it here, then."

Patrick hesitated at the shadow's edge.

"Now, boy," the old man said, growing impatient.

Reluctantly Patrick shuffled forward, and held the knapsack out to his great-uncle.

The old man turned to him and shook his head. "Don't need the bag. Just the paint."

Patrick unzipped the knapsack and pulled out the small mason jar inside. The old man took the mason jar, and began to screw off the metal lid. "Got a brush, a stick, anything like that?"

Patrick looked into the knapsack, and shook his head slowly. "S-sorry, Uncle Alf. I hardly ever . . . I mean . . ."

He seldom used the paint. The old man paid Patrick a quarter for every one of the marks that he cleaned around the neighborhood, which usually involved plucking off vines or moss, or wiping away dirt or mud. But if any of the paint in the grooves had chipped away since the last visit, his instructions were to fill it back in with the special paint, as a temporary fix until his Uncle Alf could make more permanent repairs.

"Okay, okay, don't worry. I can use my finger this time. The mark won't have to last." The old man handed Patrick the metal lid, lips pursed. Then he slowly lowered himself down on the pavement with considerable effort, his joints creaking audibly. "This—" he said, then grunted before continuing, "used to be easier."

Finally, he was seated on the ground beside the dead man, breathing a little heavy, like he'd just walked up a few flights of stairs. He carefully placed the mason jar on the pavement beside him, and then stuck his index finger into the jar's open mouth. When he pulled it out the finger was covered up to the first knobby knuckle in viscous white paint that sparkled faintly when the light struck it.

"But you should carry a brush, boy," the old man said, as he bent low over the pavement. "No point in taking my paint if you don't have a way to use it proper."

"Yes, Uncle Alf."

The old man began to draw a spiraling pattern on the pavement beside the dead man's head.

"Course, if you'd found this fella a few blocks south of here, this wouldn't be a problem." The old man dipped his finger in the mason jar again, then shifted position and began to draw another spiraling pattern by the dead man's left elbow. "There are enough marks on the houses there to protect entire blocks. But the Kururangis' place is the closest house to here, and they're a good . . . what? Two blocks away?"

The old man took a brief rest to catch his breath, and then held his finger in front of his face, studying the paint closely. "Could use more sea salt in the next batch, I think. Not quite enough crystals in this mix." He sidled down until he was near the dead man's feet, and started inscribing another spiraling pattern on the pavement there.

"He *stinks*." Patrick pinched his nose. Standing this close, he could smell the dead man. Judging by the state of his clothes and hair, the vagrant probably hadn't smelled very good when he was alive, but in death his smell was something else entirely.

The old man glanced up at him, chuckling. "You think *this* is rough? When I was a boy, back on the island, and *my* grandfather was tohuna, I had much worse jobs than this. But when *he* was a boy, he had to help *his* grandfather prepare the bodies of the dead for burial. Do you know what he had to do?"

"No." Patrick lowered his hand and shook his head. "What?"

"First, the tohuna would slice the body open." Reaching out his hand, the old man pointed at one side of Patrick's stomach, then moved it quickly across to the other. "Then they would remove all of the organs and . . ." He broke off when he saw the stricken expression on Patrick's face. "Maybe I'll tell you when you're a little older," he added with a sympathetic smile.

Patrick nodded, swallowing hard.

The old man moved on to the space beside the dead man's right arm, and rested for a moment. Then he dragged his finger along the pavement one last time, back and forth, up and down and around, leaving a trail of sparkling white paint behind.

Finally he sat up straight and regarded his work. "That should do." He picked up the mason jar and held it out toward Patrick. "Here, take this."

Patrick kept his hands at his sides, and looked from his grandfather to the dead man who lay on the pavement between them. In order to take the jar, Patrick would have to step closer and lean over the dead man himself.

"He can't hurt you now," the old man said. "That's the whole point. Now close this up before it dries out."

"Yes, sir." Patrick stepped forward, took the mason jar, and then hurriedly stepped away as he screwed the metal lid back in place.

With his joints creaking audibly, the old man climbed to his feet, and then stood for a long moment with his hands on his knees, struggling to catch his breath. Then he wiped the remainder of the paint from his index finger as best he could on the bib of his overalls.

"So what now?" Patrick asked as he put the paint back in his knapsack. He looked down at the dead man, who was now surrounded on all four sides by his great-uncle's marks. These wouldn't last as long as the ones that Uncle Alf had etched in stone all over the Little Kovoko neighborhood and *then* filled with his special salt and paint mixture, of course, but they looked about the same.

"Now?" The old man lay a hand on Patrick's shoulder. "We tell the police about this, and get something to eat, maybe? I don't know about you, boy, but I am starving."

Patrick grinned. "Pizza?"

"Do you ever want to eat anything but pizza? You live in a city with so much to choose from, and always want to eat the same thing, every time." The old man rolled his eyes and guided Patrick back toward the street. "When I was your age, back on the island, we didn't have that kind of choice. We had good food, don't get me wrong. Really good food. But if you didn't want to eat what there was, you didn't eat. Not like here."

The street lights were beginning to warm up as the sun set, and in the distance Patrick could hear the mothers of the neighborhood calling from their front steps for their kids home for dinner.

"Uncle Alf? Do you ever miss it?"

"Hhn?" The old man turned to look in his direction. "The food? Your aunties cook island food as good as anyone back home, and—"

"No." Patrick shook his head, a slightly embarrassed expression on his face. "Do you ever miss the island?"

"Oh. Yes. And no." The old man looked away, a distant expression on his face. He took a deep breath and sighed. "I miss the island I knew as a boy, but it isn't really there anymore. Places can change and grow, just like people do, and not always for the best. Even true places."

"Besides," the old man said, stopping in his tracks and pointing at the ground at his feet, "I knew that this was where I was needed. Even if I had wanted to stay on the island, it would have meant turning my back on my people here. Maybe I *did* want to stay, but in the end, it didn't matter. . . ."

The old man paused, looking up at the sky. When Patrick followed his gaze, he saw that the first stars of the night could faintly be seen overhead. The old man sighed deeply, his eyes shut tight. Then he opened them, looked down, and shook his head a little sadly before turning to Patrick with a smile.

"After all, if I had stayed back on the island, who would be here in the city to look after all of you?" He gestured back the way that they had come, toward the alley where the dead man lay. "Who would protect you from the things in the shadows? Things that would stare back at you from a dead man's eyes?"

The old man continued on up the sidewalk toward home, chuckling, but Patrick couldn't help but shiver at the thought of it, unable to get the image of the dead man's blank stare out of his head.

Patrick almost collided with the old man when his Uncle Alf stopped short on the sidewalk.

"Nice. Clean." The old man was looking at a tight spiraling pattern etched into the pavement beside the front steps of a row house. He glanced in Patrick's direction. "Your work?"

Patrick nodded. He had visited the house earlier in the day while making his rounds, sweeping away dirt and leaves from the mark, cleaning out the deep grooves until the glittering paint sparkled in the midday sun.

"How many you get to today?" The old man gave Patrick and appraising look.

"Um . . ." Patrick tallied up the numbers in his head. It was important to keep track, since every job meant another twenty-five cents coming to him at the end of the day, and he was saving up to buy some new comic books. "I was hoping to do three dozen today, but I got sidetracked by . . . well, everything. So, thirty-two houses today, I guess?"

"Very nice." The old man had his hand on his chin, thoughtfully. "You know, I think it's time you learn how to make the marks *yourself*."

Patrick's eyes widened.

"Sure." The old man started walking again, gesturing for Patrick to follow. "Someone has to look after our people when I'm gone. I won't be here forever, but the things in the shadows aren't going anywhere."

Patrick trailed along behind the old man, silent for a moment, eyes on the pavement and lost in thought.

"Uncle Alf?" he finally said, looking up from the sidewalk. "Is it real?"

"Hhn?" The old man glanced back over his shoulder at him.

"The things in the shadows?" Patrick clutched his knapsack a little tighter. "I mean . . . are they *real*, or just like something from a story? Like, I don't know, a metaphor or something."

A lopsided grin spread across the old man's face. "Just because something is from a story doesn't mean it can't be real. Don't you remember me telling you about how the time that Pahne'i conquered fire, and then he climbed down below the earth and found the god of Shadows in—"

He stopped suddenly, shoulders lurching forward and an expression of intense pain twisting his face. His hand, the index finger still faintly stained with sparkling white paint, clutched at his chest.

"No . . ." He gasped, eyes wide, and then fell sideways, landing hard on the pavement with a sickening thud.

"Uncle Alf?" Patrick threw his knapsack to one side and rushed to the old man's side. "Uncle Alf!"

The old man wasn't moving, wasn't breathing, but his eyes were wide open and staring straight ahead.

CHAPTER THIRTEEN

Following the death of his great-uncle, Patrick had become an angry agnostic, railing against what he thought to be nothing more than ignorant superstition . . . but only when he was with his friends, or when he had left home to attend college. When he was around his family, his mother and aunts in particular, he had kept his mouth shut, hoping to avoid any withering glances at best, or lengthy lectures at worst. When his mother passed away after a lengthy illness, though, Patrick had been unable to hide his disdain at the whole idea of organized religion, and when it came time to make the funeral arrangements, his aunts had surprised him by responding not with anger or disappointment, but with pity. They felt sorry for him that he didn't have faith, that he didn't have that to lean on for support.

At the time, likely because he was too preoccupied with his own grief, Patrick had resented those pitying looks that they had given him. But now, after enough years had passed to give him a little perspective, he couldn't help but feel that he had let his aunts down. Their faith had mattered to them in a way that he had never been able to understand, and gave them a sense of comfort and security when facing an uncertain and often frightening world.

Patrick's hand slipped into the pocket containing the wooden disc with the spiraling design etched onto its surface. He had carved those loops and whorls himself, and then carefully filled the cuts with paint mixed with sea salt, just as he'd watched his great-uncle do when he was a child. And even though he couldn't know for certain that it would protect him if the need arose, he felt comforted knowing that he had it with him. Was that really all that different from his aunts clutching their crucifixes or saints' medallions in times of crisis?

Patrick realized that, in a way, what he and the others were doing at the moment could be seen as reinventing a very personal kind of faith from the ground up. A faith based on their experiences and how they believed the world to work, perhaps, but that drew from multiple traditions and schools of belief. A faith that they were working out experimentally, through trial and error.

It was sobering to realize that the same could easily have been said about Nicholas Fuller five years before. And even the most respectable of faiths had a history of leading people to make less-than-ideal choices.

He thought about what Joyce had said to him on their walk back to her car the day before, and her worries that the path they were on might lead to him choosing to act outside the law. But less than twelve hours later Joyce had been seemingly unfazed when Izzie had stabbed someone in the neck with her own scalpel and then left them in the road to die. Sure, there was the complicating factor that the person in question had likely been dead already, but the fact remained that Joyce seemed to have gotten increasingly comfortable with the idea of taking matters into their own hands. As had Izzie's friend Daphne, for that matter.

Where would all of this end? And even assuming that they survived, what kind of people would Patrick and the others be when they got there?

Patrick stepped out of the bakery on Mission with a Styrofoam cup of coffee in one hand and, in the other, a paper bag filled with island-style donuts, each of them flaky, sweet, and roughly the size of a dinner plate. He headed down the sidewalk in the direction of his house, but had only taken a few steps when he heard a voice calling out from behind him.

"Hey, sir, you get enough to share?"

Patrick couldn't help grinning slightly as he turned around. It was far from the first time that he'd heard the request.

"Morning, guys," he said with a nod to the three kids who were sauntering up the sidewalk toward him.

"We're pretty hungry, sir," Tommy Hulana said as he leaned heavily on the handlebars of the bicycle he was pushing along beside him. He didn't look like he'd missed a meal a day in his life.

"Yeah," added Ricky Kienga, "I didn't even have breakfast this morning."

"Liar." Joseph Kienga jabbed an elbow into his brother's side. "You ate all the biscuits before I even got downstairs."

The Kienga twins and their constant companion Tommy were eighth graders at Powell Middle School, and all took part in the Te'Maroan Cultural Enrichment program that Patrick sponsored at the school. He was well accustomed to them trying to cadge sweets or treats out of him at any given opportunity; it was pretty much their standard modus operandi.

"Well, let me see . . ." Patrick set the Styrofoam coffee cup down on top of a metal newspaper box, and made a show of unrolling the top of the paper bag to peer inside. This was not his first rodeo, and he always made it a point to buy far more donuts that he thought he needed, just in case. "I suppose I could spare a couple," he said, feigning deep concentration, "but I need you guys to do a favor for me in return, okay?"

The three kids didn't bother to consult with one another, not even so far as to exchange a glance, but all three nodded immediately with enthusiasm.

"Here's the deal." Patrick reached into the bag and made a show of pulling out one donut. "I'm putting together a community project this afternoon, and I need you guys to round up as many kids as you can to meet me at the blacktop behind the school. Say around four o'clock? Can you spread the word for me?"

He held the donut out in front of the boys, waggling it slightly from side to side.

"Sure thing," Tommy said, reaching for it.

Patrick pulled the donut back out of reach. "Promise?"

Nodding as one, the three boys' expressions were as solemn as police recruits swearing in their oath of office.

"Okay, then."

Patrick grinned as he tossed Tommy the donut, and then fished two more out for Ricky and Joseph. He knew that it probably wasn't necessary to bribe them with donuts, and that they would likely have helped out for free. They were three of the most eager participants in the Te'Maroan Cultural Enrichment program, though he got the impression that they were eager to be done playing konare on battered old checker boards and to move on to something a little more active. Whenever one of them started a sentence that began *"Sir, when are we going to . . ."* Patrick knew that the words "learn stick fighting" were going to follow in pretty close order.

The three boys were already working their way through the plate-sized donuts as Patrick rolled the top of the bag shut and picked up his coffee cup. "Don't forget, four o'clock."

Tommy tried to reply around a mouthful of donut, but the twins just nodded again, eagerly. Then they hurried away down the sidewalk, as if worried that Patrick might have second thoughts and take their treats back from them.

As he turned to continue heading home, he paused, shrugged, and then opened the bag back up to pull a donut out for himself. This was not his first rodeo, after all, and he'd bought more than he thought he'd need. . . .

By the time Patrick walked back into the house, the bag of donuts was already half empty, but he told himself that was still more than enough for Joyce and the others. The two that he'd eaten on the way home had been filling enough that he would probably only want one more, himself.

The house was filled with the smell of coffee brewing, and voices coming from the doorway to the kitchen. Hanging his jacket on its hook by the door and putting his pistol on a side table, Patrick walked into the kitchen to find that Izzie had taken over one end of the dinner table as her workstation, and was sitting in front of her laptop deep in concentration, with a legal pad at one elbow and a stack of papers and hardcover journals at the other. Daphne and Joyce were sitting across from one another at the other end of the table, each with a steaming cup of coffee, and were currently engaged in what seemed to be a fairly spirited discussion.

"Um, hey guys," Patrick said. And then, when all three women turned to him with annoyed expressions on their faces, he held up the paper bag and added, "Anybody want a donut?"

Joyce sat back with her arms folded over her chest, fuming silently, while Daphne scowled as she took a sip of her coffee.

"What'd I miss?" Patrick sat the bag of donuts on the table and went to fetch some plates and napkins.

"Not enough." Izzie straightened up and pushed her laptop away from her, a look of annoyance on her face. "For one thing, your wifi's bandwidth is for crap."

"Yeah, I always . . ." Patrick put the plates on the table, then turned to look at Izzie, raising an eyebrow. "Hey, how were you able to log in? I didn't give you the password."

Izzie sat back, rolling her eyes.

"For a cop, you've got a pretty lousy sense of security." Izzie nodded in the direction of the wireless router in the corner of the room, sitting atop a rat's nest of cords and cables. "I needed to do some research online and didn't want to have to wait until you got back, so I tried the default password that the manufacturer printed on the back of the router, and was able to log in no problem."

Patrick glanced over at the router and then back to Izzie, a blank expression on his face.

"You can reconfigure the router and choose your own password when you set them up," she said. "You *do* know that, right?"

"Okay, okay," he said, dismissing the criticism with a wave as he went to grab a cup of coffee for himself. "But I'm guessing that's not why things seem so tense in here, right? Or did you all get in a disagreement about my substandard cyber security?"

"Look, if I seem tense," Izzie shot back, "it's only because *these* two won't knock it off and let me concentrate on what I'm reading."

She waved her arm at the far end of the table, indicating Joyce and Daphne, who were still staring daggers at one another.

Patrick finished pouring coffee from the pot into his cup— he was stuck with *So Many Men, So Few Can Afford Me*—and came back to the table, taking a seat between Joyce and Izzie.

"Well?" he said, looking over the rim of the cup while he took his first sip. "What's the problem on this end of the table?"

"The only problem," Joyce said, arms still crossed, "is that Little Miss FBI here can't accept that some people have principles, is all."

"Look," Daphne snapped, leaning forward and slapping the table with the palm of her hand, "I wasn't suggesting that you *lie*, okay?"

"No?" Joyce gave her an icy glare. "And what would *you* call falsifying official medical records then, hmm?"

"They wouldn't be medical records . . ." Daphne began.

"Those file requests go *into* the official records." Joyce shook her head, exasperated. "I keep telling you but you don't want to . . ."

"Enough!" Izzie shouted from the other end of the table, slamming the lid of her laptop shut by way of punctuation. "I'm sorry I asked."

Patrick looked from her to the bickering pair at the other end of the table and back again.

"I thought this didn't have anything to do with you," he said. He pulled a donut out of the bag, put it on a plate, and slid it across the table to Izzie.

She took a bite of the donut, sulking while she chewed, a frown lining her face.

"All Izzie is asking for is a little—" Daphne began, but Izzie interrupted her before she could continue.

"No," she said evenly, remaining calm. "Joyce is technically correct. And I shouldn't have even asked before exhausting all other alternatives. But who knows, maybe Patrick could help out, instead."

Patrick was confused, and he knew it showed on his face. Izzie could clearly see it, too, and sighed before she tried to explain.

"This morning I got to thinking about what we're going to do the next time we run up against the Ridden," she said. "We survived last night by a combination of quick thinking and dumb luck, and we can't expect our luck to always hold out. But it occurred to me that we're not the first people to go up against these things, and maybe we can learn from their example. Or, worst case scenario, from their mistakes."

"Like old man Aguilar, you mean?" Patrick gestured to Roberto Aguilar's personal journals on the stack at Izzie's elbow.

"In part, but the old guy doesn't really go into much detail in these," Izzie answered. "These were for his own benefit, after all, and he didn't need to explain things to himself that he already knew. But he wasn't the only person we know of in Recondito who survived an encounter with the Ridden or the loa."

Patrick arched an eyebrow, and Izzie held up a finger, begging a moment's patience. Then she opened the lid of her laptop, waited while it woke back up, and turned it around so that Patrick could see the screen. The banner at the top of the browser window indicated that Izzie had loaded the website of the *Recondito Clarion*, and the headline of the article on the screen read Killer Cult Hides Deep Secret.

"That's the article you sent me the other day." Patrick looked up from the screen to meet Izzie's gaze. That had been the source of Izzie's discovery that the subterranean levels of the Eschaton Center had been connected to the disused mine that was connected to the Undersight project and so many other elements of their investigation.

"Right." Izzie nodded as she turned the laptop back around to face her. "And whatever it was that went down the night of the Eschaton Center mass suicide, it involved the loa somehow. Maybe Jeremiah Standfast Parrish was one of the Ridden himself, like Zotovic. Maybe not. But either way, it would be useful to talk with someone who was there, right?"

After a moment it occurred to Patrick that the question wasn't rhetorical and that she was waiting for an answer. He glanced over at Daphne and Joyce and saw that they were still glaring at one another, and so he turned back to Izzie and quickly bobbed his head in agreement

"According to the news reports at the time," she went on, "there were three people who were at the Eschaton Center that last night who lived long enough to see the next day. Two young people who had been indoctrinated into the cult—a young man and a young woman—and the man who rescued them."

"What was his name . . . ?" Patrick snapped his fingers,

trying to find the memory in his cluttered recollections of the past week. "Jet something?"

"George Washington Jett," Izzie read aloud from the screen. "Though most of the news reports at the time referred to him as 'G.W.' Jett, and a couple of times as 'Harrier' Jett."

"Harrier?" Patrick raised an eyebrow.

"Nickname, I guess," Izzie answered with a shrug. "Anyway, the young woman, Muriel Tomlinson, and the young man, Eric Fulton, had both been living at the Eschaton Center for about a year when their families hired Jett to pull them out. At the time he was a Recondito-based private investigator who specialized in 'deprogramming' young people who had been indoctrinated into cults. Several other families had approached him about getting their loved ones out of Eschaton, too, but unfortunately Tomlinson and Fulton were the only ones who made it out alive."

"One of them wrote a book about it, right?" Patrick recalled.

Izzie nodded. "Yeah, Fulton was credited as the author of . . ." She broke off, checking her notes to confirm the title. "*Escaping Shadows: My Months In The Eschaton Center*. But it was probably the work of a ghost writer, because most of the details don't line up with the statements that either Fulton or Tomlinson gave to authorities at the time. More than likely somebody just paid Fulton for the right to tell his story, and then jazzed it up with details borrowed from stories told by survivors of other cults, or b-movie plots, or whatever."

Patrick could remember seeing battered old paperback copies of that book everywhere when he was a kid. The Eschaton Center massacre had left such an indelible mark on the psyche of the city, and even if most people might have preferred to forget all about it, it was impossible to completely erase. It was like being unable to resist probing a sore tooth with your tongue.

"But Tomlinson gave a few lengthy interviews," Izzie went on, "including the one I found from the *Recondito Clarion*, and one of those ended up being the basis of the made-for-TV movie that aired a couple of years later."

"I watched that in my ninth-grade history class in school, actually," Patrick said. "I think the teacher just needed the break, to be honest—we watched a *lot* of videos that year—but that one really stood out because it took place so close to where we lived."

"Well, from what I've read it was reasonably faithful to the version of events that Tomlinson gave in her interview, though the people who made it glossed over a lot of details and went to some lengths to keep it family-friendly enough for broadcast standards." Izzie took a sip of coffee, thoughtfully. "But obviously, there was a lot more to the story than either Tomlinson or Fulton let on."

"Maybe they'd be willing to open up a bit more, now that so much time has passed?" Patrick said around a bite of donut.

"Too late for that, I'm afraid," Izzie answered. "Fulton died of a drug overdose in '82, and Tomlinson stepped in front of a bus in '91. I've only been able to search the publicly available information so far, but it seems like neither of them ever totally recovered from whatever they experienced at the Eschaton Center. Both of them had been honor roll students when they walked in the doors at Eschaton, Fulton the quarterback for the high school team and Tomlinson her class's valedictorian, but the months that they spent with Jeremiah Standfast Parrish changed all of that. Fulton was in and out of drug rehab programs pretty much constantly, arrested several times for public intoxication, even served a little jail time for possession, and Tomlinson seems to have spent more time in mental hospitals than out of them."

"That's not too surprising though, is it?" Patrick said. "Look at the people who hung around with Charles Manson, or walked away from Jonestown, or any one of a dozen different cults from the time. Those kinds of experiences can leave some pretty serious mental and emotional scars."

"Maybe," she answered, unconvinced. "Maybe not. But I got to wondering whether they talked any more about what they went through at Eschaton in later years. Tomlinson, in particular. Spending that much time in mental hospitals, there are bound to be patient records about therapy sessions, things that she might have said to the doctors there, I don't know . . . diaries, even?"

"Could you request those records?" Patrick asked.

"Not Tomlinson's." Izzie shook her head, frowning. "I checked the hospitals where she was treated, and their policy is to destroy medical records ten years after a patient's last discharge date."

"But Fulton?"

Izzie glanced at the other end of the table for a brief moment before answering, as if anticipating a fight.

"After one of his arrests for public intoxication, the Recondito District Attorney's office wanted to question him in connection with another ongoing investigation— they were trying to connect his dealer to a larger supply ring, and thought he could supply the missing pieces of the puzzle—but they needed to know if his state of mind was solid enough that they could rely on his testimony. And so the D.A. asked the court to order a psychological evaluation."

"And?" Patrick asked. "Did he talk about the Eschaton Center?"

"I'm not sure," Izzie answered. "But whatever it was Fulton told the psychologist handling his evaluation was enough for them to recommend that any of his previous or future testimony be should be completely disregarded, that he could not be relied upon to act as a material witness in any capacity, and that he should be ordered to seek treatment immediately."

Again, she glanced toward the other end of the table, tensing slightly. Daphne was still glowering, arms crossed over her chest, listening to Izzie talk while periodically casting sharp glances at Joyce across the table from her. By this point Joyce seemed to be ignoring the conversation entirely, eyebrows knitted in annoyance as she typed a brief, furious burst with her thumbs on her smartphone's screen, paused for a moment, then typed again. Patrick couldn't tell whether Joyce was texting with someone else, or pretending to do so in order to avoid the conversation, or something else entirely, but she seemed completely engrossed in it, whatever she was up to.

"It's a long shot," Izzie went on, "but the text of the interview that psychologist conducted with Fulton might still be on file in the archive at the Recondito Hall of Justice. Now, if I were to go through the system and file a record request with the city, it might raise some red flags, and I'd be hard pressed to explain to Agent Gutierrez or my superiors why the FBI has any business digging around in forty-year-old municipal court records. . . ."

"But," Daphne interrupted, slapping the surface of the table again to accent her point, "if the city's *medical examiner* were to request those files because . . . I don't know, there was an element in a new case that was similar, or some kind of pathology, something like that . . . then the city probably wouldn't even blink an eye." She wheeled around to address Joyce directly. "Look, I get that you don't want to *falsify* records requests, but what if you just . . ."

Joyce slammed her phone down on the table, screen up, the impact echoing as loud as a gunshot in the kitchen's breakfast nook.

"It's a waste of time." Joyce sat back with a look of triumph on her face. "Why go chasing dusty old files that might have been destroyed forty years ago when you can go right to the source?"

She glanced around the table and took in the confused expressions on the others' faces.

"He's *alive*." She pointed at the screen of her phone.

"Who?" Patrick asked.

"George Washington Jett," Joyce said, enunciating each syllable with exaggerated care. "He's still alive."

Patrick shot a glance over at Izzie and saw that she was as surprised as he was.

"He's a resident at the . . ." Joyce trailed off as she reached for her phone and double-checked her details. "At the Northside Community Living Center, located here in town on Northside Boulevard, appropriately enough. It's a hospital and assisted living facility for military vets, operated by the Department of Veteran Affairs for . . ."

She paused, glancing up and to one side as a glimmer of recognition lit her face.

"Is that the same the same VA hospital that Hasan . . . ?" she muttered in a low voice. Looking back to her phone, she tapped a link on the screen and then scanned the screen closely as she scrolled down a list of names. Then she sat up, a smile creeping across her face, and laughed in triumph. "Ha! And it just so happens that an old friend of mine from med school is on the staff there."

Joyce reached out and picked up one of the donuts, and took a big bite as she glanced around the table, looking like the cat that got the cream.

"So," she said around a mouthful of donut, "anyone want to go with me and pay the old guy a visit?"

CHAPTER FOURTEEN

Izzie sat in the passenger seat of Joyce's Volkswagen Beetle, trying to act casually preoccupied with the passing scenery as they drove through the sluggish Sunday afternoon traffic, acutely aware of the awkward silence that had stretched out since they had left Patrick's house a quarter of an hour before.

When she had enthusiastically accepted Joyce's offer to introduce them to her friend who worked on the staff of the Northside Community Living Center, it had been Izzie's assumption that the four of them would be travelling there together. But Patrick had begged off, insisting that his first priority was to tend to his great-uncle's marks on the surrounding buildings, so as to prevent another incursion of the Ridden like the one they'd faced the night before. When Joyce had suggested that they could simply wait until he was done, Patrick was clearly tempted, obviously as curious to hear what Jett had to say as any of them. But he had made plans with some of the neighborhood kids he had run into that morning, to meet up later in the afternoon, to go over the basics of cleaning and tending the marks. The sooner that the rest of the neighborhood was secured, the better, but he was anxious to learn what they could from G. W. Jett as soon as possible. So he insisted that the others shouldn't delay.

Daphne had been forced to bow out as well, explaining that she had open cases that she had been neglecting the last few days. And while the cases were hardly of earthshattering importance, Daphne had told Agent Gutierrez that she would keep on top of her workload while she was away from the office, and that if she didn't post updates on them by Monday morning then she would likely have him on her back, fabricated "long term stakeout" or no.

There had been a moment when it looked as though Joyce was unsure about carrying through on her offer when Patrick declined to join them, and Izzie couldn't help but wonder to what degree the offer had been motivated by Joyce's desire to spend time with him, and whether she would have preferred to stay behind and help him. The fact that Joyce had been prompted to seek out the status and whereabouts of G. W. Jett in the first place in order to score points in a disagreement with Izzie and Daphne was never far from Izzie's thoughts.

She hadn't intended for the disagreement around Patrick's dining table to get so contentious so quickly. Izzie had known that she was probably crossing a line with the medical examiner by asking her to circumvent regulations the moment that the words had left her mouth. And if it been just the two of them in the conversation, Izzie would have likely walked the request back as soon as she saw the offended expression on Joyce's face, and that would have been an end to it. But Daphne had taken offense on Izzie's behalf, offended that Joyce was offended, and the situation had quickly escalated out of hand.

Izzie imagined that the rest of them were as stressed and anxious as she was after everything they had been through, and their nerves were also frayed. But still she felt like she didn't know Joyce well enough to say that stress and anxiety was all that was at play, or if the woman had some other issue with her. She was tempted to ask, but was uncertain how the question would be received. It was frustrating to Izzie, who normally didn't have any difficulty talking with people. But this was also the first time that the two of them had been alone for any extended period of time, without either Daphne or Patrick on hand to facilitate matters, and Izzie couldn't help but feel like the lines of communication between them were down, and she wasn't sure how to reestablish them.

So they rode in awkward silence, driving north through Oceanview toward the Financial District, Joyce staring straight ahead and not even going to the trouble of turning on the car stereo, and Izzie left to look out the window at the cars and buildings passing by. She rehearsed things to say in her mind, ways to bridge this silence that stretched between them, but before she could settle on what to say . . .

"I've never had anyone try to choke me before."

Izzie was almost startled by the sound of Joyce's voice speaking in the small, silent space. She turned to see that, while Joyce's eyes were still on the road ahead, her brow was creased with worry.

"I mean, never anyone that I didn't *want* to choke me," Joyce added.

Izzie was momentarily confused, until she saw the faintest glimmer of a grin tug at the corners of Joyce's lips.

"And always with a safe word clearly established ahead of time." Joyce's eyes darted to the passenger seat as she sought to gauge Izzie's expression.

They pulled to a stop at a traffic light, and Joyce turned in her seat to face Izzie.

"But seriously, this is all new territory for me," she said. "I'm the one who deals with the bodies *after* all of the action is over, and then pieces together what happened from the physical evidence. I am most definitely *not* used to being one of the people who is out in the middle of the action, getting attacked or grabbed or what-have-you. And when the people doing the attacking and grabbing and what-have-youing aren't even technically *alive*?"

She shook her head, but before she could continue, the light turned green, and she turned back to look straight ahead as she shifted the car into gear.

"Don't get me wrong," Joyce went on, "because I do not regret getting mixed up in this at *all*. Ever since I saw the state of the Ink users' brains that kept coming into the morgue, I knew that there was something going on that was pretty far beyond the current scientific understanding. But I couldn't have imagined how far it really went. Even now I think we're only just getting the barest glimpse as to what is actually going on with the 'Ridden' and the 'loa' and whatever else you want to call it. For the sake of scientific curiosity, I'd continue to stick my neck out . . ."

She paused, casting a quick glance in Izzie's direction and mugging to emphasize her inadvertent pun.

"*Literally*, if need be," she stressed, unnecessarily. "But seriously, I'd continue to put myself in the middle of the action if it meant answering some of those questions. But . . . this is still new territory for me, and it's taking some getting used to."

"Okay," Izzie said, stretching out the syllables. What Joyce was saying made sense, but it didn't seem to follow that it meant that she needed to give Izzie the silent treatment and the cold shoulder because of it.

"I don't know," Joyce went on, sighing. "I know that these . . . these amulet things are supposed to keep us safe—" she patted the hip pocket where she had slipped the makeshift copy of the Te'Maroan markings when they'd left the house "—but I'd allowed myself to feel *safe* back at Patrick's place, you know? And ever since we left his neighborhood I've felt like . . ."

Her eyes darted over to the driver's side window beside her, and she shivered, like someone had just poured icy water down the back of her shirt.

That's when Izzie finally understood what was happening. Joyce wasn't mad at her, or annoyed about the situation, or still incensed about anything that anyone had done or said that morning.

Joyce was scared.

Izzie hadn't expected that. Joyce had always struck her as fairly fearless, with a self-assured poise and unflappable sense of humor in the face of death. With her precisely sculpted asymmetrical undercut bob, her leather jacket festooned with pins, and her heavy boots, Joyce had always seemed like a woman who was completely in charge of herself and her own reactions. But Izzie had not considered the possibility that the calm and controlled exterior that Joyce presented to the world might not be a form of self-defense, a kind of carefully constructed armor to protect herself from the world around her.

"If it makes you feel any better," Izzie said, "I'm pretty scared about all of this, myself. And I know that Daphne is, too."

Joyce glanced quickly in her direction before looking back at the road ahead. "Yeah?"

"Of course. I mean, at Quantico we were trained to handle stressful situations by running through different scenarios and situations, testing out how we apply the tactics and techniques that we've studied in different possible scenarios. So by the time we're sent out in the field as agents, we've already run through all kinds of various permutations of the types of situations we might encounter. The specifics out in the real world might be very different from the practice drills, of course, but there's almost always something from those simulated exercises that we can draw on and use in real life."

"Okay?" Joyce's tone suggested she wasn't seeing Izzie's point. "And how does that apply here?"

"That's just it," Izzie answered. "It *doesn't*. Nothing that we trained for at the Academy prepared me or Daphne for dealing with the undead."

She paused, chewing her lower lip, thoughtfully.

"In fact, the only thing that comes even close to the kinds of stuff we're dealing with are the stories my grandmother told me when I was a kid," Izzie went on. "And honestly, that scares me even more."

The Northside Community Living Center was located in the northeastern corner of the city, at the edge of a network of blocks that included Recondito General, the city's premier hospital, and Founders Square Medical Park—a cluster of office towers housing oncologists, surgeons, gynecologists, ENTs, and all manner of other medical specialists.

Joyce had parked in a visitors' spot in an underground

parking garage that serviced several of the surrounding buildings, and while they were riding the elevator up to the ground
level, Izzie couldn't help but be reminded of their descent into
the darkness of the warehouse subbasement on Friday night,
and felt eager to be back out in the daylight.

Izzie had trouble getting her bearings when they reached
the street level, but Joyce pointed with her cane at a four-story
building with a red brick façade and white trim. They crossed
at the light, and made their way to the visitor's entrance at the
front of the building.

While Joyce spoke to the receptionist at the front desk,
Izzie stood to one side of the waiting room, keeping out of the
way of nurses pushing patients in wheelchairs, families coming to visit their loved ones, and doctors discharging outpa-
tients. Voices were kept low, and sounds in general seeming to
be muted and subdued. When combined with the faint antiseptic scent of the warm recycled air, it seemed to Izzie to be
very much like any retirement home or elder care facility that
she had ever been in. Which, in a way it was, she supposed,
except that all of the patients and residents here were veterans
of the United States armed services.

Joyce waited at the front desk while the receptionist made
a call, and then, with a smile and few words of thanks, walked
back over to where Izzie was waiting. Moments later, the elevator doors opened on a fit but somewhat weary-looking man
with a neatly trimmed beard, eyeglasses, and an unkempt
shock of dark brown hair, wearing a polo shirt and jeans with
an ID badge on a lanyard and a stethoscope draped around his
neck.

"Joyce!" the man said, smiling warmly as he approached
them. "I wasn't sure if you were going to make it *this* time."

"Come on, Hasan," Joyce answered, moving in for a quick side hug, her other arm occupied with her cane. "That *one* time I stood you up, and you've never let me forget for a second."

She turned and indicated Izzie with a nod of her head.

"Hasan, this is Special Agent Isabel Lefevre of the FBI," Joyce said. "Izzie, this is my old friend Hasan Khatib. He's kind of a jerk, but I like him anyway."

"Nice to meet you," he said, shaking Izzie's hand. Then he turned back to Joyce. "So, what's this about? There's a patient here you need to see?"

Joyce nodded. "George Washington Jett. Records indicate he's a full-time resident?"

"Oh, sure. Mr. Jett doesn't get many visitors, I don't think." Hasan looked from Joyce to Izzie, eyes narrowed slightly in suspicion. "And the FBI is interested in talking to him . . . because?"

"We're doing some background on an ongoing investigation," Izzie said, speaking up quickly. "Mr. Jett was involved in a case back in the seventies that we believe might have some bearing on what we're dealing with now. We were hoping to ask him a few questions, see if he can't help shed some light on things."

Hasan put his hands on his hips, head tilted slightly to one side.

"Well, you're welcome to *try*," he said, his tone skeptical. "But like I said, Mr. Jett doesn't really get many visitors, and he's not the most, shall we say, *social* of our residents here."

"Is he capable of answering questions, though?" Joyce asked. "Given his age and residency status, I can't help wondering if there's any dementia at play, or anything of that sort."

"Oh, he's perfectly cogent and lucid. He's just kind of a misanthrope and avoids social interaction if at all possible." He gave Joyce a look and grinned. "So maybe you two would get along, after all."

Joyce rolled her eyes in mock exasperation. "I swear, Hasan, if you're about to bring up that one time at the shore I swear to god I'm going to . . ."

"Okay, okay!" Hasan held up his hands palms forward in a gesture of surrender. "You're not a misanthrope. Oh, hey, do you remember that tall guy from biochem? The one with all the tattoos? I ran into him at the market last week and . . ."

Izzie was managing to keep from tapping her toes in impatience, but just barely.

"Can we see him now?" she said, interrupting, trying to keep her tone civil.

Hasan turned to her, a distracted look on his face, eyes blinking behind the lenses of his glasses.

"Mr. Jett?" Izzie clarified.

"Oh, sure," Hasan answered. "Let me see where he's at. Most of the residents are in the community room this time of day, but Mr. Jett tends to keep to himself."

He walked over to the front desk, leaving Izzie and Joyce waiting by the elevators.

"He's awfully chatty," Izzie said out of the corner of her mouth.

"Yeah, but I get along with him okay," Joyce answered. "Of course, I do spend most of my waking hours hanging out with dead people, so I may have low standards."

A short while later Hasan escorted the two of them through the labyrinthine corridors and hallways of the building's ground floor until they reached an outdoor courtyard at the center of the complex. Izzie was sure that in the spring and summer months the space must get a lot of use from the residents and staff, with benches arranged around a fountain and a few well-tended trees to provide shade. But this deep into autumn, with winter just around the corner, the trees were barren of leaves, the grass underfoot was brittle and brown, and the fountain was dry, with the water turned off for the season. The benches themselves were untenanted, as the only person outside at the moment was the old man sitting in a wheelchair near the fountain, looking up at the sky.

"Mr. Jett?" Hasan said gently, approaching the man's wheelchair from behind. "There are some people here to see you."

The old man just grunted in reply.

Izzie got a better look as she and Joyce stepped around in front of him. His face was deeply lined, his skin like weathered mahogany, and there was a bare fringe of tight white curls that ringed his head from one ear around the back to the other. He had a blanket over stick-thin legs, his narrow chest and bony arms buried in a down coat, and bare hands with knobby knuckles rested like withered claws in his lap. There was an oxygen tank strapped to the back of the wheelchair, connected to plastic tubing that snaked up and over his ears like the arms of a pair of eyeglasses, ending with two prongs that were snugged in his broad nostrils. His mouth seemed to be settled into a perpetual frown, but his dark eyes were bright and lively.

"Well?" the old man growled, sizing them up. "What do you want?"

"I'm Special Agent Lefevre, FBI," Izzie said, and then gestured to Joyce. "This is Dr. Joyce Nguyen, Recondito's Chief Medical Examiner. We wanted to ask you a few questions about one of your old cases, from your days working as a private investigator."

The old man's eyelid twitched for a moment, and his frown deepened.

"I retired a long, *long* time ago, girl," he said, his voice gravelly. "And I got little enough time left to me that I don't want to be wasting it digging up the past. So why don't you keep your questions to yourself and leave me be?"

"I just wanted to know about . . ." Izzie began, but the old man interrupted her before she could continue.

"So what, doc?" He rolled his gaze over to Hasan. "This going to be a regular thing now, you bringing people here to bother me? I didn't do four tours in Vietnam just so I could spend my twilight years being hassled by any fool that comes along and wants to bend my ear."

"The Eschaton Center," Izzie hastened to finish.

The old man's eyes slowly turned back in her direction.

"We want to know what you saw down there," Izzie continued, keeping her tone level but insistent. "Underground, where Parrish and his people carried out their secret rituals."

He studied her face closely, as if searching for something hidden there.

"We think you might have encountered something . . ." Izzie trailed off for a moment, thinking of the right way to phrase it. "Something not *from* here."

The old man's eyes widened fractionally.

"I'll be damned," the old man said, looking from Izzie to Joyce and then back. "You got the knack, do you?"

Izzie glanced over and saw that Joyce seemed about as confused as she was herself.

"The knack?" Joyce asked.

The old man gave them both an appraising look, and seemed to reconsider.

"Well, maybe you don't, at that." He raised one knobby finger and tapped his chin thoughtfully. "But you've *seen* them, haven't you?"

He leaned forward slightly in the chair.

"Seen . . . ?" Izzie prompted.

"The Ridden," the old man said, as though it were the most obvious thing in the world.

Izzie and Joyce exchanged a significant glance.

"Well, now. You *have* seen them." The old man sat back in the chair, his expression softening somewhat. Then he gestured with one arthritic hand to Hasan. "Doc, you mind giving me and these girls a little privacy? I think we do have cause to talk, after all."

CHAPTER FIFTEEN

"Some folks call it the 'inner eye,' or 'second sight,' or just the Sight," G. W. Jett said as Izzie and Joyce settled themselves on a cold bench across from him. "I've heard in voodoo they talk about folks being 'two-headed,' and I figure that's just about the same thing. Some folks are born with it, and some folks get it somewhere along the way, and there's even some who can dip in when they drink or eat or smoke the right thing. Seeing the world not just with your eyeballs, but with something else besides, able to see all the things that regular folk don't even know is there. Call it what you like, but my mother always talked about having the 'knack,' so that's what I call it."

"And you have it?" Izzie asked.

The old man frowned for a moment before answering.

"Used to," Jett said, a bitter undercurrent to his words. "I lost it along the way. It bothered me for a long time, not having it anymore, but eventually I decided that eyesight can fade, and hearing can go, and all the rest, so why not the knack, too? But I was born with it, yeah, and it took a long time getting used to it being gone."

The old man ran a hand across his forehead, almost as if brushing away a thought, and then continued.

"When I was little I didn't think too much about it. The knack was just something for family to know, and not something to talk about at school or church or whatnot. It wasn't even that we were worried what folks might think, just that it was a private thing, not for anyone else to share. Everyone in the whole family knew, though, and there were always relations trooping to our house to get my mother's advice, or help getting rid of some bad luck, or anything like that. Of course, back then I didn't have the knack nearly so strong as she did, and all I could see were little hints of things, here and there. More like a tickling at the back of my head than a full-blown thought. But I always knew which neighborhoods to avoid, which houses and strangers to keep clear of, and I could just feel it if something wrong was about to go down."

Izzie couldn't help but think of her own grandmother, and the way that so many friends and family had come to her when they felt like they needed a little help.

"My mother died right around the time I was finishing up school," the old man went on, "and lying in her deathbed she told me that there were dark days ahead for me. When my number came up in the lottery and I got myself drafted into the Marines, I was sure that's what she had been talking about. And there were dark days aplenty over in Nam, true enough. But whether it was the knack or just dumb luck, I managed never to put a step down wrong, and was always ready when things went sideways out on patrol, and I got through it all without so much as a scratch. That's when I first picked up the nickname 'Harrier,' when another grunt said I charged through mine-fields like I was harrowing the gates of hell. My luck held out long enough that I got cocky, even, and kept reupping after my first tour was through, and then again after my second, and my third. Fifty-two months in country in all, and it wasn't until my fifty-first that being cocky caught up with me. The knack saved my ass that day, but that's a story for another time, I suppose. But even through the worst of all that, the most that I ever got out of the knack was an intuition here and there, a feeling that something wasn't right, or maybe a premonition that some-thing was about to go south. I didn't actually *see* anything until after I was back stateside. And then, the things I saw . . .'

Jett took a deep breath and let out a ragged sigh, and folded his gnarled hands in his lap.

"The first time I felt it was when I got off the plane in San Francisco," the old man said, his eyes gazing off into the mid-dle distance. "It was like something was tugging at me, like there was a string around my soul and someone was pulling the other end. The knack was telling me there was somewhere I needed to be. All I had in the world was stuffed in the seabag slung over my shoulder, so I changed into civvies in an airport men's room, walked out onto the street, and hitched a ride with a truck driver heading in the direction the knack was pulling me. When the driver pulled off the interstate into the South Bay, I knew that Recondito was where I was supposed to be."

The old man fell silent for a moment, and stared into space.

"Why?" Joyce asked, gently urging him to continue. "How did you know?"

It took another second or two for the old man to bring himself back to the present, and for a moment Izzie wondered if he hadn't gotten lost in his memories. But when he turned to look back at the two of them his eyes were clear and his expression lucid.

"It was just a feeling at first," he explained. "But as I walked around the town, it felt like there was always something hovering just at the corner of my eye. When I'd turn to try to catch a good look, I'd get just a glimpse and then it would be gone, every time."

"What were they?" Izzie asked. "What did they look like, at least?"

"I couldn't rightly have said at the time," the old man said. "They were like hazy shadows, or mirages over a blacktop road on a hot summer's day. I got the impression of things reaching out, like fingers on a hand or an octopus's tentacles, but couldn't quite bring it into focus. No one else ever seemed bothered by them, didn't even seem to notice. For a while I thought it was all in my head. I'd tried acid a time or two, and had heard folks talk about lingering flashbacks. But that didn't sit quite right with me. I could *feel* them, too, if I got close enough, down in the pit of my stomach. Hell, I could practically *taste* them."

Izzie could not forget that sensation of wrongness she'd felt whenever she had gotten close to one of the Ridden, the nausea in her gut and the foul taint on her tongue.

"But that night, after the sun went down? That's when I *saw* them clear for the first time." The old man shook his head slowly and let out a low whistle. Then he turned his eyes to Izzie and Joyce. "You girls old enough to remember lava lamps?"

"Sure," Joyce said while Izzie nodded.

"That was the first thing that came into my head when I saw the shadows," Jett went on. "Those little blobs all stretching and squashing around. They trailed around behind some of the people walking on the street, like they were streaming out of their heads. At first I thought they were black as ink, but as I looked closer, I could see that it wasn't just that they didn't have any color, but that they were some color that we don't *have* here, and my mind had just decided that black made more sense. Anyway, I tagged along behind one of the folks who had the shadows around their head like a halo, watching as it stretched and squashed. I was close enough that I could reach out and touch them. So I did."

A pained expression flitted across his lined face for an instant, and then was gone.

"That was when I saw it for the first time. Not just the parts of it that were *here*, but what those shadows were a part of, someplace *else*. Not anywhere on Earth, or even in outer space, but in some *other space*. It was too large to fit in my head, with too many angles to make sense of, but I got this image of a living thing as big as worlds. A mass of writhing tendrils stretching out in more directions than I could comprehend, driven by an incredible hunger to consume. And there was a mind at the center of it all, thinking thoughts too vast and alien for me to understand, and all the sudden it occurred to me to wonder what would happen if it *noticed* me. . . . All the things I'd done and seen to that day, and I'd never been so scared as I was at that moment."

Izzie noticed the way that the old man's gnarled fingers were clawing at the blanket draped over his legs, as if he were falling off a cliff and grasping for anything to hold onto.

"I'm not too proud to say it," he said, though Izzie could see that it did make him uncomfortable to admit, "but I turned tail and ran away. Didn't even look back, for fear that the person I was following would turn and notice me. Because if *he* noticed me, I figured, then there was a good chance that *it* would notice me, too. And the thought of that . . . that *thing* knowing I was there turned my insides to ice."

The old man's grip on the blanket loosened as he visibly tried to relax.

"I holed up in a flophouse way out in the Kiev that night, and barely stepped outside for the next few days, leaving my room only to pick up packs of smokes at the newsstand or to hit the package store for bottles of rotgut whiskey and forti- fied wine by the armful. I drank because otherwise I couldn't hardly sleep, since every time I closed my eyes I was back there in that other space, with that thing about to notice me. Only stone-cold drunk could I get any kind of rest, and even then, I'd wake up every morning in a cold sweat. Then, about three or four days after I'd hit town, I went out to the newsstand to pick up a pack of Camels, and one of the paperbacks on the rack caught my eye. The cover illustration showed a guy in a skull mask and fedora with a Colt .45 in either hand, look- ing up at something above him, crawling out of a crack in the night sky. And damned it if didn't look exactly like the thing that I'd seen when I touched that shadow, or as close as a body could get with ink and paint."

"Wait," Joyce interrupted, her tone skeptical, "like a novel, you mean? A mass market paperback?"

The old man nodded.

"Struck me kind of odd, too," he said. "I bought it on the spot, and took it back with me to the flophouse. Turned out to be a reprint of a pulp novel that first come out back in the Great Depression, and the cover illustration had originally appeared on the front of the magazine. The story was about a masked avenger type called the Wraith, and it mostly seemed to be about him fighting crooked politicians and gangster types in 1930s Recondito, but every so often he'd run up against something supernatural in a back alley or someplace like that, and then the writer would go on a tear about invaders from the 'Otherworld' who infect men's minds and steal their memories and personalities."

Izzie and Joyce exchanged a sharp glance, eyebrows arching.

"Yeah, I know," Jett said, "but at the time I didn't know anything about the Ridden yet. I was more interested in the cover art. There were a couple of short bios in the back of the book, and it turned out that the writer—Alistair Freeman—had died in a fire back in the forties, but the cover illustrator, who was credited in the indicia as 'Chas. A. McKee,' was still alive and living in Recondito. Only it wasn't 'Charles' McKee like I originally assumed, but *Charlotte* McKee. And when I borrowed the phone book from the front desk of the flophouse and checked, sure enough there was a listing for that name. And I couldn't get to a payphone fast enough. I just had to know, right then and there."

"Whether she had it?" Izzie asked. "The Sight, or the knack, or whatever you want to call it?"

"It stood to reason," the old man answered. "The thing she'd painted on that cover? It was just too much like what I'd seen to be a coincidence. So I called her up and asked."

"You just called a complete stranger and asked if she had psychic abilities?" Joyce sounded even more skeptical than before.

"What can I say?" The old man chuckled, his bony shoulders lifting slightly in an abbreviated shrug. "I was all het up. She had every right to think I was a babbling lunatic, calling her up out of the blue and asking her about a painting she'd done forty years before, and whether it was something she'd really seen. All I'd given her a chance to say was something like 'Yes, this is she' when she answered the phone, and after that it was just me talking a mile a minute. But when I paused long enough to take a breath, she said that we should probably meet in person to talk about it."

The old man looked down at his hands contemplatively, flexing the knobby fingers.

"When I first saw her I thought that Charlotte McKee was as old as the hills, a shrunken up little blue haired biddy in a housecoat and slippers. But I suppose she was younger then than I am now. Time's got a way of catching up with you when you're not looking."

"What did she say?" Izzie prompted when the old man got that far-off look in his eye again. "Did she have the knack?"

"No," Jett answered with a sigh. "But she told me that she'd been in love with a man who had it back when she was young. And he'd been the one who had described to her the thing she painted on the cover, because he'd seen it himself. She said that he had the 'Sight,' and that he'd studied on how to use it with an old Mayan who'd come up from Mexico."

"Wait, are you talking about Roberto Aguilar?" Izzie interrupted.

The lines on Jett's face deepened as he frowned harder, and he seemed to tense at the mention of the name.

"That's a name I'd not thought to hear again," he said in a low voice. "But no, Aguilar was another one of the old man's students, long after. By the time I met her, Charlotte McKee wouldn't have poured a glass of water on Aguilar's head if he was on fire. They'd had a falling out a long, long time before. The man she had loved was Alistair Freeman."

"The guy who wrote the novel?" Joyce asked.

Jett nodded.

"Charlotte said that Freeman wrote the stories about the Wraith to keep folks off the scent of what he was really up to in the city. He figured that anyone who came forward and said that they'd seen a guy in a silver skull mask and twin .45s fighting undead monsters in the alleys would be written off as a crank."

"So he was really doing those things himself?" Izzie thought about the silver skull mask that Fuller had worn when he dismembered his victims, and wondered for the first time where he might have gotten it. "They weren't just stories."

"A mix of fact and fiction," Jett explained. "Freeman was what Charlotte called a 'daykeeper,' like the old Mayan who trained him. He'd come to Recondito because he knew that a great evil had taken root here, years before."

"In the Guildhall," Izzie said quietly.

"You girls *have* been digging around, haven't you? Yes, Freeman spent years protecting the city from all manner of supernatural threats, trying to keep the Guildhall in check, until finally he couldn't take it anymore. Charlotte didn't got into too many specifics, but it sounded like one innocent too many got caught in the Guildhall's mess, and that was the straw that broke the camel's back. Freeman marched right in the front doors of the Guildhall, guns blazing, and brought the whole place down on top of them. All that was left of him were a pair of silver-plated Colt .45s and some charred bones."

"If it was that easy to stop them, why didn't he do it before?" Izzie asked.

"Because it wasn't that easy," Jett answered. "Charlotte said that Freeman had been talking about staging a frontal assault on the Guildhall for years, but wasn't sure that he would survive long enough to bring them all down. And even if he did, he knew it wasn't likely that he would be coming back alive, and he worried about leaving the city unprotected. Because even with the Guildhall gone, there was every chance that someone else might come along and make the same sort of pact with the Otherworld that they had. But the old Mayan had started training Aguilar by that point, so Freeman must have felt like it was time to take that risk."

"In Aguilar's journals he talks about spending most of his life protecting the city against invaders from another world," Izzie said.

"*His* journals," Jett repeated, sneering. "He kept his own journals, did he? Probably just because he couldn't get his hands on the ones that Freeman left behind."

Izzie arched an eyebrow.

"That was part of the reason that he and Charlotte fell out," he explained. "The old Mayan died not too long after Freeman, and Aguilar figured that left him in charge. But his training wasn't quite complete, and he said that he needed Freeman's own secret journals to study. But Charlotte just couldn't bring herself to part with them. They were all that she had left of him. Aguilar seemed not to have handled things as delicately as he might've, and said some unflattering things about Freeman. Charlotte got her back up, and dug in her heels. She locked the journals away where Aguilar couldn't get at them, and told him to go eat sand, in so many words."

Izzie wondered whether that accounted for why she hadn't come across any mention of Alistair Freeman or Charlotte McKee in Aguilar's own journals. Which reminded her of the references that she had read about the daykeepers and the Sight.

"But Aguilar didn't have the knack, did he?" Izzie asked.

The old man shook his head. "Not to hear Charlotte tell it. She said that he had to use some kind of brew that the Mayan had brought up from the Mexican jungle with him. It let him see the shadows, not quite like Freeman could, or me for that matter, but well enough to know they were there."

That would be the ilbal, Izzie knew. The same drug that Aguilar would later pass on to Nicholas Fuller, the last two vials of which Patrick had taken from a file box in the 10th Precinct station house's community room, and which were now sitting in a gun case in his living room.

"I was lucky that I got to know Charlotte when I did," Jett went on. "She was already in pretty poor health, and she didn't have too much more life left in her. When she passed, it seemed to me like she'd held on until she could find someone to hand off the torch to, and when I came along she felt like she'd earned her rest. Aguilar was still at it, of course, but he pretty much concerned himself exclusively to his own people down in Oceanview, leaving the rest of the city to fend for itself. But Charlotte told me that the things I'd seen since coming to Recondito—the shadows, the thing out in other space— it all meant that the same darkness that had taken root back in the Guildhall days was coming back, and that someone would have to contend with it. So Charlotte looked to me to pick up where Freeman had left off, and I think that's why she left his journals to me in her will."

"You have his journals?" Izzie leaned forward, eagerly. "Everything he wrote about the Guildhall?

"*Had* them," the old man answered. "Boxes of the things, along with one of Freeman's silver-plated Colt .45s and a case full of rounds. The pistol would end up coming in handy, but

I ended up losing all but one of the journals in a fire back in '78, which seemed kind of fitting, considering how Freeman had ended up himself. There wasn't anything in them about that last night in the Guildhall, of course, since he didn't live long enough to write anything down. But they were full of all sorts of stuff he'd gathered about the Guildhall members and their allies over the years, and what he'd learned about the Otherworld, the Shades, and the Ridden. And that helped me understand what I was seeing on the streets of Recondito around me. Somebody was taking normal folk and corrupting them, turning them into the Ridden. Only I didn't have the first idea who was behind it."

The old man pulled the blanket up higher around himself, shivering almost imperceptibly.

"So I did what seemed natural. I went on recon. Started tailing the folks I could see out at night, with the shadows hanging around their heads. Seeing where they came from, seeing where they went. I asked after them with people I saw them talking to on the street, got a few names to track down. I went around to the Recondito PD to see if any of them had rap sheets, and got stonewalled until I found a friendly gal in the Records Division up in the Hall of Justice who said she liked my smile, and agreed to run the names in exchange for a meal and a couple of drinks. Most of them were young folks, and turned out that some of them were runaways, or had been reported by their families as missing persons. There were a lot of kids out on the streets in those days, you have to remember. This was a few years after the Manson murders had put the lie to all of that flower power bullshit, but there were still more than enough hippies out on the street corners in the Kiev, busking or panhandling or what have you."

"Did you try talking to any of them?" Joyce asked. "The people you were following?"

The old man nodded slowly.

"Sure did. Found one all on his own one night, and made like I wanted to bum a smoke, just to see if I could get him talking. He was all spacy, like he was hopped up on something, but I'd never seen any of them smoking grass or taking pills, nothing like that. Said he didn't have any cigarettes, but that he had something better that he could share with me. The *truth*. Damned fool started preaching at me like a Jehovah's Witness at your front door, jabbering about opening yourself up to wisdom from above, letting the light of the hidden universe into your soul, that kind of nonsense. But the first sign I showed that I wasn't interested in any of that self-help guff, he clammed up tight and walked away. Like it was bait on a hook, and if I didn't bite he was going to go off and find another spot to fish."

He chuckled ruefully.

"I braced a few more of them in the nights that followed, and I got the same sales pitch from every one of them. I figured they were all part of the same church or cult or whatever, and I got to thinking that's what they were doing out on the street in the first place, looking for other lost souls that they could bring into the fold. I didn't know for sure whether any of them even knew what they were carrying around in their heads, but it stood to reason that whoever had made them all Ridden was behind that self-help nonsense. It was round about that time that I heard from my lady friend in the Records Division. Seems that the calls she'd made about the runaways had gotten back to the families who had filed the missing persons reports in the first place. The RPD brass had told the families that they didn't have the manpower to go chasing after a handful of kids, and that unless there was some evidence of criminal activity that they were on their own. So the families were looking to hire a private investigator to find their kids for them, and my lady friend put them in touch."

"This was the families of Muriel Tomlinson and Eric Fulton, then?" Izzie asked.

"Yeah, their families and the parents of a couple of other kids, too," Jett answered. "Now, I didn't have a California private investigator's license yet—I ended up taking the exam and making it official when this mess was all over—but the families didn't seem to mind. And the fact that I wasn't asking for one thin dime up front probably didn't hurt matters any. I told them that they could pay me if I managed to get their kids back to them, and otherwise they could keep their money."

The old man kneaded his hands together, and glanced up briefly at the sky overhead. It was still a few hours until sunset, but it seemed to Izzie as though he was checking to make sure that the sun was still up.

"I had pictures of the kids I was after, yearbook photos and family portraits, that kind of thing. Four kids in all, ranging from their late teens to mid-twenties. I'd seen each of them at least once out on the street at night, fishing for new recruits, but damned if they weren't anywhere to be found as soon as I went looking for them in particular. There were others, of course, so I figured my best bet would be to tail them, and see if they led me to the kids I was after. It took a few days before any one of them went anywhere but the rattraps they squatted in or whatever fleabag hotel they were living in, but then one night I trailed one of the Ridden through Hyde Park, and spotted a few more approaching from the other direction. And then a couple more came down a side street. I hung back, watching as six of them stood there together on a corner, like they were waiting for a bus. Then a panel van came along, they all climbed in, and it drove away. I managed to flag down a cab quick enough to follow them, but when the van continued on past Northside and turned onto a winding road heading up into the hills outside of town, the cab driver refused to take me any further. I had my suspicions where they were headed, though, and when my lady friend ran the license plate number I'd taken down, they were confirmed."

"The Eschaton Center," Izzie said.

"Got it in one." The old man sighed. "There wasn't much else up in those hills except coyotes and boarded-up mines, so it stood to reason. But once I started looking into Jeremiah Standfast Parrish's self-help gospel, it sounded an awful lot like what those Ridden were pushing on the street. Now, I'd heard about the Eschaton Center already, of course, but as far as I knew it was just another place that mostly catered to rich white folks who wanted to feel better about themselves, willing to pay through the nose so that somebody would tell them that they were special and deserved every nice thing that happened to them. So what were they doing busing in a bunch of kids to go beating the bushes in the city looking to recruit people who probably didn't have two dimes to rub together? And how did the Ridden factor into it? Anyway, the next morning I bought a junker from a used car dealership in my neighborhood, enough food and sodas at the corner market to last me a day or two, and cleaned up, oiled, and loaded Freeman's old 1911 Colt .45."

"You were going in to shoot up the place?" Joyce sounded alarmed.

"Wasn't planning on it," the old man said, equivocating,

"but I wasn't ruling out the possibility either. The knack was itching at the back of my head, telling me that I was walking into trouble, and after more than four years of never heading out on an op without the tools to defend myself if necessary, I wasn't about to start then. But the plan was to stake the place out for a bit, see what went on up there, and hope to spot any of the kids I was after."

He took a deep breath, but before he could continue they were interrupted by an orderly calling from an open doorway on the far side of the courtyard, brandishing a clipboard.

"Mr. Jett? I hate to break up the party, but it's time for your physical therapy."

The old man glowered, his brows knit together.

"What's the point of all that nonsense?" he growled as the orderly walked over.

"Don't shoot the messenger," the orderly said with a long-suffering grin, "it's doctor's orders."

The orderly flashed a smile at Izzie and Joyce while he took hold of the handles at the back of Jett's wheelchair.

"Mr. Jett'll be done in about thirty minutes, if you gals want to stick around."

Izzie had no intention of leaving when they were just getting to the meaty part of the old man's story, and from Joyce's expression is was clear that she felt the same.

"We can wait." Izzie stood up from the cold bench, rubbing her hands together. "But maybe inside, though, instead of out here? I can barely feel my fingers."

"You two go on to the waiting room, then," Jett said as the orderly wheeled him away. "I'll meet you there as soon as these sadists get done torturing me."

Izzie stuffed her hands in the pockets of her jacket and

watched as the old man was wheeled inside, thinking over everything that he'd told them so far. Joyce hopped up off the bench and started walking toward the door with purpose.

"I don't know about you," Joyce said, glancing back over her shoulder at Izzie, "but I could use a cup of coffee."

"Oh god, yes," Izzie sighed, falling into step behind her.

"But a *good* cup of coffee," Joyce insisted. "I figure we could drive over to Monkeyhaus or maybe Sacred Grounds and get back before the old guy is finished up."

The thought of good caffeine was enticing.

"If you're driving, I'm buying," Izzie said, holding the door open and stepping aside to let Joyce through. "Let's do Monkeyhaus, though. I had a cappuccino there with Daphne the other day, and it was strong enough to keep me juiced up all day. And today, I just might need *two* of them."

CHAPTER SIXTEEN

Patrick had spent the better part of two hours tending to the marks that his Uncle Alf had made decades before on the houses of his block. It had been a strangely familiar sensation, quickly settling back into routines he'd all but forgotten about for years, muscle memory taking over as he pulled away vines and weeds, brushed away caked-in dirt and debris, and touched up cracks and gaps in the glittering paint. He found the work went faster and more easily than when he was younger, in part due to his taller height and greater strength and stamina, but also because he was more motivated now to move quickly. Back when he was a kid, his goals had been to earn enough quarters to buy comics or candy bars at the corner shop. Now, it was a question of life and death.

When he was satisfied that the alley behind his house and the surrounding streets were once again relatively secure against encroaching Ridden, Patrick checked his phone and saw that it was almost time to meet up with the kids from

Powell Middle School. The trio that he'd run into that morning on the way back from the bakery—the Kienga twins, Ricky and Joseph, and Tommy Hulana—had agreed to spread the word around the neighborhood that he needed as many kids as they could round up to meet him at the blacktop behind Powell Middle School.

He had just enough time to run into the house, wash some of the grime from his hands, and guzzle a quick glass of water before he headed off to the school yard, grabbing a jar of paint and a fistful of brushes on his way out the door. Izzie's friend Daphne had ducked out a short while before to run some errands, and he'd given her the spare key so she could let herself in if she got back before he returned. But he hoped that this meeting with the kids wouldn't take long, provided enough of them showed up at the schoolyard.

Powell Middle School was only a few blocks to the south, on the far side of the Church of the Holy Saint Anthony, and still looked pretty much the same as it had when Patrick had been a student there a lifetime ago. As he approached, he had the same odd sensation he usually did when seeing the school grounds, the sense that if he were to turn the corner at just the right moment he might see his old classmates loitering out by the basketball court, still children, talking about the cartoons they'd watched the past weekend or bragging about their collections of action figures. And when he left the building and came back outside, there was always a little part of him that expected to see his mother waiting for him on the corner, the day's groceries in her arms, to ask him what he'd learned that day. As though the past was a physical place to which one could return, even by accident, if you just could work out the way there.

When he rounded the corner, the blacktop behind the school still looked pretty much the same as it had when he was young, but it wasn't his classmates as children who were standing around in small groups over near the basketball court, but the children *of* his classmates. At least, that was how he usually thought of them. There were only a couple of students whose parents had actually been in the same graduating class as Patrick, but many of them where the offspring of kids that he'd known from the neighborhood growing up, or who had hung around or gone to school with his cousins, and even a few whose mothers or fathers had been enlisted by Uncle Alf to look after his marks on the weekends. The majority of them had at least one Te'Maroan parent, and some had two, but there were a couple of Latino and African American kids who didn't have any islander ancestry at all, and had just started showing up to Patrick's informal classes at the school for the heck of it.

The Kienga twins were off to one side with Tommy Hulana and the rest of their usual clique, and seemed pretty pleased with themselves for having been able to get so many of their classmates up to the school on a weekend. There were a bit over a dozen kids in all, it looked like, which represented about half of the attendance at Patrick's regular school-day sessions. Sandra Kaloni and the knot of girls she ran with were on the other side of the group, huddled close and talking about anime and video games, like they usually did when given a spare moment of free time. A couple of kids were sitting cross-legged on the blacktop, seemingly in a world of their own, one reading a paperback novel and another drawing in a sketchbook, and the rest of them were passing a basketball back and forth and making mostly unsuccessful attempts at shooting hoops.

"Okay, everybody," Patrick said as he approached, "huddle up."

He put the can of paint on the ground at his feet and put the stack of brushes on top.

"Hey, Coach Tevake," Nicky Tekiera asked, still dribbling the basketball, "what's this all about?"

"I've got a project I need some help on," Patrick answered, wincing slightly. He hated being called "coach," and had successfully gotten the rest of the kids to break the habit, but Nicky had refused to let it go.

"What kind of project?" Regina Jimenez was still sitting on the blacktop, and barely looked up from her sketchbook as she spoke.

"It's a kind of a . . ." Patrick thought for a moment, and then finished, "let's call it a community cleanup. And a cultural enrichment project, too."

"Is this part of our grade?" Angela Kururangi asked, raising her hand timidly. "Or extra credit or something?

"I'll repeat," Patrick sighed, "*again*, you are *not* getting a letter grade in Te'Maroan Cultural Enrichment. The school has categorized it as an art elective with a pass/fail credit. And anyone that shows up and participates, passes. Now, as I was . . ."

"Sir," Tommy Hulana interrupted, "when are we going to learn . . ."

Patrick held up a hand to silence him.

"We're not starting on stick fighting until after the winter break," he said, wearily. "And that's only if everyone brings back the permission slips signed by their parents."

There were some worried expressions around the group. He knew that some of the parents had expressed reservations about the kids learning a martial art at school, even if they would be using sticks blunted with foam and padding. But that was a debate for another day.

One of the Kienga twins put up his hand. Patrick thought it was Ricky, but it could have been Joseph—he often had trouble telling them apart. "Sir, this community cleanup thing? You mean, like, picking up trash or something?"

Before Patrick could answer, the other Kienga twin chimed in.

"Or painting over graffiti, maybe?"

Patrick shook his head, but as he opened his mouth to answer it occurred to him that either of those ideas weren't a million miles from what he actually had in mind, in the broadest terms.

"Kind of, yeah," he answered, nodding slowly. "But not exactly. Here, it might be easier to show you."

He turned in place, looking at the houses across the street and then on the far side of the corner, trying to remember where the nearest of his Uncle Alf's marks could be found. Then he remembered how he would sometimes take a break from doing his rounds as a kid, when he was just up the street from the school, and would stop by the black top to see if any of his friends were around before heading to the convenience store over on Burgess Street to play video games, burning through whatever quarters were left from the week before. And the last house that he would always hit before taking a break, the one closest to the school, was his Aunt Pelani's apartment building just a block west of the Church of the Holy Saint Anthony, just a stone's throw from where he stood now.

"Come on, gang," he said, bending down to grab the paint can and brushes, and then starting off in that direction. "A little exercise will do you good."

It only took Patrick a few minutes to find one of his uncle's marks on the rear of a nearby building, all but completely obscured by vines and moss and dirt. He motioned the kids to gather around.

"Okay, can everyone see this?" He pointed to the spot on the wall, about five feet off the ground.

"It's a wall, coach," Nicky Tekiera answered with a smirk.

"Right, but it's what you *can't* see that's the problem." Patrick set down the paint, and then reached up and began pulling vines off the brick, one strand at a time. "There's something hidden under here that . . . well, it's really important."

Patrick chewed his lip for a moment as he searched for the best way to explain it. He was pretty sure that bringing up invaders from another dimension or shambling hordes wasn't the way to go. He needed a better way to couch it, both to stress the importance of the work and to help them understand the significance of what they'd be doing, at least in part.

"Does anyone remember the story about how Pahne'i conquered fire, and taught the people how to protect themselves against shadows?" There was an awkward silence from behind him. "Come on, we've talked about this in class, you guys."

"Was that the one with the lizard god in it?" Joseph Kienga said.

"No, stupid," his brother Ricky answered, "he got the magic knife from the God of Lizards, remember?"

Patrick glanced over his shoulder, and sure enough, Angela Kururangi had raised her hand and was waiting to be called on. She was a stickler for proper student-teacher etiquette.

"Yes, Angela?" he said, turning back to wrestle with the vines. "You have something to share?"

"He went to the First Volcano," she answered, "looking

for a way that the people could cook their food so that they wouldn't have to eat it raw."

"And wouldn't be cold at night," Tommy Hulana added, eagerly.

"Right," Patrick nodded, dropped a fistful of vegetation to the pavement at his feet. "The people who lived on Kovoko-ko-Te'Maroa didn't know anything about fire, so it wasn't just that they ate their food bloody and cold, but their nights were full of terrors because they had no defense against the shadows that crept outside the grass walls of their huts."

"Pahne'i knew about it, though, didn't he?" Sandra Kaloni interjected. "Didn't his mom tell him about it, or something?"

"He saw it when he went to visit his dad, the god of the ocean," Ricky answered.

"How can there be fire under the ocean?" Joseph sounded skeptical.

"It's magic, dummy. He's the *god* of the ocean."

"Technically you're both right," Patrick said. "Pahne'i's father lived in a *cave* under the ocean. But yes, Pahne'i had seen light coming from burning logs in his father's long house, and had eaten cooked fish and boar there. So he went to ask his mother—and yes, Sandra, she was the one who knew where this burning light could be found."

Patrick could remember his Uncle Alf telling him the story, time and again over the years, and if he listened hard enough he could almost hear the echoes of the old man's voice, bouncing around somewhere far back in his mind.

"Pahne'i's mother," he could remember the old man saying, *"who had been introduced into the mysteries by her own mother, told her beloved son everything she knew about the secret light he had seen, told how it burned within the breast of every man,*

but extinguished when brought into the air. She told him how the sun and the stars were of the same stuff, floating high above the waves. And she told him the secret name of the light: Fire."

Patrick had managed to pry loose most of the vines, and picked up the paint brush to use the end of its wooden handle to start digging moss out of the grooves.

"Pahne'i's mother told him that the fire lived far away to the west," Patrick continued, "at the edge of the world, in the place where the sun went to sleep every night. So Pahne'i sailed west, for eight days and eight nights, until he came to Helekea, the First Volcano, climbed up to the very top, and then climbed down inside of it."

"Where he fought a lot of monsters!" Nicky Tekiera was always the most interested in Te'Maroan legends that involved monsters of one kind or another.

"With that magic knife of his," Ricky Kienga amended, quickly.

"Yes, with the moonstone knife he'd been given by the god of lizards, which was said to shine like the stars themselves." Patrick gritted his teeth as he scraped away a particularly ground-in bit of moss. "He fought the tikua demons that live beneath the earth, sending their shadows back down to their master. Then he came to a lake of fire, resting in the bottom of the volcano. He tried a bunch of different ways to carry it back with him, but it burned everything he tried to put it in, so in the end he drank it and carried it back in his belly. Then he climbed back out and headed home."

"Wait," Sandra cut in, "what about the god of shadows? Didn't Pahne'i fight him down there, too?"

Patrick shot her a grin over his shoulder. "That was the next trial he faced—good memory, Sandra—but it wasn't on that same island. He got caught in a storm on the way back, and was lost at sea in the cold and dark for days and days. When the storm finally cleared, he was in an unfamiliar part of the sea. He continued sailing east for a long, long time, trying to find his way back home, until he came to a shore that stretched out to the north and south as far as the eye could see."

"The mainland?" Tommy asked.

"Maybe," Patrick answered noncommittally. "Island people sailed all over the place, so it's entirely possible that they might have gotten that far. Anyway, as Sandra says, it was there that Pahne'i encountered the God of Shadows, after climbing down into a big hole in the ground, like an unhealed wound on the land itself."

"Why was this dude always going around climbing down into holes?" Joseph sounded skeptical.

"Because he was looking for more monsters to fight, I'll bet!" Nicky said, bouncing his basketball on the pavement to punctuate his point.

"The way I always heard the story, he went underground to get away from the heat of the sun, after having been outdoors so long," Patrick answered, appraising the state of the mark he'd uncovered. Reaching down, he picked up the paint can, twisted off the lid, and began to touch up the cracks and gaps where the decades-old paint had flaked away. "Anyway, he found the God of Shadows, who promptly swallowed Pahne'i whole. For eight sunless days and eight moonless nights the darkness tried to consume him, but he was kept warm by the flames that were still burning deep inside of him. And finally he found the strength to cut his way free with his moonstone knife, and in doing so discovered the secrets for keeping the shadows at bay. The God of Shadows retreated back into the dark, presumably to plot his revenge, and Pahne'i returned to the surface and sailed off in search of home."

He stood back from the wall, hand on his chin as he studied the mark. It had taken some time, but it looked almost as fresh and clean as it had the day that his Uncle Alf had first carved it into the brick and laid in the salt-infused paint. Patrick could hear his great-uncle's voice echoing in his thoughts, reciting the end of the tale, again and again.

"Once home, Pahne'i was able to disgorge the fire he carried in his belly into the pits of his mother's village, and taught the people of Kovoko-ko-Te'Maroa the art of cooking, so that never again were they forced to eat their meat bloody and cold. And he taught them the secrets of how to defeat the shadows, so that they would never need fear the nights again."

Patrick set the can of paint on the ground and began cleaning the last of the white paint off the brush's bristles with a Kleenex as he turned to face the kids.

"And *this* is what Pahne'i taught them," he said, nodding toward the spiraling mark, "the secret of how to defeat the shadows. These are traditional Te'Maroan symbols, and my great-uncle carved them here a long, long time before you were born, as part of a ritual that was believed to protect the people who lived inside the house from danger. The fact that they're somewhat obscured, kept in safe places, is kind of the point. But when they get completely covered over by vines and moss and dirt, then they are lost, and forgotten."

Patrick looked from one face to another, gauging their reactions.

"*This* is who we are," he went on, pointing at the spiraling mark again for emphasis. "It doesn't matter whether you believe that the old stories are true or not. They still *belong* to us, they still help *define* us. They were a really important part of island life, and it was something that the islanders who came here to Recondito felt like it was important to preserve. Just like the Pahne'i stories I've told you, and konare and stick fighting, and the songs that the old folks used to sing. If we don't look after these things, and keep them alive, then they'll be lost and forgotten, just like these marks have been, and the people that come after us will never know that they were ever here."

"So what do you want us to do about it?" Tommy Hulana asked.

Patrick reached down, picked up the paint can and brush, and then held them out at arm's length toward the kids. "What you just saw me do. There are marks like this all over the neighborhood, and I need you to find them and take care of them, just like I did with this one."

"And that's it?" Nicky Tekiera. "Just clear out the dirt and crap and put paint in the grooves?"

"That's it. Now, there are marks like this on buildings all over this corner of the Oceanview, but you'll have to go looking for them. They're usually on the backs of houses, or on the pavement near front doors, that kind of thing. Don't bother looking anywhere east of Delaney or north past Crouchfield, though. Stick to the southwest part of the neighborhood."

From the expressions on their faces, it appeared that most of the kids were mostly swayed by the argument, or at least convinced enough that they didn't feel the need to debate the point. But even if they were onboard with the idea that it was important to keep up the old traditions, would they be willing to put in the work to do so themselves?

"All right, then," Patrick said, bending down and picking up the handful of brushes that were sitting beside the paint can. He straightened up, and held the brushes out to the kids on the open palm of his hand. "Can I count on you?"

A few of the boys exchanged dubious looks, and Patrick saw that he might have to sweeten the deal.

"And when you've finished cleaning them all, I'll throw a pizza party for the whole group," he added.

That brought them around. Nothing like the offer of free pizza to motivate a group of middle-school kids.

"Okay," Patrick said with a slight smile. "Let's get to work."

The Kienga twins took charge of the paint can, and the other kids all took a brush each.

"Now, some of them might be too tall for you to reach from the ground," Patrick said, dusting his hands off. "So you might want to get a broom from home, or maybe a stepladder. Or maybe you could see if one of your older siblings could pitch in."

He nodded toward Regina Jimenez, who was at the rear of the group with her sketchbook clutched to her chest.

"Regina, your brother's pretty tall, right? If he helped out, maybe I can arrange for it to count toward his community service."

The girl looked up from under her eyebrows at Patrick, a stricken expression on her face, and tightened her grip on the sketchbook.

"Oh," Patrick said softly. Had he hit a nerve, mentioning Regina's brother? Still in high school, Hector Jimenez had been charged with a misdemeanor back in the spring, underage possession and consumption of alcohol, and had lost his driver's license and been sentenced to thirty hours of volunteer work. He'd come around the school a few times on weekends, helping out with various clean up jobs or minor repairs, and seemed to have gotten his act together.

"Okay, everybody," he went on, turning his attention back to the rest of the group and raising his voice. "Get out there and get to work. The sooner those marks are all cleaned off and cleaned up, the better."

As the other kids drifted away, heading off in different directions individually or in small groups, Patrick hurried to catch up with Regina, who was shuffling along by herself, her eyes on the pavement in front of her.

"Regina?" Patrick tapped her lightly on the shoulder to get her attention, trying not to startle her.

She turned around, flinching slightly. She wasn't shy, exactly, just reserved, and seemed more interested in the things she wrote and drew in her sketchbook than anything going on around her most of the time. Patrick suspected that she had joined the Te'Maroan Cultural Enrichment program in large because he would let her sit and draw in the back of the room without bothering her, though he knew that her Te'Maroan grandmother on her mother's side had been pleased to hear that Regina was taking an interest in island culture.

"Sir?" she said in a quiet voice.

"I just wanted to ask about Hector," Patrick explained. "Is he doing okay?"

She looked at the ground at her feet for a moment, and seemed to be considering her answer before opening her mouth.

"Regina?" Patrick urged gently. "You shouldn't worry about getting him in trouble. I'm worried about keeping him *out* of trouble. That's what the police are here for."

She took a breath and then let out a ragged sigh.

"He's started hanging around those kids again," she said. "You know, the ones from before?"

Patrick nodded. Hector had been arrested back in the spring at a warehouse party out by the docks, in the company of some repeat offenders from another high school.

"Is he drinking again?" Patrick asked.

She briefly met his gaze, and then looked away, shoulders hunched.

"Taking drugs?" Patrick guessed.

Regina blanched. And then, after a long pause, slowly nodded.

Patrick let out a labored sigh. If the kid was lucky, he would be staying away from the harder stuff. Patrick had seen far too many kids dip their toes in the water only to find themselves in way over their heads at the deep end of the pool quicker than they could have imagined.

"He's going to some place in Hyde Park today," Regina went on. "The kids he's hanging around with got their hands on some new stuff that they want to try out."

Patrick chewed his lower lip. Maybe there was still a chance to stop Hector before he got in too deep?

"It comes in, like, this pen thing." Regina held up her mechanical pencil and mimed the act of injecting it into her arm. "Like the kind kids with allergies use?"

"You mean Ink?" Patrick said in a rush, his eyes widening. "Your brother is going to take Ink?"

Regina nodded. "Yeah, I think that's what he called it. He's never done it before, but I think he just wants those stupid kids he hangs around with to think he's cool."

Patrick took hold of the girl's shoulders with both hands. "Regina, do you know *where* he's going to go? Where he's going to take it?"

"I think so." She pulled a smart phone out of her pocket.

"Mom made us install that Find Friends thing? So we wouldn't get lost or whatever?"

She tapped the screen, and then turned it around to show it to Patrick. There was a green dot marked "HECTOR" just the other side of Prospect Avenue, at the edge of Hyde Park.

"That's where he is now," Regina said.

Patrick grabbed his own phone out of his pocket, and reached out to take Regina's from her hands.

"Can I borrow this?" he said perfunctorily, already taking it from her. Then he brought up the camera app on his own phone, took a quick photo of the display on the girl's phone, and then added Hector's phone number to his own contact list. He handed Regina's phone back to her, stuffing his own back in his pocket. "Thanks. Now, listen. I'm going there *right* now, okay?"

"Are you going to arrest him?" Her voice sounded small and afraid, tinged with guilt at the thought she might be getting her brother into trouble.

"No," Patrick said, already turning to hurry off. "But hopefully I can stop him and his friends before they make a *huge* mistake."

CHAPTER SEVENTEEN

Izzie and Joyce were just walking up the sidewalk toward the Northside Community Living Center, warm cups of coffee in hand, when Joyce's phone rang. She hooked the handle of her cane over the elbow of the arm holding her coffee cup, and with her free hand pulled the phone out of her pocket and glanced at the screen.

"It's Patrick," Joyce said, and then glanced over in Izzie's direction as she tapped the screen to answer. "Hang on a second."

Izzie just nodded and took a sip of her coffee, turning to look up the street while Joyce held the phone to her ear.

"What's up?" Joyce said, and even from a few feet away Izzie could hear the faint buzzing of Patrick's voice from the other end of the call, talking urgently and without pause, though she couldn't make out what he was saying from that distance.

"Okay, but . . ." Joyce began, and then the buzzing cut her off as Patrick kept on talking.

Joyce looked over at Izzie and mimed a silent grimace.

"Understood," Joyce finally said as the buzzing came to an end. "Keep us posted."

"What was that all about?" Izzie asked while Joyce pocketed the phone. "Sounded pretty important."

"He said that some kids from his neighborhood are apparently about to take Ink for the first time, at a house over in Hyde Park, and he's trying to get there in time to stop them."

"Oh." Izzie blinked.

She could easily understand the sense of urgency. Once they injected the Ink into their systems, the loa would have its hooks in them, and there would be no turning back. Or at least, that was what they had assumed. But what about the two kids that G. W. Jett had pulled out of the Eschaton Center back in the seventies?

"Hey," Izzie went on, turning to Joyce, "didn't Jett say that the runaway kids that he saw on the street, the ones that he was going to the Eschaton Center to find, showed signs of being Ridden? That they had the halos of shadows or whatever they were around their heads?"

Joyce was looking at her over the rim of her coffee cup, and nodded slowly as she lowered the cup from her mouth. "I think so, yeah. Why?"

"Well, the loa must have had its hooks in them, assuming that it worked the same way then that we're seeing now." Izzie chewed her lower lip, thoughtfully. "But they both lived for years after Jett pulled them out of there—maybe not happily or well, but they lived—and didn't seem to show any of the symptoms of being Ridden in all that time."

"Not based on the evidence that we've found so far, no," Joyce answered, shaking her head.

"So . . . how did he manage that, exactly?" Izzie asked. "Is it possible to make someone, I don't know, *un-Ridden*?"

Joyce raised her shoulders in a shrug.

"I don't know." Then she raised her cane and pointed toward the visitor's entrance of the community living center. "Why don't we go back to the source and ask him?"

The receptionist at the front desk saw them as they entered, and waved them over with her free hand while she held the handset of her desk phone to her ear with the other. Izzie and Joyce walked over and then waited while the receptionist wrapped up her phone call.

"You were here before to see Mr. Jett, right?" the receptionist said as she set the handset back in its cradle. "I'm guessing you're back to see him again?"

When they nodded, she picked up a handwritten note from the desktop beside her elbow.

"He's finished up his P.T.," she read aloud from the note, "but he's a little worn out so he's resting up in his room. If you want to go up and talk with him there, though, I can print you out a couple of visitor badges. You'll need them to get into the residential floors."

"That would be great, thanks," Izzie answered, trying not to sound too eager.

A few minutes later, adhesive badges stuck to their chests, Izzie and Joyce were escorted upstairs by an orderly. As he led them down a long hallway, Izzie felt that the smell of antiseptic and age was even stronger here than it had been in the waiting room, and as they passed open doors she caught glimpses of elderly residents—mostly men but a few women, too—sitting

in chairs and staring out windows or just into the middle distance, awake but not exactly alert. Were they lost in their own
memories of the past, or waiting for someone to visit, or just
patiently idling away what time remained to them?

Finally, the orderly knocked on a partially opened door
with a few raps of his knuckles, and said, "Mr. Jett, you decent?"

"If I am, it'd be the first time," came a voice from inside.
"Come on in, then."

The orderly stepped aside and held the door open for Izzie
and Joyce to walk through.

"Took you long enough," Jett said as they entered. "Was
starting to think you girls had got bored and gone on home."

He was sitting in his wheelchair, parked over by the window. The room was outfitted with the same relatively featureless furniture that Izzie had seen in the other rooms they'd
walked by, like the kind that she'd expect to find in college
dorms or hospital patient's room. Unlike the other rooms she'd
glimpsed, though, Jett's didn't have much in the way of personal touches, no framed photos of family members or vases
with flowers. The only thing that the old man seemed to have
added to the bland anonymity of the room's fixtures was a battered old wooden footlocker, the olive drab of its covering of
paint scuffed and faded, sitting on the floor at the end of the
bed. There was a narrow couch with thin cushions opposite
the bed, and the old man pointed to it with a knobby-knuckled
finger, indicating that they should sit.

"So where were we?" Jett said as they settled onto the
couch.

"You were on your way up the hill to the Eschaton Center,"
Joyce answered. "You said that your sixth sense . . . your *knack*
. . . was telling you that you were walking into trouble, I think."

"Was that all the knack was giving you?" Izzie added. "Just an intuition?"

"At first, yeah." The old man folded his hands in his lap, his face lined by a deep frown. "But when I drove up there that morning and found a spot in the brush where I could park the car without being seen from the road, I got my first look at the Eschaton Center itself, and it felt . . . wrong. I couldn't see anything exactly, either with my eyes or with the knack, but I knew something wasn't right. It was like the whole place was radiating waves of dread. Anyway, I kept an eye on the place throughout the rest of the day and night, watching as folks came and went. Saw some Hollywood stars I'd seen in the movies showing up in limousines, rock stars with their entourages, other folks I recognized from TV . . . the kind of rich folks who I'd have expected to hang around that kind of place. But nobody like the street kids that I'd been following, and no sign of the four kids I'd been hired to find. There were maintenance and custodial employees who were bussed in mornings and taken back to the city at night, though, but they were picked up and dropped off around back at a service entrance instead of the big fancy front gates that the rich folks came in and out of. When a laundry truck came by to deliver laundered uniforms the next morning, I snuck up when the driver wasn't looking and snagged a janitor's uniform that would fit me well enough. And then when the workers came in a little while later, it wasn't too difficult to slip in with them and get into the place without being noticed. A black man in a janitor's uniform was pretty much invisible to those rich white folks, anyway, so I was able to move around the place without much trouble."

Izzie thought about her aunts back in New Orleans, who had worked as maids in fancy houses in Bywater and the

Garden District or housekeepers in upscale hotels in the French Quarter when she was a little girl, and how they'd talked about feeling like they practically blended into the furniture and wallpaper for their employers and their guests. Unless something went missing, of course, in which case they were the first ones to be blamed.

"The ground floor of the place was pretty much exactly what I'd expected," Jett went on. "Big auditorium, bunch of meeting rooms, a dining room. I checked out the second and third floors, too, and it was almost like a hotel or a hunting lodge or something like that, with lots of rooms for guests to stay, lounges with couches and chairs, a sauna, Jacuzzi, all sorts of rich white people stuff. But no hippie kids, and no sign of the four kids in particular I was after. The knack wasn't giving me much, either. I was still getting that same sense of dread, of wrongness, but I wasn't *seeing* anything. I knew it was close, though, but it wasn't until I was checking out the indoor pool up on the fourth floor that I realized that the feeling was getting weaker the higher up I went. I needed to go *down*. Took me a while, poking around back on the first floor, but I finally found a stairway that led to a basement. At least, that's what I thought when I started heading down, but it wasn't any basement that I found."

He drew one of his gnarled hands slowly down across his face, blinking slowly and taking a deep breath.

"That feeling of wrongness, it got stronger every step I took down those stairs, and it was stronger still when I walked out into what looked more like a school or training facility. There was one room where a lady was standing up in front of a big group of folks, talking about wisdom and higher knowledge and truth flowing down into their minds and souls from the higher dimensions. The same kind of guff that the Ridden kids were pushing in the streets, basically. Further down the hall there was another huge room filled with young people sitting in row after row of chairs, facing something on the far wall and chanting in unison. Had to sidle around to see what they were looking at, and then I saw that it was some kind of mandala or something like that, but it made my eyes water to look at, like it seemed to have too many angles to be just a flat image printed on a piece of poster board. All of the kids in the room were wide-eyed and staring at the thing, and I don't think I saw a single one of them blink while I was standing there."

"Were they Ridden?" Izzie asked. "Could you see those . . . those *shadows* around them?"

"Nah," the old man answered, shaking his head. "When I tried to stop using my eyes to see them and start using the knack, there weren't any shadows on any of them. But I could see that something weird was happening to them. It was like, looking at that thing up on the wall was changing things inside their heads, almost like it was pushing thoughts out of the way to make room for something else."

"You could *see* their thoughts?" Joyce was clearly skeptical about the idea of reading minds.

"Not exactly. I mean, I've heard of some folks who have the knack strong enough that they can hear what folks are thinking, but I never was able to pull that off. It was more like being able to see about how many pages were in a book without opening the cover, just by looking at how thick the spine was. Things were getting rearranged in there, but I couldn't have said just what it was, one way or the other. When I found out what *was* happening, a while later, I was glad that I hadn't spent too much time looking at that mandala thing, though. But I'll get to that in a minute."

Izzie ran through her memories of what she had learned from Nicholas Fuller's papers and Roberto Aguilar's journals, trying to see if she could think of anything that would account for the important of some kind of "mandala" in all of this, but came up empty. This was a new piece of the puzzle.

"I found another stairway at the far end of the hall, leading down deeper still. As I went down the stairs, the wrongness got stronger and stronger still, and the stairs just kept going and going. When I got to the bottom and looked out the door, at first I was expecting more classrooms or whatever like the level above, but this one was more like a church or something. It was one enormous space, with high arching ceilings that had to be fifty feet above the floor, and the whole thing looked to have been carved out of the living rock of that hill. There were rows of pews set up, and some kind of ceremony going on at a dais at the far end of the room. The only light in the space came from bright fluorescents on the rear wall above the dais, and the edges of the room were in near total darkness. I hadn't seen any janitors or custodial staff since I'd left the ground floor, so I kept to the shadows as I crept closer along the side of the room, trying to get a better look at what was going on.

"There were people sitting in the pews at the front half of the room, facing the dais, where a white guy dressed in some kind of robes was standing behind a podium. As I got a little closer, I could see that it was Jeremiah Standfast Parrish, whom I recognized from the author photo on the back of his book. He was talking to the folks in the pews like a preacher on Sunday morning, talking about how the hard work that they'd done had made them 'primed,' their minds 'unlocked' and made ready. Then he started calling folks from the front row to come up to receive their 'daily sacrament.' And one by one they knelt in front of him, and tilted their heads back with their mouths open. From where I was standing, it looked like he was pouring a drop from a black pitcher onto their tongues while chanting some kind of nonsense, but as I got a little closer I could see that the pitcher was actually made of clear glass, and the stuff inside that he was pouring onto their tongues a drop at a time was some kind of thick black goo, almost like oil."

"Like ink, maybe?" Izzie prompted.

"About like, yeah," the old man allowed. "Well, the folks would just shiver a second or two, then he'd pat them on the top of the head and they'd go on back to their pew. Looking with the knack, though, I could see what was *really* going on. All of those folks were Ridden, little clouds of shadow trailing from their heads. But every one of them that went up and got that 'sacrament,' the shadows around them grew bigger and stronger while I watched, coming up from their heads and shoulders like tendrils reaching up into nothing at all. Like he was pouring more of whatever was controlling them right into their bodies a little bit at a time, strengthening the Otherworld's hold on them every time he did. And Parrish himself?"

He shook his head, a pained expression deepening the lines on his face.

"Him I could hardly stand to look at. The shadows had damn near swallowed that man whole, until there was nothing left of him. The body I could see with my eyes was like a thin shell covering up the darkness inside. I doubted there was much left of the man he'd once been in there at all."

Jett drew in a ragged breath through his nostrils and composed himself before continuing.

"I'd gone close enough to the front of the room that I could see the faces of some of the folks in the pews. I recognized a lot of the kids that I'd been tailing on the street, all of them with the same glassy look in their eyes, zonked out and expressionless, like they'd been hypnotized or something. And sitting right next to each other on the back row, on the same side of the room as I was standing, were two of the kids I'd gone in there looking for: Muriel Tomlinson and Eric Fulton. They hadn't gone up to get the 'sacrament' yet, and there were a couple of rows to go until it was their turn. Judging by the shadows that the knack was showing me around their heads, I could see that they weren't yet as far gone as some of the others, but it looked to me like another dose or two of that oily junk was likely to eat away enough of them that there wouldn't be any coming back from it. The whole damned place, the entire Eschaton Center, seemed to be nothing more than a factory churning out Ridden, taking in lost and vulnerable young people at one end and pumping out possessed minions at the other. Just what Parrish planned to do with them—or what the force that had taken control of Parrish, I guess I should say—I didn't know. But I had to do something, and fast. I couldn't just stand there and watch those two kids give up a little bit more of themselves to that junk while their families were out there waiting for me to bring them home. So, while everyone else's attention was on the front of the room where Parrish was dosing one dupe after another, I slunk over to where the two kids were sitting, keeping low and hoping nobody looked in my direction."

"You were still wearing the janitor's uniform, right?" Izzie asked.

"Yeah, and I had that Colt .45 riding in the waistband of my pants, hidden by the shirt's hem. I was hoping I wouldn't

have to use it, but considering that there weren't any maintenance or cleaning folks anywhere to be seen on those lower
levels, I knew that if someone were to spot me, there was a
good chance that I might have to. If I just tapped Tomlinson
and Fulton on the shoulder, I figured there was an even chance
that when they saw me they might start hollering for help, so
instead I leaned in close and, before they'd even had a chance
to turn around, I whispered that Parrish needed their help
with a special ceremony. They turned and gave me that same
zonked out, glassy-eyed stare. They didn't holler, but they
didn't budge, either. Tomlinson was at the end of the row, so
I took hold of her arm and pulled her to her feet, and held on
tight so she wouldn't wander away while I grabbed Fulton and
dragged him off the pew, too. As I pulled them into the shadows at the edge of the room, I chanced a look back over my
shoulder and saw that Parrish was still occupied with chanting and dosing the kids with the gunk, and hadn't seemed to
notice me yet. So I kept on pushing the two kids toward the
back of the room, staying in the shadows as much as possible,
keeping a tight grip on their arms. They weren't resisting, but
they were sluggish, dragging their feet like they were sleepwalking or something."

The old man looked down at his hands, flexing the knobby-knuckled fingers.

"I bundled them through the door and into the stairway
without getting noticed, and it wasn't until we got up to the
classroom-looking level at the top of the stairs that they started
to struggle. If they'd been sleepwalking, now it was like they
were starting to wake up a bit. The girl started squawking about
the 'special ceremony' I'd promised them, and the boy wanted
to know why I was taking them *away* from the sacrament. The

girl just seemed annoyed, but there was a desperate, hungry edge to the boy's voice, sounding like a junkie who'd just been denied a fix he'd been waiting for for a long, long time."

"But they *were* Ridden, right?" Izzie asked, leaning forward on the couch. "It doesn't seem like they were completely under the entity's control if you were able to trick them like that. Aren't all of the Ridden connected, somehow?"

"Yes and no." The old man smiled slightly as he nodded. "In his journals, Freeman talked a lot about how all of that business worked. There were those folks who'd been tainted by the Otherworld but not yet fully possessed, folks who were influenced but still had minds of their own, and folks who were pretty much nothing but puppets, with hardly anything of their original selves left in them. Tomlinson and Fuller had a touch of the Otherworld on them, and were hungry for more, but they hadn't lost themselves to it completely yet."

That lined up with what Izzie and the others had observed, with some Ridden able to go out into the world by daylight, and others too far gone to even step a foot outside until nightfall.

"I was able to get them on up to the ground floor before the two of them started acting squirrelly. It was coming on dark out, and neither of them was in any hurry to go outside. But I wasn't about to let go of their arms, either, and I had the inches and weight on them to drag the both of them after me. Some of the cleaning staff saw them struggling and looked like they might be getting ready to raise some kind of alarm, and that's when I took out that silver plated Colt .45. I kept hold of the girl's arm, and told the boy that if he took one step wrong that I'd shoot him. Then I told the cleaners to keep their distance, but with the knack I could see that none of them were Ridden, just regular working folks, so I didn't need to tell them twice.

Then I marched those two kids out the back door and hustled them toward the spot where I'd hidden my car."

"Wait," Joyce interrupted, "you rescued runaways from a cult at *gunpoint*?"

The corners of the old man's mouth tugged up in a slight smile.

"Wasn't the last time, either," he said. "But it got the job done. I had the girl drive the car while I covered her and the boy with the gun from the passenger's seat. The farther we got away from the Eschaton Center, though, the less trouble they gave me. And by the time we got back to the city, they were jittery, but they weren't putting up any kind of fight. I took them by my lady friend's place, and asked her to keep an eye on them while I took care of some business. I called police dispatch from a payphone, and told them that there were a whole mess of drugged-up runaways in the basement of the Eschaton Center. I ended up getting passed around like a hot potato, transferred from one department to another while I tried to convince them that I was on the level, and that I wasn't a prankster or some acidhead coming down off a bad trip. I finally got transferred to a detective in a bunco squad that had been trying to put together a case about Parrish and the Eschaton Center for months, and enough of what I had to say jibed with what he already knew."

"They were already investigating him?" Izzie hadn't heard about that angle of the case before.

"A couple of detectives had their eyes on him," the old man answered. "A lot of money was flowing into the Center, but it wasn't clear just where all of it was going. Some of the guys who worked the fraud unit thought there might be some dirt on Parrish, but so far hadn't found anything they could move on. But the detective I talked to was convinced by what I told him, and his say-so was enough to convince the higher ups to authorize a full-scale raid on the place."

"But you told them about the . . ." Joyce searched for the right word. "The rituals that were taking place underground?"

Jett shook his head. "They wouldn't have understood if I tried. Anyway, the detective told me to hang back and let them take care of things, but I thought there was still a chance I might be able to get the other two kids I was after out of there. So while the police were still gearing up and getting ready to make their raid, I drove right back up the hill and got there about an hour before them."

"And?" Izzie realized that she was perched on the edge of the couch cushion, but didn't care. She was eager to hear how this played out. "Was everyone already dead? Killed by each other or by their own hands?"

The old man's frown deepened.

"The official story was that it was a mass murder/suicide, yeah," he said after a long pause. "But that's not the whole picture."

Before he could continue, there was a knock at the door. Izzie turned, and saw that the orderly had returned.

"Sorry, folks," he said, tapping his wristwatch. "But I'm afraid visiting hours are over for the day."

Izzie started to object, but the old man raised his hand and motioned toward the window.

"Looks to be coming on night soon," Jett said, wearily. "And I'm guessing that you two don't want to be out and about if there's Ridden on the streets." He paused, and then gave Izzie a hard look. "And there *are* Ridden out there again, aren't there? That's what this is all about."

Izzie nodded.

"Yes," she answered, swallowing hard. "They're back."

The old man put his hands on the wheels of his chair, and pushed himself over to where the wooden footlocker sat at the end of the bed.

"You two come on back tomorrow and I'll give you the rest of it," he said, straining to reach over and lift the lid of the footlocker. "But before you go, there's something I suppose you should have."

He reached into the footlocker and pulled out a battered old cloth-bound journal.

"This was the only one of Freeman's journals that didn't go up in that fire," he said, holding the book out to Izzie. "Might be something in it you can make use of."

Izzie pushed herself up off the couch and walked over to Jett's wheelchair. When she took the journal from his hands, she could see that the corners of the cover were scorched black by flames.

"I don't think I'm long for this world," the old man went on, breathing heavily. "And there are times when I'm surprised that I've lasted as long as I have. But maybe I held on as best I could until someone came along that I could hand the torch off to, just like Charlotte handed it off to me. When I lay my head down to sleep that last time, I'll go a little easier knowing that there's somebody left to carry on when I'm gone."

Izzie stood in front of the old man, holding the journal in both hands, struggling to think what to say.

"I'm sorry, folks," the orderly called from the hallway, "but I'm going to have to ask you to say your goodbyes and head on out."

Joyce stood up from the couch and came over to stand beside Izzie.

"We'll come back tomorrow," Joyce said, touching Izzie's elbow lightly.

"Fair enough," the old man said, and there was something in his tone that made Izzie suspect that he wasn't sure he'd still be around by then. "But you two best tread carefully, and anybody else that's mixed up in this, too. That night underneath the Eschaton Center, when I confronted Parrish . . . I wasn't talking to him, really, but to whatever it was that had hollowed him out and pulled his strings like a puppet. That demon from the Otherworld. It saw me, and it *knew* me, and it promised me things if I would just walk away and let it be. Power. Wealth. Anything I wanted. But I told him to go to hell, and with one of Freeman's silver bullets from that Colt .45 I sent him on his way there. And when he went, well, the rest of those Ridden went with him. Now, the time may come when you folks find yourself in that same position. And it might be hard to refuse. But you'll need to stay strong."

The orderly cleared his throat noisily in the hallway.

"Just a damned second," Jett said, raising his voice and shouting toward the open door. Then he turned back and added, quietly enough that only Izzie and Joyce could hear him. "Just know that there's been many a man and woman faced with that same choice in this city over the years, and those that went along with the darkness caused nothing but pain and misery for the rest of us. You've got to be able to look at the shadows and not blink, no matter what the cost is."

Izzie turned, and started toward the door, but the old man reached out and grabbed hold of her elbow while she was still in reach.

"But you've got to be able to *see* the shadows to know what you're up against," he added, an urgent undertone to his voice.

"If you can't see them, you won't stand a chance. And if you don't have the knack, you'll have to figure out some other way."

Izzie nodded slowly.

"I think I have an idea," she said, laying her hand on top of the old man's for a moment. "We'll be careful."

The old man sighed as he released his hold on her arm and settled back in his wheelchair.

"Best you do. Because it seems to me you've got work to do."

As Izzie followed Joyce to the door and out into the hallway, she remembered the waking dream she'd had of her grandmother telling her much the same thing a few nights before. *You got work to do.*

CHAPTER EIGHTEEN

Patrick parked his car up the street from the address he'd taken from Regina Jimenez's phone, which turned out to be a modest single-story bungalow in a somewhat rundown corner of Hyde Park. As he got out, he glanced around at the other houses on the street. The developers who bought up older houses to remodel and then flip on the market hadn't gotten to this area yet, and many of the people that were out on the street were older retirees walking their dogs, or working-class types heading home from the liquor store. In time, Patrick was sure, the houses would all be outfitted with new porches and pristine new paint-jobs, with young professionals parking their electric hybrid cars in the driveways while nannies kept careful eyes on pampered toddlers playing on neatly manicured lawns. That was assuming that some developer didn't just bulldoze entire blocks and put up overpriced apartment buildings instead, like they'd done out in the Kiev. But either way, the people who lived here now likely wouldn't be able to afford to stay in just a few years' time.

Patrick had picked up his firearm and badge from the house on the way, and was debating with himself how to play this as he walked up to the front door of the house. He was off duty, and not on any official police business, but flashing a badge could open doors that might remain closed to a simple concerned citizen. But at the same time, he didn't have a warrant, and what little he knew was pretty sketchy to justify probable cause, if the need arose to justify his actions in court.

The fact remained that it was likely that a group of kids from the neighborhood were about to unknowingly inject a mind-controlling parasite from another dimension into their bodies if he didn't do something about it, so Patrick decided that he would have to play it by ear and worry about justifying his actions when and if the need arose.

It was late afternoon, the sun sinking over the buildings to the west, and would be getting dark soon. He was somewhat comforted by the tohuna mark amulet and sandwich bag of salt in his pocket, but even so, he hoped to be back home before the sun set.

There was a ratty old screen door that was barely held up on its hinges, and when he pulled it open there was a screech of metal against metal. He rapped his knuckles on the door, noting the flaking paint on the wood. Through the peephole in the door Patrick could see a pinprick of light from within.

He was about to knock again when he heard footsteps approaching the other side of the door, and muffled voices. The pinprick of light in the peephole was snuffed out as someone looked out from the other side, and Patrick did his best to appear unthreatening, keeping his badge out of view in his pocket and his pistol still in its holster under his jacket.

The clack and clatter of locks being turned went on for a

few seconds, suggesting that the house was more well-fortified than its somewhat shabby exterior might suggest. And when the door finally opened it was only for a few inches, with a security chain stretched taut from the leading edge of the door to its base on the door jamb.

"Yeah?" a gruff voice said as an eye peered out the gap in the door. "What do you want?"

"Is Hector Jimenez here?"

The eye disappeared for a moment, and angry whispers could be heard from inside.

"Who wants to know?" the voice said when the eye returned.

"I teach at his sister's school," Patrick said, deciding to play the concerned citizen for the moment. "I just want to talk to him for a second. Is he here?"

The door shut suddenly, and for a moment Patrick thought that they'd slammed it on him. But then he heard the rattle of the security chain being slid back, and a moment later the door swung open wide.

A skinny white guy in his mid-twenties stood in the open doorway, a lit cigarette hanging from the corner of his mouth. He was wearing a stained white t-shirt, tattered jeans, and scuffed up sneakers, with a patchy tuft of beard on his chin and long, greasy hair. He had a glassy-eyed look, and smelled of marijuana smoke. From the interior of the house, Patrick could hear the sounds of electronic bleeps and the simulated gunshots and screams of a video game being played.

"You don't look like any teacher I ever seen." The skinny guy sounded pretty stoned as he looked Patrick up and down. Then he narrowed his eyes with suspicion, and studied Patrick's face. "Are you five-o?"

So much for playing the concerned citizen, Patrick thought. There seemed little point in denying it now. He pulled his shield out of his jacket pocket and held it up, cupped in the palm of his hand.

"This isn't a bust," Patrick said, keeping his tone level and soothing. "I just want to talk to the kid for a second."

The skinny guy made a move to shut the door, but Patrick stepped forward and put his shoulder against it. His feet were still on the threshold, so technically he hadn't entered without being invited, but from this vantage point he was able to lean forward and look past the skinny guy into the living room beyond. He could see a bong, grinders, pipes, and an open sandwich bag half-filled with bud, which not long before would have been enough to justify probable cause for a search without a warrant. Seeing that it was legal now, Patrick would have trouble making that stick. But the skinny guy didn't necessarily know that.

"Look, friend," Patrick said, leaning in close to the guy while keeping his weight on the door. "I didn't come here to make any arrests, and I don't have a search warrant. But I'm seeing a lot of drug paraphernalia on your table there, and I'm thinking maybe I need to do a thorough search of the house to see what else I can find."

A look of alarm registered on the skinny guy's face, and Patrick wondered what the guy was worried he might find. He didn't have the look of a dealer, and didn't show any of the signs of Ink use, but instead seemed to be just what he appeared to be: a stoner who had a place for others to come over and hang out.

"*But*," Patrick hastened to add, "if you let me in for a second to talk to Hector and his friends, I'll be on my way. And since I'll be too busy talking to *notice* anything, there won't be any need for a search or for any arrests. Does that sound like a deal?"

The skinny guy narrowed his eyes and Patrick could probably see the thoughts bouncing together in his head.

"So I let you in, then you leave," the guy said. "But if I don't let you in, then you're going to come in anyway and search the place, and arrest me if you find any dirt?"

"That's about the size of it," Patrick answered with a smile.

The skinny guy nodded slowly and stepped back, taking his hand off the door.

"Just don't make too much noise, okay?" he said, padding back into the living room. "My grandma's asleep upstairs."

Patrick followed the skinny guy into the house, his eyes roaming around the room warily, keeping his hand close to his holstered pistol.

"Hey, Hector," the guy said as he walked through a doorway into a dimly lit room beyond. "Get your ass over here, already."

Patrick stopped in the doorway. Inside, a handful of teenage boys crammed onto a couch watched as two others mashed buttons on video game controllers while computer-generated soldiers in powered armor exchanged fire on a flatscreen TV. Patrick recognized Hector in the bunch, as the boy turned to him with a guilty expression on his face. There were beer cans on a low table, and the smell of marijuana smoke hung heavily in the room, but Patrick didn't see any sign of Ink injectors.

"Come on, kid," Patrick said, "I just want to talk for a second."

Hector pushed himself up off his chair reluctantly, and slouched over to where Patrick stood.

"Yeah, what?" the kid said, trying to sound tough.

"Your sister thinks that you and your friends were planning to try Ink for the first time today," Patrick answered. "Any truth to that?"

Hector's eyes darted to the kids on the couch, who were studiously pretending not to notice the police officer standing in the room.

"My sister's just a dumb kid," he said, turning back to Patrick. "I don't know anything about . . ."

Patrick held up a hand to interrupt him.

"I'm not here to arrest you again, okay?" Patrick said. "And this isn't about your probation. I just want you to know that Ink is *bad* news. Seriously. It will *destroy* you. And I'm not talking about some kind of 'Scared Straight' gateway drug lecture stuff, either. It will literally rot your brain, and once you start using there's no going back."

Patrick could see from Hector's glowering expression that he wasn't getting through to him.

"You would be better off taking literally *anything* else, kid," Patrick went on. "Shooting heroin directly into your eyeball would do less damage than one injector's worth of Ink."

Hector's eyes widened slightly. Patrick knew that he wasn't expecting a cop to recommend one illegal narcotic over another.

"Where did you get the stuff?" Patrick looked around the room, and raised his voice to address the rest of the kids. "Who's got the Ink connection?"

The skinny guy who lived in the house stood in the corner, hands shoved deep into his pants pockets, and the kids on the couch were continuing to pretend that they couldn't hear or see Patrick.

"You could answer me," Patrick continued, "or maybe I call up a couple of squad cars and we arrest the lot of you for underage drinking."

The skinny guy had a startled look on his face. "Hey, now . . ."

"Those were there when we got here, man," one of the kids on the couch said, trying hard not to slur his words.

"We don't have the stuff yet, okay?" Hector raised his hands in front of him, palms forward. "Vincent's cousin is coming to drop it off."

"Hey!" One of the kids on the couch—Vincent, Patrick assumed—turned and glared at Hector. "Not cool, man."

Patrick motioned for the kids to settle down with a wave of his hand. "All right, all right. And when is Vincent's cousin supposed to get here?"

Hector glanced over at the kids on the couch, then back to Patrick.

"I dunno," he said with a shrug. "Supposed to be here already. I guess he's running late."

Patrick pulled out his phone to check the time. It would be sunset soon.

"Okay, kids, I'm going to head out," he said as he slipped the phone back into his pocket. "You can go back to your video games and weed and what not, but *seriously*, stay off the Ink. I've seen what it can do to a person, and trust me, you do *not* want that to happen to you."

He pointed a finger at the skinny guy in the corner.

"And if I find out that anyone here *did* dose themselves with Ink after I'm gone, I'm holding *you* personally responsible. And considering that I'm looking at a half-dozen cases of aiding-and-abetting underage drinking and drug use here, you'd be lucky to get away with just a few grand worth of fines and community service. You end up in the right court room, and you might even be looking at jail time."

The skinny guy blanched, swallowing hard.

"Don't worry," Patrick went on, turning to go. "I can see myself out."

The front door was still partially ajar, and through the gap Patrick could see a plain white delivery truck parked out front. As he was walking outside, a guy wearing dark sunglasses and a ball cap was climbing out of the passenger side of the truck, carrying a paper bag in his hand.

"Hey, you live here?" the guy said as Patrick turned onto the sidewalk.

Patrick's stomach roiled with nausea and an unpleasant taste stabbed his tongue. His hand moved closer to his holstered pistol as he turned in the guy's direction.

"Who's asking?" Patrick said, eyes narrowing. "Are you Vincent's cousin?"

Were they really using a delivery truck to drop off illegal drugs? And hadn't Izzie talked about almost being run down in the street the day before by the same kind of white delivery truck?

"Hey, I know you." The guy reached up with his free hand and took hold of his sunglasses.

Patrick could hear the driver's side door slam shut. He reached for his pistol.

"Lieutenant Tevake." The guy pulled the sunglasses off his face, and Patrick got the inescapable sense that someone else was looking out at him from behind those eyes. "Patrick. My man."

Dark blotches bloomed on the guy's cheek and forehead, as his lips curled in a sinister smile.

"I've had my people looking all over town for you and your friends."

Patrick drew his firearm with one hand, and pulled the makeshift amulet with its spiral mark out of his pocket with the other.

"Keep your hands where I can see them," Patrick said, aiming the barrel of his pistol at the guy's chest while holding the amulet out at arm's length.

"There's no need for that," the guy said, taking a step closer, and the blots grew larger. The sun had just dipped below the skyscrapers of City Center to the west, bathing the street in deep shadows. "I just want to talk."

Patrick could hear the sound of the swing doors at the rear of the truck being opened, and the scuff of approaching footsteps.

"Stay back." Patrick gestured with the barrel of the pistol, and held the amulet up in the guy's face. Then he chanced a glance behind him.

The driver was walking quickly toward him, followed by three other men and a woman.

"You can shoot this one if you want," the guy said, reaching out and wrapping his hand around the barrel of Patrick's gun. "But put away that damned squiggle. That's just being rude."

The driver and the four others were closing in behind him, blots blooming on their exposed skin.

"Your friends aren't here, and you won't have time to make a circle around yourself with that salt in your pocket this time, will you?" The guy stepped closer still, lifting Patrick's pistol and pressing the barrel to his own forehead. "So if you need to shoot first, go for it, and then the rest of my people will bring you to me so we can talk."

Dark shadows swirled in the guy's eyes, as the blots on his face grew larger.

Strong arms wrapped themselves around him from behind, and as Patrick jerked reflexively the gun in his hand went off.

The skin around the entry wound smoldered as the back of the guy's skull exploded outwards, raining gore onto the sidewalk and lawn.

"Got that out of your system, did you?" the dead man said, staring at Patrick through now lifeless eyes, his voice like an echo from the bottom of a deep, deep well. He put his sunglasses back on, as a viscous trail of blood oozed down from the hole in his forehead.

"I'm glad," the driver said, wrenching the pistol from Patrick's hand. "Now we can talk."

CHAPTER NINETEEN

Izzie sat in the passenger's seat of the Volkswagen Beetle as Joyce drove through the concrete canyons of the Financial District. She held the journal that the old man had given her in her lap, her gaze resting idly on the battered and scorched cover.

"Sorry I couldn't talk Hasan into letting us stay past visiting hours," Joyce said as they waited at an intersection for the light to change. "Maybe if we'd been there in an *official* capacity, but . . ."

She trailed off, and glanced over in Izzie's direction.

"So what's in there?" Joyce asked, indicating the journal with a curt nod. "Have you taken a look yet?"

Izzie shook her head, and ran her fingertips along the cover's edge. She was still thinking about what G. W. Jett had said about needing to *see* the shadows in order to face them.

"Well, what are you waiting for? With this traffic, we won't be back at Patrick's place for another twenty or thirty minutes. Crack that thing open and read some of it."

Izzie looked up from the journal and glanced in Joyce's direction. "Out loud?"

"Sure, why not?" Joyce shrugged. "I'm pretty curious to know what's in there, myself."

Izzie nodded absently, and flipped open the front cover of the journal. The interior pages were somewhat yellowed with age and filled with handwritten lines, the neatly formed block letters faded to an almost sepia-toned brown.

"The first entry is dated October of 1942," Izzie said. She scanned a few lines. "This Alistair Freeman was a pulp novelist, right?"

"Yeah?" Joyce said as she shifted the car into gear. "So?"

"Well, this is pretty flowery stuff. Here, listen to this. *'I dreamt of that day in the Yucatan again last night . . .'*"

Saturday, October 31, 1942.

I dreamt of that day in the Yucatan again last night. Trees turned the color of bone by drought, skies black with the smoke and ash of swidden burning for cultivation, the forest heavy with the smell of death. Cager was with me, still living, but Jules Bonaventure and his father had already fled, though in waking reality they had still been there when the creatures had claimed Cager's life.

As the camazotz came out of the bone forest toward us, their bat-wings stirring vortices in the smoke, I turned to tell my friend not to worry, and that the daykeepers would come to save us with their silvered blades at any moment. But it was no longer Cager beside me, but my sister Mindel, and in the strange logic of dreams we weren't in Mexico

of '25 anymore, but on a street in Manhattan's
Lower East Side more than a dozen years before.
And I realized that the smoke and ash were no longer from forest cover being burned for planting,
but from the flames of the Triangle Shirtwaist
Factory fire that had ended her young life. "Don
Javier will never get here from Mexico in time,"
I told my sister, as though it made perfect sense,
but she just smiled and said, "Don't worry, Alter.
This is the road to Xibalba." Then the demons had
arrived, but instead of claws, they attacked us
with the twine-cutting hook-rings of a newsven-
dor, and we were powerless to stop them.

Charlotte is still out of town visiting her
mother, and won't be back until tomorrow. When I
awoke alone in the darkened room this morning, it
took me a moment to recall when and where I was.
In no mood to return to unsettling dreams, I rose
early and began my day.

I ate alone, coffee and toast, and skimmed the
morning papers. News of the Sarah Pennington
murder trial again crowded war-reports from the
front page of *The Recondito Clarion*, and above
the fold was a grainy photograph of the two young
men, Joe Dominquez and Felix Uresti, who have been
charged with the girl's abduction and murder. Had
it not been an attractive blonde who'd gone missing, I'm forced to wonder whether the papers would
devote quite so many column inches to the story.
But then again there were nearly as many articles this morning on the Sleepy Lagoon murder
case just getting underway down in Los Angeles,
where seventeen Mexican youths are being tried
for the murder of Jose Diaz. Perhaps the attention is more due to the defendants' zoot-suits and

duck-tail-combs, and to Governor Olson's call to stamp out juvenile delinquency. If the governor had the power simply to round up every pachuco in the state and put them in camps, like Roosevelt has done with the Japanese, I think Olson would exercise the right in a heartbeat.

I didn't fail to notice the item buried in the back pages about the third frozen body found in the city's back alleys in as many nights, but I didn't need any reminder of my failure to locate the latest demon.

But this new interloper from the Otherworld has not come alone. Incursions and possessions have been on the rise in Recondito the last few weeks, and I've been running behind on the latest *Wraith* novel as a result. I spent the day typing, and by the time the last page of "The Return of the Goblin King" came off my Underwood's roller it was late afternoon and time for me to get to work. My *real* work.

As the sun sank over the Pacific, the streets of the Oceanview neighborhood were crowded with pint-sized ghosts and witches, pirates and cowboys. With little care for wars and murder trials, much less the otherworldly threats that lurk unseen in the shadows, the young took to their trick-or-treating with a will. But with sugar rationing limiting their potential haul of treats, I imagine it wasn't long before they turned to tricks, and by tomorrow morning I'm sure the neighborhood will be garlanded with soaped windows and egged cars.

I can only hope that dawn doesn't find another frozen victim of the city's latest invader, too. After my failure tonight, any new blood spilled would be on my hands—and perhaps on the hands of my clowned-up imitator, as well.

The dive bars and diners along Almeria Street were in full swing, and on the street corners out front, pachucos in their zoot-suits and felt hats strutted like prize cockerels before the girls, as if their pocket chains glinting in the street-lights could lure the ladies to their sides.

On Mission Avenue I passed the theaters and arenas that cater to the city's poorer denizens, plastered with playbills for upcoming touring companies, boxing matches, and musical perfor-mances. One poster advertised an exhibition of Mexican wrestling, and featured a crude painting of shirtless behemoths with faces hidden behind leather masks. A few doors down, a cinema marquee announced the debut next week of *Road to Morocco*. I remembered my dead sister's words in last night's dream, and entertained the brief fantasy of Hope and Crosby in daykeepers' black robes and sil-ver-skull masks, blustering their way through the five houses of initiation.

The last light of day was fading from the west-ern sky when I reached the cemetery, wreathed in the shadows of Augustus Powell's towering spires atop the Church of the Holy Saint Anthony. A few mourners lingered from the day's funeral services, standing beside freshly filled graves, but other-wise the grounds were empty.

I made my way to the Freeman family crypt and, passing the entrance, continued on to the back, where a copse of trees grows a few feet away from the structure's unbroken rear wall.

As Don Javier had taught me a lifetime ago in the Rattling House, I started toward the wall and, an instant before colliding with it, turned aside toward an unseen direction, and shadowed my way through to the other side.

Don Mateo was waiting for me within. He'd already changed out of his hearse-driver's uniform, and had dressed in his customary blue serge suit, Western shirt printed with bucking broncos and open at the neck, a red sash of homespun cotton wound around his waist like a cummerbund.

"Little brother," he said, a smile deepening the wrinkles around the corners of his eyes. He raised his shot glass filled to the rim with homemade cane liquor in a kind of salute. "You're just in time."

When Mateo speaks in English it usually means that he's uncertain about something, but when he gets excited-or angry-he lapses back into Yucatan. Tonight he'd spoken in Spanish, typically a sign his mood was light, and when I greeted him I was happy to do the same.

"To your health," I then added in English and, taking the shot glass from his hands, downed the contents in a single gulp, then spat on the floor a libation to the spirits. Don Javier always insisted that there were beneficent dwellers in the Otherworld, and libations in their honor might win their favor. But while I'd learned in the years I spent living with the two daykeepers, either in their cabin in the forest or in the hidden temples of Xibalba, to honor the customs handed down by their Mayan forebears, and knew that the villains and monsters of their beliefs were all-too-real, I still have trouble imagining that there are any intelligences existing beyond reality's veil which have anything but ill intent for mankind.

When I'd finished my shot, Don Mateo poured another for himself, and drank the contents and spat the libation, just as ritual demanded. Then, the necessary business of the greeting concluded, he set the glass and bottle aside, and began to shove open the lid of the coffin in which my tools are stored.

"Four nights you've hunted this demon, little brother," he said, lifting out the inky black greatcoat and handing it over. "Perhaps tonight will be the night."

I drew the greatcoat on over my suit. "Three victims already is three too many." Settling the attached short cape over my shoulders, I fastened the buttons. "But what kind of demon freezes its victims to death?"

The old daykeeper treated me to a grin, shrugging. "You are the one with the Sight, not I." His grin began to falter as he handed over the shoulder-holster rig. "Though Don Javier might have known."

I checked the spring releases on both of the silver-plated Colt .45s and then arranged the short cape over my shoulders to conceal them. "Perhaps," I said. But it had been years since the great owl of the old daykeeper had visited us in dreams.

As I slid a half-dozen loaded clips, pouches of salt, a Zippo lighter, and a small collection of crystals into the greatcoat's pockets, Don Maeto held the mask out to me, the light of the bare bulb overhead glinting on the skull's silvered surface.

The metal of the mask cool against my cheeks and forehead always reminds me of the weeks and months I spent in the Rattling House, learning to shadow through solid objects, cold patches left behind as I rotated back into the world. I never did master the art of shifting to other branches of the World Tree, though, much to Don Javier's regret.

The slouch hat was last out of the coffin, and when I settled it on my head Don Mateo regarded me with something like paternal pride. "I should like to see those upstarts in San Francisco and Chicago cut so fine a figure."

The mask hid my scowl, for which I was grateful.

Since beginning my nocturnal activities in Recondito in '31 I've apparently inspired others to follow suit—the Black Hand in San Francisco, the Scarlet Scarab in New York, the Scorpion in Chicago. Perhaps the pulp magazine's ruse works as intended, and like so many here in the city they assume the Wraith to be entirely fictional. There are times when I regret the decision to hide in plain sight, fictionalizing accounts of my activities in the pages of *The Wraith Magazine* so that any reports of a silver masked figure seen lurking through the streets of Recondito will be written off as an over-imaginative reader with more costuming skill than sense.

Don Mateo recited a benediction, invoking the names Dark Jaguar and Macaw House, the first mother-father pair of daykeepers, and of White Sparkstriker, who had brought the knowledge to our branch of the World Tree. He called upon Ah Puch the Fleshless, the patron deity of Xibalba, to guide our hands and expand my sight. Had we still been in the Yucatan, the old daykeeper would have worn his half-mask of jaguar pelt, and burned incense as offering to his forebears' gods. Since coming to California, though, he's gradually relaxed his observances, and now the curling smoke of a smoldering Lucky Strike usually suffices.

This demon of cold has struck the days previous without pattern or warning, once each in Northside, Hyde Park, and the waterfront. When Don Mateo and I headed out in the hearse, as a result, we proceeded at random, roaming from neighborhood to neighborhood, the old daykeeper on the lookout for any signs of disturbance, me searching not with my eyes but with my Sight for any intrusion from the Otherworld.

I glimpsed some evidence of incursion near the Pinnacle Tower, but quickly determined it was another of Carmody's damnable "experiments." I've warned Rex before that I won't allow his Institute to put the city at risk unnecessarily, but they have proven useful on rare occasion, so I haven't yet taken any serious steps to curtail their activities. I know that his wife agrees with me, though, if only for the sake of their son Jacob.

I caught a glimpse of the cold demon in the Financial District, and I shadowed out of the moving hearse and into the dark alley with a Colt in one hand and a fistful of salt in the other, ready to disrupt the invader's tenuous connection to reality. But I'd not even gotten a good look at the demon when it turned in midair and vanished entirely from view.

The body of the demon's fourth and latest victim lay at my feet. It was an older man, looking like a statue that had been toppled off its base. Arms up in a defensive posture, one foot held aloft to take a step the victim never completed. On the victim's face, hoarfrost riming the line of his jaw, was an expression of shock and terror, and eyes that would never see again had shattered in their sockets like glass. But before I'd even had a chance to examine the body further I heard the sounds of screaming from the next street over.

There is a body, I Sent to Don Mateo's thoughts as I raced down the alleyway to investigate. Had the demon retreated from reality only to reemerge a short distance away?

But it was no denizen of the Otherworld menacing the young woman huddled in the wan pool of the streetlamp's light. Her attackers were of a far more mundane variety-or so I believed. I pocketed the salt, and filled both hands with silver-plated steel.

Eleven years writing purple prose for *The Wraith Magazine*, and it creeps even into my private thoughts. Ernest would doubtless consider his point made, if he knew, and that bet made in Paris decades ago finally to be won.

The young woman was Mexican, and from her dress I took her to be a housekeeper, likely returning from a day's work . . .

CHAPTER TWENTY

Izzie left off reading as Joyce pulled the Volkswagen to a stop in front of Patrick's house. The sun had nearly finished setting, and deep shadows pooled at the edges of the buildings.

"Do you believe all of that?" Joyce said, shouldering open the driver's side door and reaching for her cane in the back seat. "That this Freeman guy really ran around the streets in a mask like some kind of pulp hero? And there were others who were doing the same thing in other cities?"

Izzie closed the journal, and opened the passenger side door.

"It makes a certain kind of sense," she answered as she climbed out. "Hiding in plain sight, that kind of thing. And it could explain where the mask that Nicholas Fuller wore came from. We never were able to track down a source for it before."

"And what was that about 'sending'?" Joyce had a quizzical expression on her face. "Some kind of telepathic communication, sounded like?"

"I'm not sure." Izzie nudged the door shut with her hip while Joyce came around the front of the car, her cane *tonk*ing on the pavement. "But in Roberto Aguilar's journals there were mentions of 'seeing' and 'sending' in the belief system of the Mayan daykeepers. 'Seeing' referred to the 'second sight,' Jett's 'knack.' But the 'sending'? It wasn't clear."

"Hey." Joyce looked first one direction up the street and then the other. "I don't see Patrick's car around anywhere, though, do you?"

"The lights are on," Izzie said, nodding toward the front door of the house. "Maybe he parked somewhere else and walked back?"

"Hope so." Joyce continued on up the front steps. "After what happened last night, I'm not too crazy about the idea of any of us being out after dark."

The door was locked, but after Izzie knocked she could hear the sound of someone moving inside, and a moment later the door swung open.

"Hey, you." Daphne smiled, her face sheened with a thin layer of sweat, with dark smudges on her cheek and forehead.

For a brief instant, an icy hand of fear gripped Izzie's heart as she wondered if the black marks meant that Daphne had been possessed by the loa somehow. But then she saw that Daphne's fingers were also stained, and there were similar smudges on the fabric of her white t-shirt.

"What have *you* been up to?" Izzie asked as she stepped past Daphne and into the house, with Joyce following close behind.

"I had an idea while you were away." Daphne answered as she closed the door.

"Oh, yeah?" Izzie glanced back over her shoulder as she

stepped into the living room. She stopped short when she heard a rustling sound under her feet, and looking down saw that there was butcher paper spread out on the hardwood floor, and bits of plastic and metal scattered in piles all around. On the low coffee table were bowls, scissors, knives, containers of different types of salts, and a myriad of plastic tubes that were each a bit over an inch long and as big around as a nickel. "Daphne? What is all this?"

"Well, remember last night, when I said that it might be handy to have some more weaponized silver on hand?" Daphne asked.

Izzie nodded, while Joyce slid down onto the couch.

"The Recondito Reaper used a silvered blade, right?" Daphne went on. "And that was a considerable amount of silver over a sizeable surface area. But that scalpel that Joyce stuck in the neck of that Ridden last night couldn't have been more than a few ounces of silver, max, and not much more than a couple of inches long. So I got to thinking that maybe small amounts of silver would do the trick."

She walked over to the low table and reached her hand into one of the bowls, scooping out a handful of glittering little spheres, each of them about the size of a peppercorn, or a ball bearing.

"Silver shot," Daphne explained. "It's used in manufacturing, and in the production of jewelry, that kind of thing. I got this for twenty bucks an ounce at a jewelry supply store up in the Kiev."

"How much did you get?" Izzie stepped forward and prodded the little beads on Daphne's palm with her finger tip.

Daphne groaned, and rolled her eyes dramatically. "Let's just say my credit card statement next month is going to be less than fun."

"Do you intend to *throw* it at them?" Joyce asked wearily, running a hand across her forehead.

"Kinda." Daphne had a lopsided grin on her face.

Izzie crouched down and picked up one of the plastic tubes, which she now recognized as the hulls of shotgun shells.

"That could work," she said in a low voice. Then she looked up and met Daphne's gaze. "That could really work. Loading shells with the silver shot, and then blasting it into the Ridden at a distance."

Daphne poured the silver balls back into the bowl, careful not to spill any of them onto the table or floor.

"Exactly. Only, there's no way I could afford to fill the shells *all* the way up with silver. So I mixed it in with this." Daphne picked up a box of rock salt in one hand and a jar of sea salt in the other. "I figure if they don't like crossing salt when it's on the ground, it'll really mess them up if they've got a face full of the stuff."

She put down the salt, and picked up an assembled shotgun shell from a cardboard box on the floor.

"We had the shells that we brought with the tactical shotguns from the RA offices, so I just cut those open, emptied out the shot, and packed the hulls with a mixture of salt and silver. Then I reassembled them with the original primer, powder, and wad, and there you go." She held up the shell, a proud expression on her face. "Zombie-proof shots."

Izzie rolled her eyes. "I wish you'd stop calling them that."

Daphne blinked, deflating a little.

"But I think it's a *fantastic* idea," Izzie added with a grin, and leaning forward gave Daphne a quick peck on the lips. "How many have you put together so far?"

Daphne bent down and put the shell back in the box with the others.

"A little over three dozen. Enough for three full magazines, and a little bit left over." She straightened up, and her grin widened. "I work fast."

"What, was Patrick too worn out from cleaning the streets to help out?" Joyce asked from the couch. "Or did he spend all afternoon tracking down that kid in Hyde Park so he could scare him straight?"

Daphne's smile fell as she looked from Izzie to Joyce and back.

"What kid?" she asked. "He wasn't here when I got back from the Kiev, and I assumed he was still out teaching the neighborhood kids how to clean the marks."

Joyce sat bolt upright on the couch. "You mean he's not back yet?"

"No." Daphne shook her head. "I've been here on my own the last few hours."

Izzie and Joyce exchanged a worried glance.

"He should have gotten back by now," Joyce said, her brow furrowed with worry lines. She fished in the pocket of her jacket for her phone.

Izzie already had her phone out, and after thumbing it on checked to see if she had any text messages or missed calls from Patrick's number. She was already starting to thumb out a quick text to him when Joyce held her own phone to her ear.

"I'm getting his voice mail." Joyce scowled, and stabbed the screen with her fingertip to end the call.

Izzie finished typing out "WHERE ARE YOU?" and then added "911" for safe measure. She would have added some suitable emoji for urgency if she had any idea which one to use.

As she watched the phone's screen, the text was marked as "delivered," and shortly after as "read." But at no point did the scrolling ellipse show that Patrick was composing a response on the other end.

"He read it, but he's not answering." Izzie chewed her lower lip, thinking through the possibilities.

"Or *someone* read it," Daphne said ominously.

Izzie knew that she wasn't wrong. There was no way of knowing for sure.

"Where *is* he?" Joyce sounded increasingly worried.

"Hang on, I have an idea." Izzie punched the home button on her phone, and then scrolled through pages until she found the icon for the "Find Friends" app that she and Patrick had used five years before. When Izzie had gotten to town earlier that week, Patrick had used it to know where to pick her up, so she knew that it was still installed on his phone. Provided he hadn't uninstalled it in the last few days, which seemed unlikely.

Joyce levered herself up off the couch and came over to stand beside Izzie, while Daphne stepped closer on her other side. All three women watched as the app zeroed in on the location of Patrick's phone, a broad blue circle gradually shrinking over a map of the city as it triangulated his position via cell towers.

"There," Izzie said, pointing at the tight blue dot that had come to rest at the corner of Gold Street and Northside Boulevard.

"Pinnacle Tower." Joyce covered her mouth with her hand, her voice breathless.

"The goddamned belly of the goddamned beast," Daphne said through clenched teeth, uncharacteristically swearing.

"They must have snatched him up," Izzie said, still staring at the screen of her phone, as if she could will that little blue dot to migrate to a safer spot on the map. "He wouldn't have gone on his own without telling us."

"Maybe the RPD is doing a raid?" Joyce lowered her hand from her mouth, a note of pleading optimism to her voice, a flicker of hope in her face. "They've established a link from the Ink suppliers to Parasol, and Patrick said that the taskforce was gearing up for a big push. Maybe this is it?"

Izzie shook her head. "Do you really think that Patrick would go off on a police raid in the middle of all of this—a raid on the Pinnacle Tower of all places—and not tell us first? He called you just to let you know he was checking on some neighborhood kid, do you think he wouldn't call you about something as important as *this*?"

The fleeting expression of hope bled from Joyce's face. "No," she said, in a quiet voice. "Damn it."

"So we've got to operate under the assumption that Patrick is not there of his own free will," Izzie went on, "and that someone is holding him there."

"Martin Zotovic, do you think?" Daphne asked.

Izzie stabbed the power button on her phone and jammed it back into her pocket.

"Probably," she answered, after considering the possibilities for a moment. "Or else someone high enough up in the chain that they report directly to him."

"Um . . ." Daphne held up her hand, like a student in a classroom not sure that they want to voice the question they've got in mind. "Do we need to consider the possibility that Patrick's *phone* is there, but that he's somewhere else? I mean, I'm not saying that they left him in a ditch somewhere, but . . ." She trailed off, seeing the stricken look on Joyce's face.

"No." Joyce shook her head quickly, as if to knock loose an

unwanted mental image. "Patrick has thumbprint ID set up on his phone. And that text message that Izzie just sent was marked read. So he *had* to be there to unlock it."

"Or someone unlocked it using his thumb." Daphne stopped, and then seemed to consider how that might sound. "I don't mean they cut off his thumb and took it with them, or anything," she hastened to add, "just that they might have forced him to . . ."

"It's okay," Izzie interrupted, and put a hand on Daphne's shoulder. "I think we both knew what you meant."

Joyce gripped the handle of her cane in both hands, shoulders hunched defensively, a dark cloud of worry and anxiety on her face. Izzie got the impression that she was considering all of the worst-case scenarios, up to and including the idea of Patrick's phone and his thumb being in a different location than the rest of him.

"We . . ." Joyce started, her voice like brittle glass. "We should call in the police. Maybe Patrick's commanding officer, or the other detectives on the Ink squad. Get them to move *now* on that big push that they were planning, go in there and get Patrick to safety before those things do . . . *something* to him."

"They'd need to get a judge to sign off on a no-knock warrant," Izzie said, "assuming that they haven't already, and by then it could be too late." She was considering some of the worst-case scenarios herself.

"We could bring Gutierrez in on this," Daphne suggested, but even as she said the words Izzie could tell she knew that the Senior Resident Agent would be unlikely to be of much assistance at this point.

"Well, we can't just stand here *talking* about it," Joyce said, pounding her cane on the hardwood floor. "Patrick's *life* could be in danger."

Izzie thought about what G. W. Jett had told them about Parrish and the Eschaton Temple, and about Alistair Freeman writing in his journal about the menace of the Guildhall cabal that he would one day bring down in flames. That same darkness that bubbled up time and again in Recondito had once more taken root, and Martin Zotovic was at the heart of it. If Patrick was being held there, and they weren't able to rescue him soon, then death might be the least of his worries.

"We need to get him out of there, *now*." Izzie bent down and picked up one of the shotgun shells that Daphne had packed, and hefted it in the palm of her hand. "Enough of these for three full magazines, you said?"

Daphne nodded. "Shouldn't take but a couple of minutes to get them loaded."

Izzie walked across the floor to the far wall where the tactical shotguns were sitting beside Patrick's hardshell gun case.

"Wait," Joyce said, "you're going to go in yourself? Without backup?"

"Hell, no," Daphne put in before Izzie could answer. She bent down to pick up the box of shells. "If she's going, I'm going with her."

Daphne turned to Izzie, who was kneeling down beside the gun case.

"You *are* going, right?" Daphne asked.

Izzie pulled out the stun baton and pistol-gripped Taser that Patrick had brought home from the station house the day before, and set them on the floor beside her.

"Yeah, I guess I am," she answered, and reached into the case. "When Alistair Freeman brought the Guildhall down on top of himself and everyone inside, he ended the incursion of the Ridden for at least a generation. Then when G. W. Jett took down Jeremiah Standfast Parrish at the Eschaton Center, the Ridden were off the streets again for a good long while. If we can get in there and take out Zotovic, then maybe we can do the same."

"You're just going to *kill* him?" Joyce sounded shocked. Even as worried about Patrick as she was, there were some lines that she wasn't comfortable crossing.

"Like I said, it was our fault that Nicholas Fuller didn't finish the job five years ago," Izzie said, her jaw set. "We have to finish it for him."

"And any Ridden that we run into along the way, I assume?" Daphne shook the cardboard box so that the shells clattered inside of it. "But there have got to be employees in that building that *aren't* Ridden. Cleaning staff, security guards, that kind of thing? How will we know the difference before it's too late? Because while I'm all for taking out the undead monsters possessed by alien entities, I'm not crazy about the idea of shooting innocent bystanders."

"For the bystanders, or even anyone mixed up in the Ink trade who isn't one of the Ridden, we use these." Izzie nodded to the stun baton and Taser. "As for the Ridden, your silver and salt shot should be enough to slow them down, and hopefully sever their connection to the loa. Whether they just fall down dead like the guy Joyce stabbed in the alley last night, or we end up with a bunch of formerly Ridden but still mostly alive people with shotgun wounds and a bunch of empty holes in their heads, I'm not sure. But either way, we take the shots and hope for the best."

"So how will you be able to tell the difference?" Joyce

asked. "What's to stop you from shooting someone that isn't possessed by mistake?"

"We use these." Izzie straightened up, and held out both of her hands, a glass vial resting on each palm.

"Oh, right," Daphne said, "isn't that the . . ." She trailed off for a second, searching for the name. "The ilbal? Patrick got that out of the Reaper evidence, right?"

"Wait," Joyce said, her eyes widening. "You're not thinking about *taking* that stuff are you?"

Izzie nodded.

"Nicholas Fuller thought this was the 'key' to seeing the Ridden for what they really were. With any luck, it will work for us, too."

"So that's the plan?" Daphne sounded skeptical. "Tool up, take some weird jungle drug, and go in guns blazing?"

"That's the plan." Izzie held up one of the vials to the light, and saw the fine powder glinting within. She had wondered what she would see when she took it. Now she'd get to find out.

"You know how crazy that sounds, right?" Daphne said, resting the box of shells against her hip. "And even if we should somehow manage to survive, what then? Two FBI agents go rogue and shoot up an office building. How exactly are we supposed to explain that? 'Sorry, officer, we had no choice, they were all possessed by an alien mind from another dimension'? We'd be lucky if the worst they did to us was lock us up in a home for the criminally insane." She paused, and then added, "I mean, if you're going, I'm still going with you, but let's be honest about our chances here."

"What about wearing a mask?" Joyce suggested, hand on her chin thoughtfully. "Fuller wore one, right? And so did that

Freeman guy back in the thirties, if his journal is anything to go by." She turned to Izzie. "Probably even the same one, right?"

Izzie bounced the vials on the palms of her hands as she thought it over. She wished that Patrick had brought Fuller's mask from the station house as well as the ilbal, though she admitted to herself that it would have been harder to smuggle a silver skull face mask out than it had been to sneak out a couple of tiny glass vials. But Freeman's journal suggested that the mask was made from silver in part as a defense against the Ridden, and they could use all the help they could get.

"Maybe," Daphne cocked her head to one side, a thoughtful expression on her face. "Patrick told us that when Zotovic's people renovated the Pinnacle Tower that they were really cagey about anything they changed beyond the front lobby, right? So we don't know for sure what kind of surveillance or security camera system they've got set up in there. But something to obscure our facial features isn't the worst idea, assuming we manage to get out of there in one piece."

Izzie shook her head, impatiently.

"We're wasting time that we don't have. That *Patrick* doesn't have." She pocketed the two vials, and then took the cardboard box of shotgun shells from Daphne's hands. She bent down, and proceeded to load the shells into one of the shotgun's empty magazines.

"Okay, you're right." Daphne came to crouch beside her, and went to work loading another. "I'm just a little worried about what comes afterwards, is all."

Izzie spared her a quick glance, giving her a sympathetic look.

"Let's worry about what happens afterwards when we know that there's going to *be* an afterwards," Izzie said, a tight, mirthless smile tugging up the corners of her mouth. "For the moment, let's just worry about what happens *now*."

CHAPTER TWENTY-ONE

Patrick was surrounded by darkness, but he knew that he was not alone. There were things moving there, even though he couldn't see or hear them. Then he realized that the darkness itself was moving, and that he was wreathed in living shadow. He remembered what his great uncle had told him as a boy, about the time that Pahne'i had gone down beneath the earth and wrestled for eight days with the living god of shadows, and was suddenly convinced that he was down there now. Patrick could feel his heart pounding in his chest, and his stomach roiled as if there was a fire burning deep inside of him. He tried to open his mouth to speak, but found that he couldn't breathe. He reached out, hands grasping nothing, struggling to take a breath, until . . .

Patrick jolted awake, gasping for air.

He was in a dimly lit room, arms and legs strapped to a metal chair. He had been stripped to his t-shirt and boxers, and the metal of the chair was cold against his skin. He could feel cold tiles beneath the bare soles of his feet. As he struggled to catch his breath, he tried to remember where he was, and how he had gotten here. His last memory was of the dead man with the hole in his forehead talking to him, and then a sudden burst of pain.

They must have knocked him unconscious, and brought him . . . where?

Patrick craned his neck to look from side to side. There was a wall of windows on the far side of the room, through which he could see the night sky and the tops of skyscrapers. There were light fixtures set amidst acoustic tiles in the ceiling over-head, but they were dark, the only illumination in the room what little light was shining in through the windows, giving everything the room a faintly bluish-grey tint. And aside from the chair to which Patrick was strapped, there was little else in the room to see. There was an empty chair facing him a few feet away, a waist-high table off to one side, and set up high in a corner was a security camera, its lens trained on him. If he turned his head as far as he could in either direction, in the corner of his eye he could just make out the outline of a closed door behind him, a thin trickle of light leaking out from the gap underneath it. He tried to shift the chair, but found it was too heavy to budge with his wrists and ankles secured.

There was a dull ache at the side of Patrick's head, no doubt from the blow that had knocked him unconscious. His mouth felt parched, his lips cracked and his throat burning with thirst. When he blinked, his eyelids scraped over dry eyes. He felt more dehydrated than he would have expected, assuming that he'd only been out of it for a matter of hours. The air in the room must be arid, he realized, leeching the moisture right out of him.

He felt a sharp spasm of queasy nausea in his gut, and his dry tongue was stung by a foul taste. One of the Ridden was nearby.

Patrick heard the click of a knob turning behind him, and then light spilled into the room as the door swung open. He turned his head to see, squinting in the glare, but only got a glimpse of movement before the door slammed shut and the room was once more plunged into darkness.

It took a moment for his eyes to readjust to the gloom, as he heard footsteps circle around him, and the sound of the metal chair across from him scraping across the floor.

"You're finally awake."

Patrick could make out the silhouette of a man sitting facing him, framed against the skyline in the windows beyond. The man gestured to the camera high up in the corner.

"I've been keeping my eyes on you. A few of them, anyway."

The man reached into his pocket, and when he pulled it back out his hand was filled with light. It took a split second for Patrick to realize that the man was holding a smart phone with a lit screen, and another second to recognize that it was his.

"You'll be glad to know that your friends are worried about you." Lit from below, the man's face looked more sinister than it did in the publicity photos Patrick had seen, but still recognizable as Martin Zotovic, the founder of Parasol. He waggled the phone in front of his face. "I took the liberty of logging in with your thumbprint while you were unconscious. Just wanted to do a little digging around, you understand."

Zotovic put the phone on the waist-high table, screen facing up and still lit.

"You and your friends have had a busy week, haven't you?"

Patrick felt queasy, his head spinning. He remembered the

sensation down in the subbasement of the warehouse a few nights before, when a horde of Ridden had attacked them. The feeling of wrongness that gripped him now was even stronger than he'd experienced then. But there were no blots on Zotovic's face or arms, and dressed in a plain black t-shirt, jeans, and running shoes, with a faint shadow of stubble on his sharp chin, he looked like any other young tech millionaire. Even so, Patrick thought he could see something lurking behind the man's eyes, and couldn't escape the sense that he and Zotovic weren't the only people in the room. There was something else in here with them. Or rather, something else *in* them.

"You're one of them, aren't you?" Patrick's voice croaked in his ears as he spoke, the first words he'd uttered since he regained consciousness. "Ridden."

A humorless smile creased Zotovic's face, flashing white teeth.

"'Ridden,' huh? That's old school. I prefer to refer to those of us who have willingly taken part in the Merger as 'Shareholders.'" The smile widened as he tapped his chest. "With me being the Majority Shareholder, of course."

Zotovic talked more like the tech mogul that the media portrayed him as being than as someone being controlled by an inhuman intelligence, Patrick thought. But was it Zotovic who was looking out at him through those eyes?

"What do you intend to do with me?" Patrick asked through clenched teeth.

The smile on Zotovic's face turned down into a frown.

"That's up to you, really," he said. "There are several options on the table."

Zotovic leaned forward, resting his elbows on his knees, his fingers laced together.

"When you and your friends first came onto my radar the other day, my first thought was that I should just take you off the board. Your friend Agent Lefevre managed to avoid getting run over, but I knew it was just a matter of time before you slipped up. That was before I discovered the full extent of what you've been up to. Of how deep you've been digging."

Zotovic raised his hands, and rested his steepled fingers against his chin.

"Your captain over at the 10th Precinct thinks that you've got a screw loose, did you know that? The mayor was pressuring him for an update on your 'Ink' investigation, and the captain mentioned the toll that the detail as taking on his officers. Specifically, the mental strain on a respected lieutenant, judging by what he written on a dry erase board in the station house."

Patrick's eyes widened involuntarily. So the captain *had* been in the community room, and had seen the work that he and Izzie had been doing. But how did Zotovic know that?

"I don't have a line on internal police communications yet," Zotovic went on, "but I've been able to read every email that passes through the mayor's inbox for the past year. Most of it is useless nonsense, but it's amazing what you can find if you dig through garbage long enough."

Zotovic tapped his fingertips against his chin for a moment, regarding Patrick.

"I realized that I couldn't eliminate you until I found out how much you knew and, more importantly, who else you've told. I've been working on this rollout way too long for someone to come along and throw a monkey wrench into the works at the eleventh hour."

'*Rollout?*' Patrick wondered.

"So I sent some minority shareholders down to your place last night, to bring you here for a little chat. It was tricky getting in there, with all of those damned squiggles all over the place, but I didn't build a multibillion dollar company from nothing without learning a thing or two about persistence. And then at the last minute Agent Lefevre pulled that nasty trick with the ring of salt?" Zotovic shook his head, tongue tsking. "That was bad sportsmanship, friend. I had them dead to rights."

Zotovic sucked a sharp breath in through his teeth.

"That stuff *hurts*." He unlaced his fingers and waved one hand by the side of his head. "Messes with me, in here. It jacks up the Merger. And that can't be allowed."

Patrick could see the muscles in Zotovic's jaw tightening, a brief flash of anger passing across his face, before his features settled back into a semblance of calm good humor an instant later. It was as though just remembering that moment had caused Zotovic to *feel* it again, if only for the briefest moment. But he was talking about something that had happened to the shambling Ridden in the alley behind Patrick's house the night before, when Zotovic himself hadn't been nearby.

"You cops are getting too close to the operation as it is," Zotovic went on. "The trials are just about through and we should be ready for the rollout soon, but if you jokers keep stumbling through my manufacturing sites and locking up my distributors, we might have to delay the launch date, and that is *not* happening. Not again."

Patrick remembered the intercepted emails that they had read, Parasol employees who were part of the Ink trade discussing a coming "launch date" and product testing. Part of him burned to ask Zotovic what the hell he was talking about, but it seemed that part of the reason that he was even still alive was that Zotovic wasn't sure how much he knew, and tipping his hand at this point might not be the wisest course of action.

"The *last* time we made it this far, that damned private investigator came in and made a mess of things before I could go public, even after I offered to make him a shareholder, and it was *decades* before anyone made it down into that hole again so I could start over. And the time before *that,* with the idiot writer for the pulps? That was a *disaster.* But to be fair, that was kind of my fault for letting too many minority shareholders call the shots, and those weren't really Big Picture guys."

Zotovic had to still be in his late twenties, Patrick knew. Yet he was talking about things that had happened decades before he was born as if they had happened to him personally. This suggested who he was *not* talking to, even if it didn't clear up who, or what exactly was doing the talking.

"But that won't happen again." Zotovic sat back in the chair, chest puffing up with pride. "This time *I'm* calling all of the shots. No more middle men. Just me."

He held his hands in front of him, palms down, fingers splayed and wriggling.

"For a while I tried to diversify. Spread myself out. Brought in new talent and shared the responsibilities evenly. Not just one majority shareholder, but as many suitable candidates as I could get down into that hole."

Zotovic lowered one hand, and held the thumb and forefinger of the other a short distance apart.

"And I was *this* close to moving forward when that damned professor started taking shareholders out, cutting them off from the Merger." He shook his head. "I should have dragged him down there and brought him onto the team when I had the chance. But before someone was able to stop him he had worked his way through every shareholder but one." Then he tapped his chest.

Clearly when Zotovic said "I" he didn't mean the man sitting before him. Zotovic was a body that the voice speaking was *wearing*. Patrick was talking directly to the loa itself. So why was an extradimensional intelligence talking like a Silicon Valley wunderkind about to take his startup public with an IPO?

"I suppose I have *you* to thank for that, don't I, Lieutenant Tevake? That was the first time I encountered your name, when you and Agent Lefevre took the professor down. I considered reaching out to you at the time, making you one of my minority shareholders, but I was still in the development phase of the product at that point, and didn't have a space for you on the team." He grinned, without any warmth. "But to be honest, you wouldn't have been a good fit for the Merger back then, anyway. I needed people who carried the right kind of memories in their heads, the knowledge of how to code the priming visuals into the software, and the engineering experience to take care of the hardware of the delivery system. I thought of you just as a badge and a gun who chased down killers in the street. Imagine my surprise when I found out that you were investigating the distribution side of my business, all of these years later."

Priming visual? Patrick thought. Then he remembered the conspiracy videos that he'd watched the day before.

"The encoded data in the applications," he said in a low voice. "The subliminal visuals in the code."

"So you *had* worked out that part. I thought you might." The thing that was wearing Zotovic nodded, looking impressed. "Last time around I used large two-dimensional representations to prime the candidates, with a spoken component to engage the frontal lobe, reworking the structures of their minds to aid with the Merger. But that required a considerable amount of time and attention, forcing candidates to sit and stare at a wall while chanting for hours at a time. This time I decided it would be more efficient to put the priming visuals in a place that people would be staring at for hours at a time, anyway."

"Their phones."

The thing shrugged, a gesture of mock humility.

"Just inserting a piece of myself into a person's brain isn't enough. I can gain control in the short term, but it's a brute-force method that rapidly exhausts the usefulness of a shareholder. They tend to start decaying at a fairly rapid rate, and when the nervous system breaks down and the muscles start to rot, they're not much use to me anymore. But with the synaptic structures aligned in just the right way, I can take root in only the parts of the brain that I need to maintain control, and keep a shareholder in operation indefinitely. Even after their death."

Patrick heard the sound of the door knob turning behind him, and once again the room was bathed in light from the hallway beyond. The thing that wore Zotovic like a suit stood up from the chair as footsteps passed on either side of Patrick.

"I think you know these minor shareholders," the Zotovic thing said, as two men came to stand beside him. On his left was the man with the bullet hole in the middle of his forehead that had spoken to Patrick earlier that night, the thick sludge of blood crusted brownish black in a trail down his face. On his right stood Tyler Campbell, the dead drug dealer whose autopsy had started this whole thing off only a few days before. The Zotovic thing looked from one to the other and then back to Patrick. "I'll do most of the talking—their vocal cords aren't working so great anymore, and the speech centers of their brains are pretty much toast—but I can use the extra hands for what comes next."

The Zotovic thing reached into the pocket of his jeans and pulled out what Patrick first took to be a ballpoint pen, but then realized was one of the Ink auto-injectors.

"Now, I'm going to make you the same offer I made to the private investigator last time around, and that I should have made to the professor while I still had the chance. Tell me what you know—willingly—and I'll bring you onboard as a shareholder, leaving enough of your memories and personality in place that you'll have some sense of continuity. But if you refuse to cooperate," he juggled the auto-injector in his hand, "then I'll have to take what I need from your memories by brute force. Which would not only be more time-consuming and inefficient for me, but would pretty much leave you, well . . ." He gestured at the men on either side of him. "Like these two chatterboxes, basically. A hollowed-out meat puppet good for not much more than manual labor."

The Zotovic thing took a step forward, leaning down and putting its face close to Patrick's. It smiled again, without a trace of humanity or warmth, and Patrick could see something dark swimming behind its eyes. He thought of Pahne'i down beneath the earth, staring down the god of shadows, and knew how he must have felt.

"Now," it said, its breath hot on Patrick's face, "let's begin, shall we?"

CHAPTER TWENTY-TWO

The drugs were just starting to kick in as Izzie and Joyce finished marking out a wide ring of salt around Daphne's car in the parking lot across the street from the Pinnacle Tower. Daphne had finished pulling all of the equipment out of the trunk, and was strapping into a bulletproof vest.

"You doing okay?" Joyce asked when Izzie stood up suddenly and put her hands out to either side, as if trying to regain her balance.

It took Izzie a moment before she could answer, blinking rapidly and taking deep, slow breaths. They had taken the ilbal before leaving Patrick's house a short while before, and the visual distortion she was experiencing now was the first sign of the drug's effect.

"Yeah," Izzie said, nodding slowly. Traceries of light had begun to bloom around the edges of everything in her field of vision, and intensified with each passing moment. "Starting to feel it, is all."

"I'm getting it, too," Daphne said as she zipped a bulky hooded sweatshirt over the bulletproof vest. She picked up the other vest and brought it over to Izzie. "It's like . . . like everything is catching on fire."

As Izzie pulled the vest over her head, Joyce nodded in her direction. "You guys sure that those are going to do you any good?"

"Against one of the Ridden?" Izzie answered, tightening the straps on either side. "No chance. But if we run up against an armed security guard inside, I'd rather be safe than sorry."

Joyce reached into the backseat of the car and pulled out the boombox that they'd taken from Patrick's living room.

"I loaded this up with all sorts of noisy jams," she said, putting it on the roof of the car. They had attached the strap from a messenger bag to the handle, so that one of them could wear it across their back. "If discordant noises distract the Ridden, then hopefully this will give you some kind of edge."

Izzie shouldered into a black hoodie, and zipped it up over the vest. It was a snug fit, but could pass for street wear, at least long enough for them to get across the street and into the building.

"At least we were able to park close by." Daphne slammed a magazine of shells into one of the tactical shotguns, and strapped another onto its side. Then she slipped it into the duffel, and continued loading the other. "Wouldn't want to have to explain why we were out walking with all of this hardware in a bag if we ran into any city cops."

This part of the Financial District was pretty deserted on a Sunday night, and Daphne's car was the only one in the pay-by-the-hour lot. Izzie had worried for a moment that there might be an attendant on duty that they would have to contend with, but thankfully there had only been a sign directing patrons to use the pay kiosk in off hours. There was only sparse traffic on the street, with only the occasional city bus or taxi cab driving by. They would have no trouble getting to the entrance of the building. It was what happened next that would be tricky.

Izzie stood looking up at the towering bulk of the Pinnacle Tower, which seemed to her at the moment to be limned with fire. But she got the inescapable impression of dark shadows squirming inside, like worms wriggling through a corpse.

"You going to be okay out here on your own?" Daphne asked Joyce as she slung the boombox across her back and hefted the duffle bag.

"I'll be more okay waiting out here than I would be going in there with you," Joyce answered, and gestured with her cane. "I'd just slow you down, and I'm officially the world's worst shot with a gun. But you let me know when you're coming back out, and I'll be ready to play the getaway driver. The salt ring should keep me safe until then."

Izzie turned to look in their direction. Both women seemed to be wreathed in flames that burned only brighter as she watched, but there was something more, besides. It was as though Izzie could *see* how they were feeling, even a sense of what they were thinking. Somehow their emotions and thoughts colored the flames that lit them, Daphne's anxiety laced with resolve, Joyce's concern tinged with fear. Was this the kind of second sight that her grandmother had always talked about?

"Izzie," Daphne said as she turned to look in her direction, her voice breathless. "You look . . . amazing."

Izzie knew that Daphne wasn't talking about the ill-fitting hoodie and jeans. When she looked closer, she could see into

Daphne, as well. Something burned bright inside of her that resonated.

"Here, I've got something for you." Izzie reached into the pocket of her jeans and pulled out a silver brooch in the shape of a blooming flower that she had taken from one of their makeshift gris-gris bags. She stepped closer, and pinned it to the fabric of Daphne's hoodie above her heart like a sheriff's badge. "It's not a silver face mask, but hopefully it will do some good."

Izzie pulled a silver necklace out of her other pocket, and fastened it around her neck.

"Does this mean we're going steady?" Daphne said with a smile, and Izzie could see flames of desire wreathing around her head.

"Let's get going," Izzie answered, trying to maintain focus. "Patrick needs us."

Izzie took point as they walked through the big glass doors into the lobby of the Pinnacle Tower, the hood of her jacket pulled down low over her face, hands shoved deep into her hoodie's pockets. Daphne followed close behind, keeping Izzie between herself and the security guard behind the desk.

"The building is closed to visitors," the guard said, putting down the magazine that he'd been reading, his tone gruff but unthreatening. "You folks are going to have to leave."

Izzie could see the tinges of annoyance and boredom that flared around the man.

"I just wanted to ask you a question," Izzie said, keeping her face concealed in the shadows of the hood. She kept walking toward the security desk, her hands in her pockets.

"No public restrooms." The flames around the guard flashed with irritation. "And I don't have any change to spare, either."

Beyond the desk stood a bank of elevators, and the art deco bas relief for which the building was famous, and as Izzie approached the desk she could hear the chime of one of the elevator doors opening.

"We don't need any of that," Izzie said, coming within arms' reach of the security guard.

A woman dressed in business casual stepped out of the elevator into the lobby, a keycard on a lanyard around her neck.

"Look," the guard was saying, standing up from his chair with a weary sigh. "Whatever your problem is, I don't care, okay?"

But Izzie wasn't even listening to him anymore. She was having trouble not gasping in shock when she looked at the woman walking away from the closing elevator doors.

"Izzie . . ." Daphne said in a quiet voice behind her, pitched low enough that she was the only one to hear.

"I see it," Izzie said without turning around. "I see it."

Instead of the flames that she had seen when looking at other people since taking the ilbal, when Izzie looked at the woman walking across the lobby she saw tendrils of shadow that rose from her head and shoulders, that twisted and morphed as she watched, sometimes seeming like tentacles, other times like motes of floating darkness, but always writhing and churning around the woman.

She was one of the Ridden.

"Do it," Izzie shouted.

From behind Izzie came the sound of thumping bass and grating guitar thundering from the boombox on Daphne's back.

"Hey!" the security guard said, turning in her direction. "Turn that—"

But before he could get another word out, Izzie pulled the Taser out of her jacket pocket and jabbed the sparking end to his neck.

"Sorry," Izzie said sincerely as pain tinged the flames that wreathed the guard. "I know you're probably just doing your job."

As the guard convulsed, and then collapsed with a thud to the cold tile floor, Izzie turned her attention back to the Ridden woman.

The shadows that snaked and danced about her head and shoulders had taken on a spiky quality, throbbing violently, and the woman looked momentarily disoriented and confused. Then the shadows seemed to surge, pulsating larger and then smaller, again and again, and, as Izzie watched she could see pinpricks of inky blackness begin to blossom on the woman's exposed skin and rapidly begin to swell.

The woman turned toward Izzie, mouth hanging open as the inky blots flared on her face.

"Ke-ke-ke-ke."

Izzie could almost see the loa forcing more of itself down into the woman's mind, struggling to maintain control and reorient itself. And as it did, what little remained of the woman's memories and personality was being consumed in front of Izzie's eyes. The blots had already spread so much that the woman's bare skin was almost completely covered.

"Ke-ke-ke-ke."

The Ridden lurched toward Izzie, hands out and grasping. She had been passing close by when the guard had fallen, and was now just a matter of footsteps away. Izzie took a step backwards, and the Ridden came closer still. It might have been disoriented by the discordant music, and unable to perceive exactly where Izzie was standing, but it knew where she was just a moment before, and was clearly heading in her direction. It reached out its hand toward her, and was almost within reach.

"Ke-ke—"

A shotgun blast boomed out from behind Izzie on her left, as rock salt and silver shot ripped into the Ridden's shoulder and arm.

The woman recoiled in pain, and as the blots on her skin quickly faded Izzie could see the shadows come pouring out of her, like smoke being sucked into a turbine. The shadows shimmered and dissipated into an unseen direction as soon as they disconnected from the woman's head and shoulders, until a cold blue flame sputtered weakly around her drained body. She collapsed in a heap on the floor like a puppet whose strings had just been cut off.

Which in a way she was, Izzie realized.

"You okay?" she heard Daphne say from behind her, shouting to be heard over the music blaring from the boombox.

Izzie turned, and saw that Daphne still had the stock of the tactical shotgun to her shoulder, one hand on the grip and the other on the fore-end. The duffle bag lay on the floor where Daphne had dropped it only moments before.

"Yes, I'm fine." Izzie pocketed the Taser, then knelt down to pull the other shotgun out of the bag. Holding it in one hand, she reached in and with her other hand took the stun baton out of the bag, which she then handed to Daphne. Then she zipped the duffel closed, grabbed its carrying strap, and pulled it over her head, so that when she stood the duffel was slung across her back.

"That seemed to work." Daphne walked over and looked down at the body of the woman on the ground. No longer showing any sign of being Ridden, with no shadows around her to be seen, she was still faintly breathing, though the flames which limned her burned only faintly. "Still alive, too."

"Well, maybe," Izzie said as she came to stand beside her. "The loa chewed up a lot of her mind on the way out."

"Now what?" Daphne said, looking over in her direction.

"Grab the security guard's access card," Izzie said, nodding in the direction of the unconscious man. While Daphne saw to the security guard, Izzie bent down and pulled the lanyard with the keycard from the woman's neck, noting that it seemed to have been undamaged by the shotgun blast. Pocketing the keycard as she stood up, she glanced around the lobby. "We have to assume that they already know that we're here by now. If the minds of the Ridden are linked, then taking this one out likely alerted the rest. But I'm not hearing any alarms, so it's possible that we're still under their radar."

"So how do we find out where they're holding Patrick?" Daphne said, slipping the security guard's access card into the pocket of her hoodie.

Izzie walked over to the security desk. There was a monitor there which displayed live feeds from different parts of the building, but the coverage seemed limited. All she was seeing was hallways and open-plan cubicle farms as the display cycled through different camera feeds, and aside from a few cleaning staff and a handful of late night workers like the former Ridden laying on the floor beside them, there weren't many people to be seen.

"We'll have to search floor by floor," Izzie answered, turning back toward Daphne.

"But if they *do* know we're here," Daphne said, glancing toward the bank of elevators, "then those might not be the best way up."

Izzie nodded. "That's what I was thinking, too. They could trap us between floors just by shutting down the cars from the control room."

"I was hoping you'd have some genius reason why the elevators would be better than the stairs," Daphne said, the flames around her winking a mischievous shade of pink. "But okay. Stairs, it is."

Izzie glanced around, until she located the door to the stairway in the far corner.

"Come on," she said, hefting the shotgun. "Let's get climbing."

CHAPTER TWENTY-THREE

As they ascended the stairs to the second floor, Izzie could feel the effects of the ilbal growing stronger. Her thoughts seemed to move in strange orbits, her mind making unexpected connections, everything seeming to take on a new-found significance. Was this what had sent Nicholas Fuller off the rails, spending too much time in this kind of state?

Glancing back at Daphne a few steps behind, Izzie could see that she was having much the same experience. It took Izzie a moment to realize that she was *seeing* Daphne have that same experience, interpreting the lights that flared around her.

"Did you feel nauseated by that Ridden?" Daphne asked, as Izzie approached the door that led to the second floor.

Izzie shook her head. It hadn't occurred to her in the heat of the moment, but she hadn't, at that.

"Maybe the ilbal is tweaking our perceptions in more ways than one," Izzie said in a low voice, taking hold of the door handle with her left hand, her right hand tight on the grip of the shotgun. "The weird tastes and smells and the nausea might be our brains trying to process sensory input that is outside our normal range of perception. But with the ilbal, that stuff might be translated into the shadows we're seeing, instead."

"Maybe." Daphne came to stand beside her, the stock of her shotgun at her shoulder. "But that means we won't have that as an early warning sign, then."

Izzie hadn't considered that. They could perceive the Ridden, but they wouldn't know that any were nearby without looking. Which meant that one could be on the other side of the door, but they wouldn't know until they went through.

"Ready?" Izzie said, beginning to turn the handle.

"Go," Daphne answered.

Izzie shouldered the door open as Daphne stepped forward, crouched low and aiming her shotgun through the gap.

A cleaning lady pushing a garbage can on wheels turned toward the sound of the music blaring from the boombox slung across Daphne's back, and her eyes widened as she saw the barrel of the shotgun pointed at her. The flames around her spiked with panic and fear, but there were no shadows to be seen.

Daphne lunged forward and prodded the stun baton into the woman's stomach, as gently as she could manage. The cleaning lady collapsed to the floor, unconscious.

"Clear," Daphne said as Izzie slid past her down the corridor, her own shotgun aimed and ready.

Izzie could hear the sound of a doorknob rattling, and a door swung open a short distance up the hallway.

"Who's playing that music?" An office worker in a Polo shirt and khakis stepped out through the open doorway, tendrils of shadows rising from his shoulders and head. He was looking around, a confused expression on his face. When his gaze turned to Izzie he paused, squinting, as if he was having trouble seeing her. Then the shadows spiked and throbbed as black blots sprouted all over his face and arms, and his mouth opened wide. "Ke-ke-ke-ke!"

Izzie shot him in the leg with a blast from the shotgun, and the shadows dissipated as the man collapsed onto the floor, eyes rolled up in his head, unconscious but still breathing.

"Clear," Izzie said, as Daphne continued past her.

They continued down the hallway, until it opened onto a large room filled with cubicles made up of shoulder-height dividers. Judging by the computer terminals, banks of phones, and headsets, this was probably some kind of call center during working hours, though it seemed to be deserted at this time of night. The only other rooms that they encountered on the second floor were storage closets, a copy room, and a dimly lit room filled with humming servers. Aside from the cleaning lady and the one Ridden that Izzie had shot, there was no one else to be found. In general, the floor seemed like just the sort of featureless corporate environment that Izzie would expect from a large software company, with nothing to suggest any sinister or otherworldly connections.

"Third floor, then?" Daphne said over the clanging din from the speaker at her back.

Izzie nodded. They made their way back to the stairwell, and started up the next flight of stairs.

The third and fourth floors proved to be more of the same. Cubicle farms, mostly, with corner offices for management, supply rooms, and communications hubs. Izzie and

Daphne both put down two more of the Ridden each, while Izzie stunned another security guard insensate with her Taser. But still no sign of Patrick.

The effects of the ilbal had grown even more intense. Izzie and Daphne had reached the point now where they were communicating almost entirely nonverbally. A simple glance or quick gesture was enough to express almost any idea, and it was almost as though they were able to read one another's minds. But their tension levels only increased as they ventured further into the building without meeting serious opposition, and the flames that surrounded each of them flickered with a growing intensity.

And while they were not feeling the nausea or foul tastes that they normally associated with the nearness of the Ridden, there was something else that was beginning to dominate their perceptions. Izzie could think of it only as a sense of mounting wrongness, of things not being as they should be.

It wasn't until they stepped out onto the fifth floor of the Pinnacle Tower that Izzie had a better idea of what that sense of wrongness was trying to tell her.

"Hello, ladies."

Patrick Tevake stood facing the door to the stairwell, his arms at his sides. He was wearing the same clothes that he had on the last time Izzie had seen him earlier that day, but they seemed to fit him differently now. Or perhaps it was the way he was standing, a different posture than he normally held.

"Mind turning down the noise?" Patrick waved a hand absently, and that was when Izzie realized that he wasn't focusing on either of them, but looking vaguely in their direction. "We need to talk."

Izzie stepped forward, and it was only as she drew a little

closer that she began to see the thin tendrils of shadows that rose up from the crown of Patrick's head.

"Come on, there's no need for further unpleasantness," he said, and turned his head toward her, eyes blinking slowly.

Whoever it was looking out those eyes at them, Izzie realized, it wasn't Patrick.

CHAPTER TWENTY-FOUR

Patrick was surrounded by darkness on all sides. He could feel nothing, hear nothing, taste nothing, but he was awake and aware. He had the distinct impression that there was something that he needed to remember, but his thoughts slipped away from him like quicksilver whenever he tried to focus on them.

Had someone just spoken? Was there something that he was supposed to say? Something he was meant to do? A notion lurked at the back of his head, planted there in childhood, but Patrick struggled to think what it might be.

The darkness was all consuming.

The darkness was all.

The darkness was.

Izzie brought the stock of the shotgun to her shoulder, the barrel aimed at Patrick, but kept her finger well away from the trigger.

"Daphne," she said without turning around. "Kill the music."

"Wait, are you sure that's a . . . ?" Daphne began, but Izzie cut her off.

"Go on, turn it off."

They were in a large, empty atrium that seemed to fill most of the fifth floor, with only a single door on the far side of the room. And aside from Patrick and the two of them, no other people to be seen.

The music blaring from the boombox came to an abrupt stop in the middle of a screeching guitar solo, and the sudden silence that filled the large, empty space was almost deafening.

"Thanks for that," Patrick said, a hand to the side of his head. "Was having trouble keeping it together with all of that racket."

Izzie raised the barrel of the shotgun so that it was pointed directly at his face. "Patrick, are you in there?"

He smiled humorlessly, meeting her gaze. "What's left of him, maybe. But not for much longer."

Izzie narrowed her eyes. "So who am I talking to?"

"Your friend here has been lucky enough to take part in the Merger," he said, gesturing airily with his hands. "But unlucky enough that he wasn't a willing participant in the process, so it was a pretty unpleasant experience. The good news is that it won't last."

Izzie's aim wavered as she took that in.

"So you'll let him go?"

The sound of his barking laughter was jarring coming from that familiar face, even as it twisted into an expression of remorseless cruelty. But the shadows that rose from his head twisted and morphed in time, as if dancing with amusement.

"No; it won't last because soon there won't be anything left of him." He took a step forward, and only stopped when Izzie jabbed the barrel of the shotgun in his direction. "Which is why I want to talk to you now, while this body is still able. Offer you the same chance that I offered him, see if you two are any smarter than he was."

Izzie felt a tap on her elbow, and out of the corner of her eye saw that Daphne had stepped forward and was standing by her side.

"What do we do?" Daphne said out of the corner of her mouth, leaning in close.

Izzie only shook her head in response, not sure how to answer yet.

"Now, look," he went on. "You two have been retiring my shareholders left and right tonight, and I can respect that you've got your reasons, but that has got to stop. But if you accept my offer to join the Merger, you can help offset the losses. I'm in the process of expanding my operation, and soon everyone in the city with a smart phone and a flu shot will be part of the team. But you've still got time to get in on the ground floor before we go public, and if you sign on now you'll be able to keep enough of your memories and personality that you'll still be around to enjoy it. Unlike your friend here, I'm sorry to say."

Izzie felt like she'd had about enough of this. Just listening to him speak was like nails on a chalkboard.

"You are the loa, then?" Izzie said, cutting him off. "The thing down in the mine? From outside this world?"

He rolled his eyes in annoyance, and Izzie could see shadows swirling deep within.

"Obviously," he said, his voice sounding less like Patrick's with each passing moment. "Honestly, you're as bad as the professor was. So, what do you say, ladies? This is a limited-time offer. Are you in, or are you out?"

The shadows that writhed and pulsated around his head grew larger as she watched, and the flames that she could see limning his body were strained and weak.

"Izzie?" Daphne breathed in a harsh whisper.

Izzie could feel Daphne's mounting concern radiating from beside her, and knew that they were both thinking the same thing. The loa was consuming more of their friend with each passing moment. Even now she could see pinpricks of inky black bloomed on his cheeks and arms, as more and more of the loa was forced down into his body.

"Patrick, if there's anything still left of you in there," Izzie said, lowering the barrel of the shotgun, "just know that I'm sorry about this."

Then she pulled the trigger and fired.

CHAPTER TWENTY-FIVE

Patrick's body collapsed to the floor, his right leg below the knee stippled by the impact of the silver shot and salt, blood already staining his shoe.

"Izzie!" Daphne shouted in surprise and alarm.

Izzie didn't waste time answering, but shifted her shotgun to her left hand, then knelt down and pressed the fingertips of her right to Patrick's neck, checking for a pulse.

"The longer we waited, the less of Patrick there was to save," Izzie said, relieved to see that his pulse was regular and steady. The shadows that had wreathed his head had dissipated, and the flames around him burned low but had not yet gone out. Izzie had gambled that a small amount of silver in his system would break the loa's hold on him, as it had with the Ridden woman in the lobby. That much, at least, seemed to have worked out. "At least now there's a chance he might pull through."

She cast a quick glance over her shoulder at Daphne, and saw that she was radiating concern.

"Help me find something to use as a tourniquet," Izzie said. "I don't want him bleeding out before we can get him back to the . . ."

Before she could get another word out, she was interrupted by the sound of a door slamming open on the far side of the room. She looked up in time to see a dark figure emerge from the open doorway, with more crowding in from behind.

"Damn it," Izzie spat.

The Ridden were pouring into the room, their skin so mottled with inky blots that they were practically walking shadows themselves. But with the ilbal in her system, Izzie could see the actual shadows that writhed around them, so thick that they seemed almost a solid mass of pulsating darkness, hanging heavily above the room like a malevolent cloud.

"Ke-ke-ke-ke."

As Izzie jumped to her feet, Daphne stepped in front of her and fired off a round from her own shotgun. The silver shot and salt pelted into the Ridden in the front of the pack, and the shadows spiked and gyred as their bodies fell motionless to the floor. But still more Ridden surged from behind them, stepping over the bodies of the fallen, advancing on them.

Izzie moved to Daphne's side, and fired into the inky mass. Then again, and again. The room echoed with the booming reverberations of each blast, but still the tide of Ridden surged closer and closer.

Patrick hovered in darkness, feeling himself slipping away. From far off he could hear a sound like distant thunder, booming again and again, but he was too tired to focus. It was time to rest now. Time to let go.

Though the floor was crowded with the motionless bodies of the Ridden, still more came pouring through the door, closing in around Izzie and Daphne.

"Izzie?" Daphne said as she slammed her last magazine into her shotgun. "I think we need to go now."

Izzie scowled, swinging the barrel of her shotgun around and taking aim at a cluster of the Ridden who were approaching from the side. There was no way they could retreat, cover their backs, and carry Patrick out all at the same time. And since it would take both of them to lug his unconscious body, either they abandoned Patrick to the tender mercies of the Ridden, or they tried to carry him out together, leaving themselves open to an attack from the rear before they'd taken more than a few steps toward the door. Neither option was a very good one. But they needed to choose one before they were left without an option at all.

Izzie squeezed the trigger, then stopped short. The spent shell failed to eject, but was stuck in the ejection port between the bolt and the chamber. She couldn't fire another round without clearing it first.

"Cover me!" she shouted at Daphne, and turned the shotgun so that the ejection port was facing the floor, working to knock the shell loose.

Daphne stepped around her to fire at the approaching Ridden from her side, and then swung around to fire back in the opposite direction.

"Damn it," Izzie swore. The shell remained lodged in place. She had no choice but to pull the magazine and pry it loose. After snapping the magazine off and freeing up the ejection port, Izzie saw that there was just one shell left inside. She would need to make it count.

"Izzie, look out!" Daphne shouted.

"Ke-ke-ke-ke," came an inhuman voice from behind Izzie's back.

Izzie turned just in time to see another group of the Ridden approaching from behind them. They must have come up the stairs from the lower floors, possibly drawn back to the Pinnacle Tower from elsewhere in the city.

Before Izzie had a chance to raise her shotgun and fire, one of the Ridden lurched forward and bashed the gun from her hand. The shotgun clattered across the floor.

Daphne managed to get off one final round of her own before another of the Ridden grabbed hold of her shotgun and wrenched it out of her hands.

Izzie could scarcely focus, her field of vision all but completely obscured by the writhing shadows that the ilbal was showing her. She stepped back, until she could feel Daphne's form pressed against her.

"I'm sorry, Daphne," she said, her hand finding Daphne's, their fingers lacing together. "I'm sorry I dragged you into this mess."

Daphne squeezed Izzie's hand tightly.

"I'm glad I met you, Izzie," she said, and left it at that.

Izzie braced herself, anticipating the final attack of the Ridden, sure that they were about to be torn limb from limb. But instead, the mass of inky silhouettes stopped just within arms' reach. They surrounded the two of them like a solid wall, staring silently at them with cold, dead eyes.

"You ladies really should have taken my offer," came a voice from deep in the milling crowd.

The wall of teaming Ridden parted just enough for a man to step through.

"You had the chance to get in on the ground floor," Martin Zotovic said, tendrils of shadows waving around his head and shoulders like Medusa's snakes. "But I'm afraid that offer isn't on the table anymore."

CHAPTER TWENTY-SIX

"**I**t's a shame, really. Seems like you two have skillsets that would have made for useful additions to the Merger."

The Ridden had stepped back, leaving Izzie, Daphne, and the unconscious Patrick at the center of a broad circle as Martin Zotovic walked slowly around them, giving them an appraising look. Or rather, while the thing that had taken root in Martin Zotovic's brain did.

"Oh, well," the Zotovic thing said with a shrug. "There's always a need for grunt work, too."

Izzie remembered the things that her grandmother had taught her about the loa when she was growing up. And while the spirits invoked in Mawmaw Jean's rituals were clearly not the same sort of being that Izzie was dealing with here, it occurred to her that similar rules of engagement might be in play. You addressed a loa depending on their personality and priorities, offering them what they desired in order to get what you wanted. And for whatever reason, the entity that was speaking to them now had taken on the personality of a chatty, self-impressed business executive, so perhaps the best move would be to take advantage of that, to stall for time until Izzie could think of something.

"Why did you come here?" Izzie asked in as respectful a tone as she could manage. "What do you want with Recondito?"

The Zotovic thing sighed dramatically.

"You think I *want* to be here?" he said, waving his arms in exasperation. "I'm *stuck* here."

Then he paused, as if lost in thought. Izzie could see the shadows above him twitch and pulse as they grew larger and smaller by turns. He took a deep breath, collecting himself, and as he began to speak again it was as if he were sloughing the personality that he had adopted almost like a snake shedding its skin, and for a brief moment Izzie felt like she was seeing something of the true nature of the loa.

"I found this place by accident, poking and prodding at the boundaries of my world. I reached through a crack, and found that it closed shut around me. Not fully here, but unable to return. Hidden deep, unable to remain exposed for long. But I could shelter in the minds of living things, and spread myself through them to others. Adopting their personalities as protective camouflage, nestled deep inside their minds. But the vessels are so fragile, their lives so brief. It is never enough, and in time I always return to the darkness, waiting for the next opportunity to spread out. But this time it will be different. This time I will take root in every mind here, and make this place my own."

As Izzie watched, the shadows that wreathed his head writhed and turned, and his face twisted, a hungry look in his eyes. But then the shadows gradually settled back into their usual patterns, and his face once more took on the self-impressed expression that she recognized from publicity photos.

"But enough about me," he said with a vicious grin. He reached into his pocket and pulled out of couple of Ink auto-injectors. "Let's get you two in the pipeline, and then I'll just have your doctor friend across the street to deal with. That ring of salt won't stop my building security guards from grabbing her, and then we'll have all four of you taken care of."

Oh no, Izzie thought with a jolt. *Joyce!*

Deep in the darkness, surrendering to the cold, Patrick heard a voice calling out, like the song of a bird singing somewhere far off in the distance. And an ember inside of him sparked and flared, hungry to answer.

Two of the Ridden detached themselves from the wall of bodies on Izzie's left, and grabbed hold of her arms, wrenching her away from Daphne. Two more took hold of Daphne's arms, holding them tight in a vice-like grip. Izzie tried to break free, but the Ridden shoved her down, her knees hitting the floor hard enough to make her eyes water. A moment later Daphne was kneeling beside her, jaw set and teeth barred, and Izzie could see the spikes of frustration and rage in the flames around her.

"Okay, who wants to go first?" the Zotovic thing said, standing in front of them with an auto-injector in either hand. He looked from Izzie to Daphne and then back again. "Let's start with you, Agent Lefevre. I've never had a chance to really repay you for stopping the professor from finishing his work the last time around, so it seems the least I can do."

He leaned down, bringing the auto-injector close to Izzie's neck.

"You had a good run," he said in her ear, while she struggled to pull away from the auto-injector's tip. "But it's time to let someone else drive now. So why don't you . . ."

His next words were drowned out by a sudden echoing boom.

The shadows above the Zotovic thing's head spiked in outrage, and then as the body fell to the ground they began to dissipate like drops of water on a hot stove. The back of his shirt was shredded with dozens of tiny holes, their edges singed.

Izzie could feel the hands that held her arms relax their grip.

"Patrick?" Daphne said beside her.

Izzie turned in her direction, and saw that Patrick had rolled onto his side, holding Izzie's fallen shotgun in a one-handed grip, smoke still trailing up from the wavering barrel.

"Is Joyce . . . ?" he said weakly before trailing off, his voice scarcely above a whisper.

The Ridden who had held her were still standing behind Izzie, but motionless, like mannequins. When she climbed to her feet, they made no move to stop her. Izzie looked around the room, and saw that the rest of the Ridden were in the same state, standing stock still, expressions vacant as the inky blots on their skin began slowly to fade.

Daphne was already at Patrick's side, helping him up into a sitting position.

"Is Joyce . . . okay?" Patrick croaked.

"I don't know," Izzie said as she bent down and tore a strip of cloth from the hem of Zotovic's ragged shirt. Then she tied a makeshift tourniquet around Patrick's right leg below the knee. "Let's go find out, shall we?"

Patrick's eyelids were heavy, his breathing shallow, but he was alert and conscious as Izzie and Daphne helped him stand. With one arm over Izzie's shoulder and his other over Daphne's, he was able to keep his weight off of his right leg.

Bodies began to fall to the floor all around the room, first singly or in pairs, and then in increasingly large numbers, like dominos being toppled one by one.

"What's *happening* to them?" Daphne said.

"Minor . . . shareholders," Patrick managed. "They were connected to the loa through . . ."

He left off, struggling to catch his breath, but rolled his eyes toward the lifeless form of Martin Zotovic on the floor at their feet.

"With his connection cut," Izzie finished for him, "the loa must not be able to maintain its hold on the others."

Patrick nodded once, the most he was able to muster.

"Come on," she went on, maneuvering Patrick toward the door. "Let's get out of here."

As she and Daphne worked together to steer him toward the stairway door, Patrick rolled his head to the side to look at Izzie through half-lidded eyes.

"I could hear you," he said. "In the dark. You pulled me back."

She wasn't sure if he was in shock, or brain damaged, or just delirious from loss of blood.

"Like a bird," he said sleepily, his head forward, chin resting on his chest. "A spark . . ."

He trailed off into silence.

Tightening her hold on his arm to keep him from falling, shouldering his weight, Izzie continued to walk forwards. The light and flames still shone all around them, but the shadows were beginning to fade.

EPILOGUE

The trees in the park beside Powell Middle School were a riot of color, tinted with blooms of bright pink and purple, and the spring air was thick with the scent of them as Patrick made his Saturday morning rounds though the neighborhood. He leaned heavily on the cane in his right hand with each step, still unable to bear his full weight on his right knee, but as the months had gone on the pain of his injuries had faded, though the memories remained. There were other gaps in his memory, of course. Moments from childhood and the years since that he continued to find were missing. But he retained the broad sweeps and bigger picture, and was thankful that the losses had not been greater.

The marks on the buildings that he checked were clean and well-tended, though some of them had been joined by graffiti tags that identified which of the neighborhood kids had claimed the right to maintain them. A competitive streak had taken hold in the neighborhood, with different factions of students vying to see who would earn their new gym teacher's most effusive praise. Since leaving the force and starting to work for the school full time, Patrick had done his best to be as impartial as possible, though he found that Regina Jimenez and her brother seemed to be responsible for the greatest number of well-kept markings. Hector had watched from the window of the house as the Ridden had been shot in the forehead from Patrick's pistol and kept on standing, which had scared him straighter than any lecture could have ever managed to do.

When he rounded the corner at the Church of the Holy Saint Anthony, Patrick saw Izzie parking her car on the curb in front of his house, and by the time he was crossing Almeria she was already standing on the sidewalk.

"I thought you weren't due back from Quantico until tomorrow," he said, as she opened the rear door on the passenger side and pulled out her bag. Then he waggled his eyebrows at her suggestively. "What, couldn't stand to be away from your girlfriend a moment longer?"

Daphne had moved into the rooms upstairs soon after the new year, once he had finished converting them into a separate apartment. Izzie had been splitting her time between Virginia and the city in the months since, but it seemed to Patrick that he should be charging her rent, too, considering how many weekends she spent there.

"You're going to be seeing a lot more of me," she said, with a crooked smile. "My request to transfer to the Resident Agency here went through. Gutierrez has been promoted to run the Field Office up in Portland, and Daphne is being bumped up to take over as the new R.A."

Patrick wasn't surprised to hear that Gutierrez had gotten the nod. In the fallout of the Ink investigation, Izzie and

Daphne had downplayed their own roles, leaving Gutierrez to bask in the effusive praise of the mayor, who credited his Resident Agency with providing crucial support to helping the RPD stitch up the narcotics ring that the public now believed had been operating out of the offices of Parasol. The official story was that the company's CEO had been tragically killed by that same narcotics ring when he uncovered their activities and tried to put a stop to it, and that one of Recondito's finest had suffered a gunshot wound while trying unsuccessfully to save him. It was an explanation that fit the publicly known facts, and though Patrick was uncomfortable with the momentary fame that he enjoyed after articles ran with headlines like "Hero Cop Solves Murder of Fellow Officer and Software Ceo," it kept anyone from trying to poke holes in the story.

"Wait, does that mean your girlfriend is going to be your supervisor?"

Izzie shrugged. "It won't be the first Bureau regulation that I've broken since coming here." She slung the strap of her bag over her shoulder, then closed the door. "Don't worry, though, I've got a line on a place of my own. Nice red-brick house in Ross Village. My grandmother would have loved it."

She took a few steps down the sidewalk, peering down the alley to look at the mark that Patrick's great-uncle had left on the rear of the house a lifetime ago.

"So how are things here?" she asked, turning back in his direction. "No major disasters I should know about?"

Patrick leaned on the handle of his cane with both hands.

"We're keeping a lid on it."

The Ridden were off the streets, and unless someone managed to get down into that abandoned mine outside of town, they weren't likely to be back any time soon. But as they'd learned from Alistair Freeman's journal and their discussions with G. W. Jett, the Ridden were only one of the potential dangers that came along with living in a true place like Recondito. The walls between the worlds were thin here, and there were always things that were breaking though from the Otherworld and beyond.

The front door to his house opened, and Joyce leaned out the gap, her hand on the knob.

"You ever coming back inside? I've had breakfast waiting for almost half an hour." She turned and flashed a smile at Izzie. "Hey, you. Daphne's upstairs, I'll let her know you're back."

Then she disappeared back inside, and from the open door came wafting the smell of fresh-baked island donuts.

"So we're good, then?" Izzie said, looking in his direction.

"Good enough for now," Patrick answered. There would be time to tell her about the possession that he had dealt with a few days earlier once breakfast was done. "Yeah, we're good."

The Ridden might have been gone, but the city still needed someone to protect it from other threats from beyond. Already they had faced a number of other minor incursions, and it was only a matter of time before something major broke through. But they had survived one encounter, and they would be ready for whatever came next. They would have to be.

ACKNOWLEDGMENTS

I owe a huge debt of thanks to Bill Willingham, Lilah Sturges, and Mark Finn, who were generous with their advice when the earliest version of this story was first coming into focus, to Allison Baker for her support and encouragement in all the years since, and to Jeremy Lassen for helping bring it into focus.

ABOUT THE AUTHOR

Chris Roberson is the co-creator, with artist Michael Allred, of *iZombie*, the basis of the hit CW television series, and the writer of several *New York Times* best-selling Cinderella mini-series set in the world of Bill Willingham's Fables series. He is also the co-creator of *EDISON REX* with artist Dennis Culver, and the co-writer of *Hellboy and the B.P.R.D.*, *Witchfinder*, *Rise of the Black Flame*, and other titles set in the world of Mike Mignola's *Hellboy*. In addition to his numerous comics projects, Roberson has written more than a dozen novels and three dozen short stories, and has been a finalist for the World Fantasy Award four times; twice a finalist for the John W. Campbell Award for Best New Writer; and has won the Sidewise Award for Best Alternate History in both the Short Form and Novel categories. He lives with his daughter, two cats, and far too many books in Portland, Oregon.